EDGAR CAYCE'S STORY OF KARMA

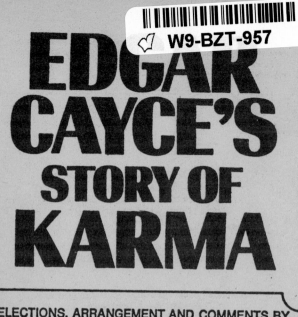

SELECTIONS, ARRANGEMENT AND COMMENTS BY
MARY ANN WOODWARD
INTRODUCTION BY
Hugh Lynn Cayce

BERKLEY BOOKS, NEW YORK

If you purchased this book without a cover you should be aware that this book is stolen property. It was reported as "unsold and destroyed" to the publisher and neither the author nor the publisher has received any payment for this "stripped book."

This Berkley book contains the complete
text of the original hardcover edition.
It has been completely reset in a typeface
designed for easy reading and was printed
from new film.

EDGAR CAYCE'S STORY OF KARMA

A Berkley Book / published by arrangement with
Coward, McCann & Geoghegan, Inc.

PRINTING HISTORY
Coward, McCann & Geoghegan, Inc. edition published 1971
Berkley Medallion edition / July 1972

All rights reserved.
Copyright © 1971 by The Edgar Cayce Foundation.
This book may not be reproduced in whole or in part,
by mimeograph or any other means, without permission.
For information address: Coward, McCann & Geoghegan, Inc.
200 Madison Avenue, New York, New York 10016.

ISBN: 0-425-10246-7

A BERKLEY BOOK ® TM 757,375
Berkley Books are published by The Berkley Publishing Group,
200 Madison Avenue, New York, New York 10016.
The name "BERKLEY" and the "B" logo
are trademarks belonging to Berkley Publishing Corporation.

PRINTED IN THE UNITED STATES OF AMERICA

30 29 28 27 26 25 24 23 22 21

The records of an entity are written upon time and space as the skein of things. They may be called as images. For thoughts are things, and as they run so are the impressions made upon what we call time and space. (1562-1)

FOREWORD

Edgar Cayce gave over fourteen thousand psychic readings, of which approximately one-third were life readings (accounts of past earth lives). These life readings reported some of the individual's former earth appearances with their consequences. The readings used the term "entity" to denote the complete individual, including the physical body, the conscious mind, the subconscious mind, the astral body, the soul, and the superconscious mind. Capitals were used in the records for emphasis, where Edgar Cayce had spoken a little louder to emphasize something.

This book has been prepared with the hope and prayer that the illustrations and the counsel given others will enable the reader to better understand himself and his purpose in life.

MARY ANN WOODWARD

INTRODUCTION

Reincarnation is a foolish belief of ignorant masses that man is reborn as an insect or animal. Rebirth is a concept which it is not necessary to consider because Jesus came to die for our sins. Reincarnation is, in various forms, a part of the beliefs of a number of major world religions and philosophies. It is intellectually stimulating. Rebirth is an acceptable idea. Karma is a universal law with which one should be working. Which of these is closest to your position?

Is man reborn in one human form after another? Does he use his bodies, his homes, through which to express the "real self" in different environments and through different hereditary strains? Is it possible that talents and abilities, as well as weaknesses and faults, are expressed and worked out from life to life as man grows toward God consciousness? Such urges, such tendencies, actually memories of the "soul," would be karmic patterns.

Mary Ann Woodward is a person who, in my opinion, has begun to work with karma as one of the important laws of life. She has taken literally Paul's admonition "Be not deceived; God is not mocked; for whatsoever a man soweth, that shall he also reap"* and examines it in the light of the psychic data in the Edgar Cayce readings on karma.

Miss Woodward knew my father, Edgar Cayce, and had information from him in readings which, in her opinion, constructively affected her life.

She did not stop there, for she has gone on to study the readings and talk with other people who have tried to apply them. After writing and lecturing over a period of years for

* Gal. 6:7.

the association which has preserved and is cataloguing, examining, and testing the readings, she is now able to bring to this book considerable new data from the Edgar Cayce files, some helpful insights, and illuminating comments on the subjects of rebirth and karma.

This volume is a welcome addition to a growing list of commentaries on Edgar Cayce's psychic data.

HUGH LYNN CAYCE

CONTENTS

MEETING SELF

CHAPTER ONE

For verily I say unto you, Till heaven and earth pass, one jot or one tittle shall in no wise pass from the law, till all be fulfilled.

—*Matthew V:18*

And it is easier for heaven and earth to pass, than one tittle of the law to fail. —*Luke XVI:17*

What is this immutable law referred to by both Luke and Matthew? Obviously, it is the law of cause and effect, called by many, particularly in the Orient, karma.

The word "karma" is used philosophically to indicate conditions in the present stemming from thoughts and actions in the past. Its Sanskrit meaning encompasses both action and reaction (or consequences). Its Hindu meaning encompasses work, or the labor of the soul seeking to attain union with God. Today we think of it as the law of cause and effect.

The psychic readings given by Edgar Cayce explained karma, in its many aspects and ramifications, as "meeting self." Most of our acts or deeds produce an immediate effect or result. We are usually aware of the effect of our acts and choices and know whether they are right or wrong. We see this at once. It might be called "cash" karma, so quickly are the consequences felt. There are, however, many circumstances or conditions for which we can see no cause or reason unless we can accept the theory of reincarnation. For example, why is one child born to riches or plenty and happy, loving surroundings, and another to poverty and rejection? What is it that attracts souls to such different environments? Why is one child a genius and another retarded or an idiot? Man often, in his misery, cries out as Job did: "Why has this been visited upon me?" Unless explained by previous existence or lives, these things seem inexplicable.

The Edgar Cayce readings maintain that each person is responsible for the circumstances in which he finds himself. He is not the innocent victim of his environment; he is simply meeting self.

13

What ye sow, ye reap. There are often experiences in which individuals apparently reap that which they have not sown, but this is only the short self vision of the entity or the one analyzing and studying purposes or ideals in relationship to those particular individuals. (2528-3)

Meeting self, according to the information given in the Edgar Cayce readings, is actually meeting the consequences of our own actions or attitudes. This meeting self also includes our previous thoughts and emotions. We reincarnate, or live again, in earth to face the results we have brought about. Not only do we daily make choices, but we have made choices in former lives for which we are responsible. We are free to choose, but we must realize that within each choice are future choices. The consequences of our choices and acts are the "jot and tittle" we must face. We cannot escape.

Cause and effect to many are the same as karma.
Karma is that brought over, while cause and effect may exist in the one material experience only. (2981-21)

A. *Most* individuals in the present misinterpret karmic influences—each soul, each entity, should gain the proper concept of destiny. Destiny is within, or is as of faith, or is as the gift of the Creative Forces. Karmic influence is, then, rebellious influence against such. When opportunities are presented, it is the entity's own *will* force that must be exercised—that which has separated it or has made it equal to the creative influences in the higher spiritual forces to make for itself that advancement. Then in *every* contact is there the opportunity for an entity, a soul, to fulfill or meet in itself or its soul self's association with the Creative Forces from the First Cause, to embrace that necessary for the entity to enter into the at-oneness with that Creative Force. Hence as for the entity's fulfilling, it is *ever* on the road. (903-23)

For life and its expressions are one. Each soul or

14

entity will and does return, or cycle, as does nature in its manifestations about man; thus leaving, making, or presenting—as it were—those infallible, indelible truths that it—Life—is continuous. And though there may be a few short years in this or that experience, they are one; the soul, the inner self, being purified, being lifted up, that it may be one with that first cause, that first purpose for its coming into existence.

And though there may be those experiences here and there, each has its relationships with that which has gone before, that is to come. And there has been given to each soul that privilege, that choice, of being one with the Creative Forces. And the patterns that have been set as marks along man's progress are plain. *None* mount higher than that which has been left in Him who made that intercession for man, that man through Him might have the advocate with the Father. And those truths, those tenets—yea, those promises—that have been set in Him are true and may be the experience of each and every soul, as each entity seeks, strives, tries, desires to become and pursues the way of becoming with Him.

Then, as there has been and is the passage of a soul through time and space, through this and that experience, it has been and is for the purpose of giving more and more opportunities to express that which justifies man in his relationships one with another; in mercy, love, patience, long-suffering, brotherly love.

For these be the fruits of the spirit, and they that would be one with Him must worship Him in spirit and in truth. (938-1)

We and we alone are responsible for what we are and our condition in this earth.

The Edgar Cayce readings indicate that the individuality is the sum total of what the entity has done about Creative and ideal forces in its various experiences in the earth. The individuality changes as the entity acts, thinks, and feels in the present about its ideals, its experiences, and its opportunities. Problems, conditions, individuals, all cause a reaction in the individuality. Each phase of the entity has its separate attributes, which may be both physical and spiritual. Also, they may be one, and to accomplish this the

15

entity must use the mind. The mind is the builder, the way in which one approaches either infinity or materiality.

For it is not by chance that each entity enters, but that the entity—as a part of the whole—may fill that place which no other soul may fill so well.

Thus with each material manifestation there is an undertaking by an entity to so manifest that it, as a part of the whole, may become more and more attuned to that consciousness, and thus glorify Him in the entity's relationships to others in any and in every experience.

Thus the urges latent or manifested are expressions of an entity in the varied phases of consciousness. In the material or earthly sojourn these find expressions or manifestations in a three-dimensional manner. Each entity, thus, finds itself body, mind, and soul. These phases represent the three spiritual attributes that are understandable or comprehended in materiality. Yet as the mental and the spiritual become more and more expressive, or controlling through the experiences in the earth, the entity becomes aware of other dimensions in its material sojourn.

While body is subject to all the influences of materiality, it may be controlled—the emotions thereof—by the mind. And the mind may be directed by spirit. Spirit is that portion of the First Cause which finds expression in all that is everlasting in the consciousness of mind OR matter.

And no urge—whether of the material sojourns or of the astrological aspects—surpasses the mental and spiritual abilities of a soul to choose its course that it, the soul and mind, may take.

In materiality, then, as may be expressed in whatever environ a body has chosen, it becomes accustomed or attuned to the environs of that particular sphere of activity. Yet these may become localized; or they may become state- or nation-minded, or spiritual- or fellow-man-minded, thereby altering the manner in which the entity may express itself, though under the same environ of others in that particular sphere of activity. (2533-1)

Each entity, each soul, enters the material experience for purposes. These are not individual or of a selfish nature, though they are very personal in their application and their practice.

Each soul meets CONSTANTLY ITSELF; not alone in what is called at times karma or karmic influences. For remember, Life is God; that which is constructive grows; that which is destructive deteriorates.

Then, karmic forces—if the life application in the experience of an individual entity GROWS to a haven of peace and harmony and understanding; or ye GROW to Heaven, rather than going to heaven; ye grow in grace, in understanding.

Remember then as this: There are promises made by the Creative Forces, or God, to the children of men, that "if ye will be my daughter, my son, my child, I will indeed be thy God."

This is an individual promise. Hence the purposes are for an entrance; the SOUL may be prepared for an indwelling with the soul, the mind, of the living God.

How, then, ye ask, are ye to know when ye are on the straight and narrow way?

My Spirit beareth witness with thy spirit that ye are indeed the children of God.

How? Thy God-Consciousness, thy soul, either condemns, rejects, or falters before conditions that exist in the experience of the mental and material self. Mind ever is the builder. (1436-1)

We often feel we are treated unjustly or that we deserve better things. This is probably only the short view, for we do reap what we sow. We must meet in the physical what we have done or thought in the mental.

So we have or meet those various aspects in the experience of each individual; for where there have been the constructive or destructive aspects in the experience of each individual, they must be met in the same sphere or plane of activity in which they have been in action in the experience of the entity—and met according to that which is to be meted. For what saith the law? As ye mete, so shall it be meted to thee in thine own experience, in thine own activity. So, as individuals in their material or mental experience in the material world

17

find that they are in the activity of being mistreated, as from their angle, from their own angle have they mistreated. If harshness has come to thine own experience, so has there been in thine own activity that which makes for same; and so is the experience in each phase. (262-81)

Learn this lesson well—the spiritual truth: Criticize not unless ye wish to be criticized. For with what measure ye mete it is measured to thee again. It may not be in the same way, but ye cannot even THINK bad of another without it affecting thee in a manner of destructive nature.

Think WELL of others, and if ye cannot speak well of them, don't speak at all—but don't think it, either!

Try to see self in the other's place. This will bring the basic spiritual forces that must be the prompting influence in the experience of each soul, if it would grow in grace, in knowledge, in understanding; not only of its relationship to God, its relationship to its fellow man, but its relationships in the home and in the social life.

For know that the Lord thy God is One. And all that ye may know of good must first be within self. All ye may know of God must be manifested through thyself. To hear of Him is not to know. To apply and live and be like Him IS to know! (2936-2)

We are constantly meeting ourselves.

For each soul must meet in its own self that which the entity or body metes to its fellow man in "its" ideal relations with such. (876-1)

Some may ask, some may say, how or when does one become aware of that mercy, grace? As the individual in the Christ is under the law of grace and mercy and not of sacrifice. Then indeed does each soul, each individual, in same become aware of the saving grace—or the purpose for which the Holy One gave within self that sacrifice such that all through Him may become aware, in the *spiritual* plane, through the grace of the Christ, of the manner in which the individual has met in the material. For He has forgiven thee already. Only in thine brother—as ye are to be judged before Him by the deed done in the body-physical. For once for all has He entered in that ye are forgiven by Him already. (262-81)

Have ye not read as He gave, that he who is guilty of one jot or tittle is guilty of it all? Have ye not read that ye shall pay to the uttermost farthing? Yet it is not the same as considered by some, that ye have builded thine own karma—and that the blood, the debt, the law of grace is of none effect. But as He has given, if thine activity is made that ye may be seen of men, or if thine purpose, thine aim, thine desire is for self-glorification, then ye are none of His. Then, the meeting of the deeds done in the body is by relying upon the faith in Him, the activity that makes for an exemplification in the flesh of that faith, of that mercy. If ye would have mercy, be ye merciful. If ye would be faithful, show thyself by thy acts that ye trust in Him. How readest thou? "Consider the lilies of the field, how they grow; they toil not, neither do they spin; yet I say unto you that even Solomon in all his glory was not arrayed like one of these." Hast thou put on the Christ, then, in thy activity with thy neighbor, with thy brother, with those of thine own house? Know ye within thyself. Hast thou met with Him in thine inner chamber of thine own temple? Ye *believe* that your body is the temple of the living God. Do ye act like that? Then begin to put same into practice, making practical application of that thou hast gained, *leaving* the results with thy God.

Thou believest He is able to keep that thou hast committed unto Him. Dost thou live like that? Dost thou cherish the thought: "*I am in Thy hands. In Thee, O God, do we live and move and have our being in the flesh: And we as Thy children will act just that*"? Speakest thou evil of thy friend, thy foe, or as thou wouldst speak if thou wert in the presence of thy God? Ye are continually in that presence, within thy self. He with the Father, He in thee. Will ye keep the faith that is accounted to thee for righteousness, that thy body in its purging—through the varied experiences in the earth—may *ever* be a channel that points to the living God?

What will ye do about same? (262-82)

Actually, our karma has many aspects and ramifications reaching into the past and also into the future if the condition or problem has not been resolved. Not only our acts and deeds but also our thoughts bring their karmic effects; for thought precedes the deed, and thoughts are things.

"From the abundance of the heart the mouth speaketh"; and thoughts are deeds, and each builds to himself that which is to be glorification, or edification, or resentment built in self. Then act in the way which is befitting and responds in yourself. (294-58)

One man asked:

Q. Have I karma from any previous existence that should be overcome?
A. Well that karma be understood, and how it is to be met. For, in various thought—whether considered philosophy or religion or whether from the scientific manner of cause and effect—karma is all of these and more. Rather it may be likened unto a piece of food, whether fish or bread, taken into the system; it is assimilated by the organs of digestion, and then those elements that are gathered from same are made into the forces that flow through the body, giving the strength and vitality to an animate object, or being, or body. So, in experiences of a soul, in a body, in an experience in the earth. Its thoughts make for that upon which the soul feeds, as do the activities that are carried on from the thought of the period make for the ability of retaining or maintaining the active force or active principle of the thought *through* the experience. Then the soul reentering into a body under a different environ either makes for the expending of that it has made through the experience in the sojourn in a form that is called in some religions as destiny of the soul, in another philosophy that which has been builded must be met in some way or manner, or in the more scientific manner that a certain cause produces a certain effect. Hence we see that karma is *all* of these and more. What more? Ever since the entering of spirit and soul into matter there has been a way of redemption

for the soul, to make an association and a connection with the Creator, *through* the love *for* the Creator that is in its experience. Hence *this*, too, must be taken into consideration; that karma may mean the development for *self*—and must be met in that way and manner; or it may mean that which has been acted upon by the cleansing influences of the way and manner through which the soul, the mind-soul, or the soul-mind is purified, or to be purified, or purifies itself and hence these changes come about—and some people term it "Lady Luck" or "The body is born under a lucky star." It's what the soul-mind has done *about* the source of redemption of the soul! Or it may be yet that of cause and effect, as related to the soul, the mind, the spirit, the body. (440-5)

We often think we have karma with other people as the questioner [1436] in the following interchange did. This is apparently a misunderstanding of the true nature of karma. We only meet ourselves. Karma is a personal thing and only with God or the Creative Forces. It is not between individuals. Other people merely provide the means or conditions for us to learn our lessons and gain self-mastery. We must attain perfection through spiritual unfoldment so that we may become companions and cocreators with God the Father.

Q. Is there some karmic debt to be worked out with either or both and should I stay with them until I have made them feel more kindly toward me?

A. Thy relationships to thy fellows through the various experiences in the earth come to be then in the light of what Creative Forces would be in thy relationships to the act *itself:* And whether it be as individual activities to those who have individualized as thy father, thy mother, thy brother, or the like, or others, it is merely self being met, in relationships to what they *themselves* are working out, and not a karmic debt *between* but a karmic debt of *self* that may be worked out *between* the associations that exist in the present!

And this is true for every soul.

"If ye will but take that that as was given thee!

21

Neither do I condemn thee—neither do I condemn thee."

WHO GAVE THAT? LIFE ITSELF! Not a personality, not an individual alone; though individually spoken to the entity, to the soul that manifests itself in the present in the name called [1436]. This becomes then not an incident but a *lesson*, that *all* may learn! This is the reason, that is the purpose, that is why in the activity much should be expected, why much shall be endured, why much may be given, by the soul that has learned that God condemns not them that seek to know His face and believe!

Then it is not karma but in HIM that the debt is paid.

For who forgave thee thy material shortcomings, thy material errors, as judged by thy superiors at that experience in the material world?

Thy Lord, thy Master—*thyself!* For He stands in thy stead, before the *willingness* of thy inner self, thy soul, to do good unto others; that willingness, that seeking, is rightness, if ye will but *see*—and *forget* the *law* that killeth but remember the spirit of forgiveness that makes alive! (1436-3)

Q. What debt do I owe J. M.?
A. Only that ye build in thine own consciousness.

For every soul, as every tub, must stand upon its own self. And the soul that holds resentment owes the soul to whom it is held—much! Hast thou forgiven him the wrong done thee? Then thou owest naught! (1298-1)

Do not attempt to be good but rather good for *something!*

Know what is thy purpose, what is thy goal! And unless these are founded in constructive, spiritual construction, they will turn again upon thyself!

For each soul is meeting day by day *self!*

Hence as has been given, *know thyself*, in whom thou believest! Not of earthly, not of material things, but mental and spiritual—and *why!* And by keeping a record of self—not as a diary, but thy purposes, what you have thought, what you have desired, the good that you have done—we will find this will bring physical and mental reactions that will be in keeping with the purposes for which each soul enters a material manifestation. (830-3)

Every incarnation is an opportunity; so is really good karma, whether we are having difficulty in learning our lesson or not. We are attracted to the environment which gives the needed lesson.

We find that there were those environs in which the attraction gave the opportunity for the entity to bring creative influences and forces in the experience, *to meet self:* and thus correct much that had been and is in the way of development for the soul-entity.

For each soul enters that it may make its path straight. They alone who walk the straight and narrow way may know themselves to be themselves, and yet one with the Creative Forces. Hence the purpose for each entrance is that the opportunities may be embraced by the entity for living, being, that which is creative and in keeping with the Way. For the Father has not willed that any soul should perish and is thus mindful that each soul has again—and yet again—the opportunity for making its paths straight. (2021-1)

What thou seest, that thou be'st
Dust, if thou seest dust
God, if thou seest God.

STUMBLING BLOCKS AND

STEPPING-STONES

And those influences in the emotions—unless they are governed by an ideal—may often become a stumbling-stone. (1599-1)

The emotions come from sojourns in the earth. The innate influences come from sojourns in the environs about the earth—the interims between earth incarnations. (1523-4)

While it is true we do have karmic urges from the past and for the future, we should remember that our many attitudes and emotions are our real karma. If we really loved our fellow man and were selfless, we would turn our karma into grace and mercy.

The stumbling block *always* lies in self-aggrandizement of power and ability stored in one's own self, in the misuse of self in relation one to another. (137-118)

For each soul seeks expression. And as it moves through the mental associations and attributes in the surrounding environs, it gives out that which becomes either for selfish reactions of the own ego—to express—or for the I AM to be at-one with the Great I AM THAT I AM. (987-4)

This woman was warned very definitely about misuse of emotions.

The entity may play upon the emotions of others or it may use them for stepping-stones or stumbling blocks. It may use opportunities to raise others to the point of anxiety or to the point where they would spend their souls for the entity, using them either as buildings or as serpents or scorpions in its emotions. It may love very deeply, either for the universal consciousness or for gratifying only of self or the physical emotions.

Again the entity may express each of the emotions in

their counterpart—as patience, long-suffering, brotherly love, kindness, gentleness. It can also look on and hate like the dickens! It can look on and smile and love to the extent of being willing to give all for the cause or purpose.

These are abilities latent and manifested in this entity. Use them, not abuse them. For the powers as of friends, the powers as of love, the powers as of patience, the powers as of the spirits that be are at thy beck and call. Use them, don't abuse them. Use them to the glory of thy ideal, and let that ideal be set in that way of the Cross.

As has been indicated well by others, indicate in thine own life in this experience—for you've shown all phases of it in others: Let others do as they may, but as for me, I will serve the living God. And I am determined to know nothing among men save Jesus the Christ and him crucified, that I might know the Father.

In mercy, in justice, in love, then, deal thy abilities to thy associates and thy fellow man. (3637-1)

Our will is the key to freedom. We must choose to do right and then exert our wills in that direction.

For *will* is that developing factor with which an entity chooses or builds that freedom, or that of being free, knowing the truth as is applicable in the experience, and in the various experiences as has been builded; for that builded must be met, whether in thought or in deed; for thoughts are deeds, and their current run is through the whole of the influence in an *entity's* experience. Hence, as was given, "He that hateth his brother has committed as great a sin as he that slayeth a man," for the deed is as of an accomplishment in the mental being, which is the builder for every entity. (243-10)

For each soul enters the material plane for the fulfilling of a purpose; that it, the soul, may be one with the Creative Forces. And when such purpose is allowed to be overridden because of the application for material gains, or for self-indulgence, or self-glorification, or for self-exaltation—then stumbling blocks are in the experience. (1849-2)

28

Fear, perhaps the most devastating of all emotions, often stems from past experiences which are buried deep in our subconscious. Some of these fears seem foolish and inexplicable in the present, yet had a very real reason in the past.

This person's fear of knives and cutting instruments was explained.

In this same place where the entity spent the days [in Persia, at the time of Croesus] was where the life was taken by the invading forces from the south and east. Hence, in the present, the aversion to cutting instruments, for in that manner the destruction came. (288-1)

We naturally cling to life; so any instrument which caused one to lose life would make a deep impression of fear, which would be difficult to overcome.

The fear may be rather indefinite, as this person's fear of impending danger.

In the one [life] before this in that of Poseidia, and in that Atlantean rule this entity then was in the household of the peasant that gave the information regarding the upheaval in the mountains that brought the destruction to the land.

As to the personalities as exhibited from the individualities of this entity:

In the first, that of the fear of impending danger. These are innate conditions.

In the second, in the rule of those who would be the master of the entity; that ability to do so.

In the next, the gift of those elements through which the entity should develop itself at present.

In the next, the love of the beautiful, yet unreserved of self, so long as those whom the entity cares for receive the best.

Then, from these, gain this understanding:

Keep in the way that the development of the soul may be such as not necessary for the return; unless the entity so desires! Then it may bring to itself those conditions in

29

its own mental forces through which the soul gains its development. (4353-4)

Here we see not only a fear which originated many lifetimes ago but also other personality traits which developed in later lives. We are the result or the sum total of all our experiences. We gain or lose in every earth life, acquiring some attitudes in one life and other attitudes in later lives, as this entity did. Moreover, we do not lose these urges, attitudes, or emotions; we have to overcome them.

This next woman's fear originated in her previous life, so was probably more definite, since it was not thousands of years old.

In the one before this, we find in those days when the first settlers came into this land. The entity was then among those who gave in the development of those lands, and came among those first settlers, in the name Sara Golden, and the entity saw all of the children of the entity taken and scourged in the fires, and the entity lived in dread through the remaining days of the entity's sojourn in the earth's plane, *gaining* in the sojourn until that wrath brought on by lack of the confidence in the Divine to protect the entity and those of her children. This, as we see, brings this dread in the life to the entity for the bearing of children, and of the consequences in same; being then a direct influence in the present existence, and made that as has brought destructive forces in the entity's sojourn. (4286-3)

All of us might have such karmic fears as these; for this woman suffered persecution from invaders.

We find in the times when the change in the rule in the forces under that of Alexander The Great was overrunning that portion of Persia that this entity was then in that country and suffered under the persecutions of the invaders. In that time, we find the name as that of Hannah, and in the household of the defender of one of the cities taken by the invaders. As to the personality as exhibited in the present sphere, we find one ever in dread of an invasion of any character, whether in physical or in mental forces. (4562-2)

This following question indicates a very vague or repressed fear.

Q. Why do I feel depressed and lonely at nightfall?
A. This is the common lot of man—these come as parts of the emotions. Very few find that period of the gloaming as the period of expectancy. Many others find it as the period in which they are being left alone. For as ye were oft—as have been many—left at eventide. (1523-32)

Nearly every individual has some innate fear. Actually, fear is a very basic emotion, for many attitudes and emotions, such as nervousness and lack of confidence, are subconsciously rooted in it. What we call anxiety is really a form of fear. This person asked how to overcome such a deep-seated fear.

Q. Career as a pianist was brought to an end through my extreme nervousness and lack of confidence, and other talents have suffered because of an overpowering fear. What am I to do?
A. No doubt overpowering fear. Right about face! Know it is within thee! Defying this has brought fear, has brought the anxieties. Turn about, and pray a little oftener. Do this oftener. Do this several weeks, yes—let a whole moon pass, or a period of a moon—28 days—and never fail to pray at two o'clock in the morning. Rise and pray—facing east! Ye will be surprised at how much peace and harmony will come into thy soul. This doesn't mean being goody-goody—it means being good for something, but let it be creative and not that which will eventually turn and rend thee. . . .
First find self and the relationships to the Creative Forces. Add to thyself brotherly love, patience, long-suffering, gentleness, kindness, and these will bring within thy experience a varied concept from that being applied in the present.
Better right-about-face while it is time, else the glory of the Lord may pass thee by. (3509-1)

31

If this entity, in this particular sojourn, would make advancements, materially, mentally, spiritually, it must first apply in self that which will wholly cast out fear: fear of others, fear of influences, fear of what may come to pass. For if the entity comes to that consciousness which is a part of the universal consciousness, that ye abide—in body, mind, and purpose—as one with the Creative Forces, you are at peace with the world and have nothing to fear. For God will not allow any soul to be tempted beyond that it is able to bear—if the soul puts its whole trust in the Creative Forces manifested in the Christ-Consciousness. (5030-1)

For being afraid is the first consciousness of sin's entering in, for he that is made afraid has lost consciousness of self's own heritage with the Son; for we are heirs through Him to that Kingdom that is beyond all of that that would make afraid, or that would cause a doubt in the heart of any. Through the recesses of the heart, then, search out that that would make afraid, casting out fear, and *He* alone may guide. (243-10)

Case 3162 is an unusual one of a four-year-old child's repeated hysteria due to nightmares. It also answers another question often asked as to how soon an entity may return. This child's terror was very real to it; for it had returned very soon after its previous life.

Here we have a quick return—from fear to fear through fear. And these bring, with those experiences of the entity, that which will require special influences to be put into the experiences of this mind; that it may be kept away from fear, away from loud noises, darkness, the scream of sirens, the shouts of individuals of fear to the entity.

For the entity was only just coming to that awareness of the beauty of association, of friendships, of the beautiful outdoors, nature, flowers, birds, and of God's manifestations to man of the beauty, of the oneness of purpose with individual activities in nature itself; and then the tramping of feet, the shouts of arms, brought destructive forces.

The entity then was only a year to two years older

than in the present experience, that finds the world such a turmoil for the entity in its dreams, its visions, its experiences, in those periods when the body-mind is active again to those fears about it.

The entity then, in the name Theresa Schwalendal, was on the coasts of Lorraine. The entity only passed out and then in less than nine months again entered a material world.

Be patient. Do not scold. Do not speak harshly. Do not fret nor condemn the body-mind. But do tell it daily of the love that Jesus had for little children, of peace and harmony; never those stories of the witch, never those of fearfulness of any great punishment; but love, patience.

This do, and we will find a great, a wonderful soul that has come again to bless many. (3162-1)

A book could be written on this one problem of fear. Books have been written about it, for psychologists recognize it as our innermost problem. Guilt, inferiority feelings, and hate (which is really love in reverse) all stem from fear. We hate what we fear or feel guilty about. Of course we are thinking of self when we indulge in such emotions. So it is no wonder that the readings said our greatest fault is self.

Another reading gave directions for overcoming fear.

Fear is the root of most of the ills of mankind, whether of self, or of what others think of self, or what self will appear to others. To overcome fear is to fill the mental, spiritual being with that which wholly casts out fear; that is as the love that is manifest in the world through Him who gave Himself the ransom for many. Such love, such faith, such understanding, casts out fear. Be ye not fearful; for that thou sowest, that thou must reap. Be more mindful of that sown! (5459-3)

A woman's rebellious nature was explained by her previous life. She apparently came to the United States seeking religious freedom.

[She] was then among those that came into the land during or just following the period known as the

33

Revolution, when those peoples from the native land of the entity in the present found in the new land a place for the establishing of those tenets, in both religious and in carrying out the truths and activities of the peoples; then in the name Kucio. In this experience the entity gained and lost. Coming into a new land with high hopes in the tender years of experience brought much material hardships, but satisfactions in the material and mental developments for the entity and those about the entity. The entity lost in the rebellions against those that would make for such tyrannical activities in the relationships of the home and the church, and the entity rebelling brought for self-discontent in the manner in which self acted in relationships to others, building up much that became not only contention but the lack of abilities to consider the activities of others as those necessary forces for the experiencing in the affairs of their individual lives that necessary for the unfoldment to the expressions of, or manifestations of, the concepts of the entities (other than self) as related to moral and spiritual relationships. In the latter portion of the experience the entity again sought, through those of the spiritual forces, that which made for the easier and greater contentment in the experience. In the present we find from those influences much that makes for those conditions that arise within self's experience, as of rebellion in relationships to those that should be in the same position which the entity occupied in the one then; and there is seen much of what is meted by that entity meted in that experience. When comparisons are drawn, as the entity did in the latter portion of that experience, the entity finds in the present that trusting in self only brings disappointments; for those that are in the position of measuring others or self, by self, become unwise, unstable. Those that measure by those forces that are innate from within, as to relationships of *Creative* Forces, are in nearer accord with that of being led by Him. (2118-1)

A reading given for a baby girl two days old (case 314) shows us possible stumbling blocks in other emotions and attitudes which were brought in with her. It also shows us karma from the Roman period.

34

In the one before this we find that the entity was in that period when there were those persecutions in that land known as the Roman, when those peoples were being persecuted for their beliefs in the spiritual lessons that were being given during those periods.

The entity then was among those of the household, or of the courtiers or *cour des aides,* of the rulers in that land; yet never wholly losing sight of the innate purposes in the experience of those that suffered physically through the activities of the rulers.

Then, though often rebuked by associates during the period, the entity led rather the life of one who courted favor and who asked for many of those experiences to be changed or altered, yet throughout the experience kept self *above* those even of its surroundings and never submitted self to those indulgences as did many of the associates through the period.

Gaining then, and losing only when the associations in the marriage were *forced* upon the entity—and the entity lost faith in those who brought about these conditions. And the entity, *rebelling* in same, brought destructive forces to her own being, through the manner of leaving the earth in that experience.

In the present, then, there may be seen in the developing years those periods of sullenness, yet of cheerfulness to carry one's own point.

In the latter portion of the present experience, these influences will make for cheerfulness, as well as the abilities to succor, aid, comfort, and bring cheer to the experience of man. (314-1)

The parents of this baby were given another warning and suggestion for training this baby.

One, then, who will be found to be innately tended (and developing) toward headstrongness; great mental abilities, and will be able—and will have those tendencies when speaking—to argue anything down in another individual; a tendency for the obtaining and retaining of all that comes in the experience of the entity. Not that selfishness will prevail, but this must of necessity be one of those things that the training and environ must be warned concerning; that this does not become a fault for the entity, Lilith Ann. . . . (314-1)

Another interesting item in this reading was the fact that Edgar Cayce named this baby. The suggested name bore a striking resemblance to a name the entity bore in a previous life, which was Ann Lilith Bewton. In a still earlier life she was named Lillila.

Case 470 was told that he had gained much during a life in ancient Egypt while he was "the armor-bearer to the king of that land, acting then in the capacity of the defender of that ruler. In that development the entity gained much, by keeping his own mouth shut and listening to others. In the present personality we find this exhibited in the entity's abilities to be a good listener."

His attitude toward the opposite sex was traced back to a still earlier life in what is now Peru.

Only failing in taking unto self too many of the opposite sex of the land, bringing then the enmity of many of the peoples in the later days. In the present we find this urge to keep and steer clear of intrigues of such nature that brings the difficulties in such relations, yet these conditions ever presenting themselves to the entity. One condition to combat. (470-2)

A little different attitude toward the opposite sex was that of a woman, 3241. This attitude came from a life in England.

Before that the entity was in the English land, during those periods when groups were selected to act in the capacity of defenders of an ideal or purpose in that called the Holy War, or the Crusades.

These brought fears to the entity respecting its associations with the opposite sex. Hence as indicated, there has come an awakening to the entity of this phase of the experience, and that it may be abused or used as the fulfilling of purposes in the experience.

The name then was Anne Stuart. The entity was the reformer when those of its own household had gone to the activities in the Holy Land. Yet the fear of men still exists in the experience, because of those activities there. (3241-1)

Another case which goes back to Bible times, "when the children of Promise passed through the lands that they were forbidden to pass through, save with permission," shows how attitudes develop toward us from our acts.

For the entity was among the descendants of Esau. Thus one that looked to the products of the field, and the abilities to use the mountainside in the interest of those things pertaining to mining, herding; though then as a leader.

The name was Jared. The entity took advantage of a group. Hence expect a group to take advantage of thee! For what ye measure, it must be, it will be measured to thee. For ye must pay every whit that ye measure to others. And this applies in the future as well as in the past. Do you wonder that your life is such a mess!

From same in the present, then, ye will find things pertaining to spirituality, a search for truth, coming nigh unto thee, even as then. Do not disregard same in the present. Lay hold on same. Seek Him while He may be found. (3063-1)

As a result of persecutions in two incarnations, 2671 now has great sympathy and love for the persecuted and a desire to help them. He was told:

There are many urges seen in the entity's present experience from the past experiences, or that builded within the spiritual entity from which the material acts when the body is acting from within.

In the one before this we find the entity among those who first settled in the country now known as Connecticut, and the entity among those who came as to escape the religious persecution in the northern portion of the country in which the peoples resided. The body gained in part and lost in part. In the attempt to give succor, aid, and help to those in the new country, the entity gained. In attempting to give those in the country to which it returned, the entity lost, in attempting to force the issue, and lost the life in the attempt to aid those for whom the entity came for aid. Then in the name John Peters. In the urge as is seen from this—that of ever being mindful of those who would express the desire to worship from the dictates of their own conscience. This is in the present entity almost as a fault.

In the one before this we find in that period when persecutions were in the Roman land. The entity among those who were of the persecuted peoples, and—though not afraid for self—went to the lands to supply foods for those who would give their lives for the peoples to whom they offered relief through their teaching. Hence there is seen in the urges the love of the land and of the fruits of the soil, especially that as supplies food for the man body, and the love of those who are persecuted, and the desire to help same, without reward or without heralding that such is being done. In the name Ewoid. (2671-4)

Perhaps this present attitude toward persecution, with its intensity, stemmed from a still earlier life because of a guilt feeling which he was trying to submerge. Other urges, or attitudes toward others, began in a life with the Medes and the Persians.

In the one before this we find in that land where the peoples were in constant rebellion against the rule, now known as the Persian. The entity then in that capacity as the (or what would be termed in the present day) banker of Media, and the entity in that period, for the entity not only served the ruler, and in this service brought to self much of the satisfaction as is found in same; and in excavations yet to be made there will be found that those stores, those records caused to be made by Artiel, will be found in the land of the Medes and Persians. In the urges as is seen from this—the ability to know the usage of individual endeavor of those outside, and a judge of human nature as manifested in individual lives.

In the one before this we find the contrariwise experience of the entity, in the land now known as the Indian country. The entity then among those who would persecute those that came down from the hill country for the fruits of the valleys. The entity being the leader, then, of the raiders that would take not only the spoils, but the bodies, and put in servitude those that fell into the hands of Abioduol, and the entity lost through this experience, through that of persecuting the fellow man, and in the urge as is seen—there riles from within as of something awakened that needs to be submerged, as almost a hatred for one who would persecute another, and often the entity finds self boiling, as it were, to seek not only the personal vengeance, but to submit or subdue such conditions. (2671-4)

As we trace this man's earth lives back through the centuries, we see how attitudes and urges develop until the entity becomes concerned and dedicated to serving others. Actually this entity appears to have come far in his evolution, for he "felt the desire to do good" and is "one that gives self to the aid of those in every walk of life. Especially does the entity ever favor the 'underdog.' " This loving consideration for others was a great part of his life. His urge to give and even his attitude toward persecution began in early Egyptian times.

In the one before this we find the entity in that period that was the changing of the conditions in the histories of the religious and the philosophical, or the war between the priest and the king, in the land known as the Egyptian. In this second rule, or in this rule wherein these conditions occurred, we find the entity then among those that were in defense of the priest who was banished, and with those of the bodyguard to that priest and taking on the cause of the exile, and among those who labored with hands to give to the strength of the followers of those in exile. Gaining in this period, yet much of that as was seen in the following was of the persecution. In the urges as seen—the abilities to give—give—in an unstinted way—to those deserving. (2671-4)

Tolerance and belief in religious freedom began in 137's first earth experience and grew further during a life in Palestine when he was associated with the Master Jesus.

. . . in the days when the Master came into the Promised Land. This entity one that followed close in the ways of the teachings as set by Him. In the personage of the brother in the flesh, Jude.

In the one before this, we find in that of the one calling the chosen people from the Assyrian lands to the building again of the walls of the Holy City, and this entity in that of the armor-bearer for Ezekiel.

In that before this, we find in the days when the Sons of God came together to reason in the elements as to the appearance of Man in physical on earth's plane, and this entity was among those chosen as the messenger to all the realm. The personalities as exhibited in the present plane from these:

In the first, that of the leniency toward all laws concerning every mode of worship to Jehovah, and of the respect to every entity's own belief. (137-4)

Resentments and rebellion are frequently of karmic origin.

Is karma the reason for present-day youth's rebellious attitude? Perhaps many of them lost their lives in recent wars, therefore are resentful of authority and war.

This woman's rebellion in a previous life is causing her trouble in her present life. We find her:

. . . during that period when there were being led a people from a land that had been as the land of bondage, for the periods of development. The entity was then among the children of the Levites, and those that later became the daughters of Gershon; the entity being then in the name Mecliah. The entity joined in with those that served in the aiding to keep the records for those peoples, as they built up their relationships with that service in the temple, or the activities about the tabernacle of the Congregation, that represented the temple later. The entity gained and lost through this experience; gained in the service that was rendered, rebelling when—with the entering in of the peoples into

40

the Promised Land, and the divisions came—there were those temptations and those rebellions against those divisions that arose for this particular branch of those that waited on the peoples. The entity then brought for self, condemnation in self, which in the present oft makes for those periods when self doubts self, as to being sufficiently strong in mental aptitudes to meet the moral and the material conditions that weigh upon self in relationships to its own ideals. Here we find also those influences arising in the experience of the entity, making for the adaptability of self as to those of any nation, clime, or tongue, and a linguist, when so desires to use same for the relationships that may be built in any of the directions for self's understanding. (2118-1)

A complete study and analysis of the Edgar Cayce readings would no doubt reveal every attitude, emotion, or urge to be karmic in some instances. In this brief space we cannot give a complete analysis. These cases have been chosen to show how things experienced in one life become a part of the personality and are carried from life to life.

Nothing has more lives than an unforgiven sin or an error we refuse to correct.

Our stumbling blocks are apt to be the urges which have become a part of our personality.

For while the body changes, for it—too—must be purified, the *soul* remains ever as one. For it is in the image of the Creator and has its birthright in Him. And if this birthright is sold for the satisfying of those urges of earthly desires, they become stumbling blocks in the experience and thus the entity finds itself constantly in each and every environ meeting itself, either mentally, materially, physically, in the environs and in the experiences which are a portion of each and every soul.

Hence we find those influences arising in the present experience. For ever is a soul, an entity, meeting itself; in its shortcomings, in that wherein it has missed or chosen in the improper direction.

For remember, the good lives on—and ON—and is

magnified. The errors become then as stumbling-stones, as to be kept or to be turned into stepping-stones—into those directions and ways as to be the more perfect way—or as expressed, "a more excellent way." (1243-1)

PHYSICAL KARMA

Though the mills of the God grind slowly, yet they grind exceedingly small; though with patience He stands waiting, with exactness grinds He all.
—FREIDRICH VON LOGAN, *Retribution*

Man's undoing, then, is within himself, by gratifying the desires and weaknesses of the flesh. (254-18)

Edgar Cayce told many seekers, in their physical readings, that their physical defect or disease (dis-ease) was a karmic condition. These readings emphasized the fact that our physical condition is directly dependent upon our mental and spiritual ideals, with their concomitant emotions, from one life to another. We do take it with us! Moreover, our daily stresses and strains, our emotional upsets, affect us physically.

Many were told they would not be well, nor would their physical condition improve, until both their mental and spiritual attitudes changed. They would have to give up such negative things as fears, hates, and resentments and become more in attunement with Creative Forces.

To be sure the attitudes oft influence the physical conditions of the body. No one can hate his neighbor and not have stomach or liver trouble. One cannot be jealous and allow anger of same and not have upset digestion or heart disorder. (4021-1)

This dependency was explained thus:

For there have arisen the acute conditions not only from physical reactions but mental conditions that have been as resentments, which have been built into mental forces of the body. These are indicated in the reacting with the physical effects upon organ centers . . . now finding reflexes in various portions of the body. (1523-9)

This body is meeting its own self. For it is meeting its own shortcomings, when judged from some moral standards.

This body, then, must first in its mental and spiritual attitude make amends, not merely promises to others but to self and the sources of health and of life itself.

These should be the beginnings and the body not merely being dependent upon the applications which must be, or may be, made by others; for there are within self the conditions here taken which now bring undesirable results in the ability of the body to function in the manner either physically or mentally as is most desirable.

But there would be first a change in mental and spiritual attitude. . . . (5283-1)

Of course, physical applications help healing and do alleviate the condition, but true healing comes from the mental and spiritual self.

And there must be taken into consideration all phases of this entity's experience in the present if the conditions would be wholly understood.

For mind is the builder, and—if there will be kept a balance—the physical mind AND the spiritual mind should cooperate, coordinate.

There are those forces which the entity, then (not merely the body but the entity—body, mind, soul), is meeting in itself, CALLED—by itself oft—karmic reactions.

But karma—

Well, these are the conditions as we find them in this body:

The body, the mind, the soul are one within the physical forces; for the body is indeed the temple of the living God. In each entity there is that portion which is a part of the Universal Force, and is that which lives on. All must co-ordinate and cooperate. (1593-1)

One individual who was losing the power of voluntary movement was told, definitely, that his condition was karmic:

For here we have an individual entity meeting its own self—the conditions in regard to the movements of the body, the locomotories, the nerve endings, the muscular forces. What ye demanded of others ye must pay yourself! Every soul should remember not to demand of others more than ye are willing to give, for ye will pay—and, as most, through thy gills! (3485-1)

Such an origin or cause of the disease is of course difficult or impossible to prove. But it is harder to ignore it today as we learn more about psychosomatics and mental hygiene. Should we reject it? 3501 was told:

Sources of these are prenatal conditions, as well as karmic. These sources of course may be rejected by many. Yet those who reject this do not supply better reason, do they? (3504-1)

We have to search our inner selves for the real source of our dis-ease or physical health, for these are a reflection of our spiritual self. The Edgar Cayce physical readings often suggested that spiritual help was more needed than physical application for healing.

Actually, health is the result of both past and present life, as in this case:

Q. Is the ill health which I have been experiencing the past years the result of mistakes of a past life or is it due to something amiss in this present life?
A. Both. For there is the law of the material, there is the law of the mental, there is the law of the spiritual. That which brought into materiality is *first* conceived in spirit. Hence, as we have indicated, all illness is sin, not necessarily of the moment, as man counts time, but as part of the whole experience. For God has not purposed or willed that any soul should perish, but purgeth everyone by illness, by prosperity, by hardships, by those things needed, in order to meet self—but in Him, by faith and works, are ye made every whit whole. (3395-2)

One of the most interesting cases of a physical condition which was attributed to a previous life was that of an eleven-year-old boy who suffered from enuresis (bedwetting).

Before this, then, the entity was in the land of the present nativity, but during the early periods when there were those disturbances wrought by the activity of the minister of a church—as of one Marshall Whittaker.

The entity then was the minister, or the associate minister, who caused the uprising and the condemnation of children who saw, who heard, who experienced the voices of those in the inter-between.

And because of the entity's condemning there was brought a hardship into the experience of the entity, especially the adopting of that rule of "ducking" others.

Hence the entity physically has experienced the ducking, from its own self, in its daily activities—which will grow to become more and more of a hindrance to self, UNLESS there will be set aright that incoordination between the mental mind, or the physical mind and the spiritual mind of the individual entity, as related to condemnation of things in others. (2779-1)

Here it seems the error was condemning others.

Fortunately, this case had a happy ending, for the advice was given that a suggestion should be made to the boy as he went to sleep. The suggestion, "You are good and kind. You are going to make many people happy. You are going to help everyone with whom you come in contact. . . . You are good and kind . . ." was given to the boy by his mother as he dropped off to sleep. True, this suggestion had to be given for many nights, but it was effective. Not only did the boy no longer wet the bed, but his disposition also became kinder and sweeter.

Note that the healing was not directed to the physical body but to the spiritual and mental. Thus a healing took place.

Contrast this boy's situation and the solution of the problem with this case, which was reported in a letter to a well-known news counselor:

Dear————:*

Please help me. I am an 11-year-old boy who is the unhappiest person in the whole world. I do something that is terrible and I just can't stop no matter how hard I try. I wet the bed. I have tried starving myself and going without water for days at a time but it doesn't help.

My mother took me to a doctor last year and the doctor said it was not serious and that I would outgrow it and not to worry. Ever since my mother knows I don't have a sickness she has been trying to disgrace me out of the habit by telling everybody that her 11-year-old baby boy still wets the bed. She even told my friends and now they all know why I never sleep at their houses.

Please tell me what I can do about this awful thing. I promise to follow your advice no matter what it is.

UNHAPPIEST BOY

Dear Boy:

It's too bad that the doctor didn't go a little further when he explained to your mother that your bed-wetting was not caused by a physical sickness. He should have told your mother that many adolescents wet the bed right up through the teen years because they are insecure and unhappy.

I suggest that your mother take you to a doctor who can help you work out your emotional problems. Ask your school counselor or your favorite teacher to recommend two or three such doctors so your mother can take her choice.

This unhappy boy was given wise counsel as an answer to his letter. We do not know whether his family cooperated or whether he overcame his difficulty. We can only wish that he, too, could have had the loving help the first boy received thirty years ago because of a Cayce reading. Obviously the second boy was also meeting self in

---

* Virginia *Pilot*, Norfolk, Va., August 27, 1966, "Ann Landers Says."

some way. Certainly he was suffering enough to be willing to resolve his problem if he could only learn its source.

Epilepsy

Epilepsy is a disease which seems to be of karmic origin. There are twenty-three cases of epilepsy in the ARE files which the readings stated were definitely due to karma. Probably the other cases are also karmic in nature, but that fact was not given in the readings.

Not only may the condition be karma for the afflicted one; several of the readings said this was also karma for the parents. Actually, the statement was made in some instances that the sins of the father were being visited upon the child. Since we tend to keep family associations throughout the ages, even to being our own ancestor, this disease provides food for thought.

These readings on epilepsy were naturally physical readings, so very little information concerning the former earth experiences which had produced the present karma was given. A few cases had life readings also, so we glean a little more information from them. The source of the trouble was almost invariably overindulgence and misuse of the Creative Forces or the sexual function.

Case 543 was told:

The entity, were it able—will it arouse within self that which will be able to subdue the passion of those influences which have become inherent from the indiscretions of the youth of the parents of the entity—there will be brought the full knowledge and understanding that the truth *in* Him makes one free indeed, and though the law says that "I will visit the afflictions of the fathers upon the children to the third and fourth generation," so also is that healing and Balm in Gilead as comes through the gift of the Son into the world, that "though thy sins be as scarlet they shall be white like wool." (543-11)

In 693 we have another case of karma from the Salem period. The physical affliction, however, is quite different from that of the boy who suffered from enuresis, for both the causes and the symptoms differ. Moreover, in this case it is karma for the parents, as well as for the boy.

Yet oft, as we find here, individuals again and again are drawn together that there may be the meeting in the experience of each that which will make them aware of wherein they, as individuals (individual entity and soul), have erred respecting experiences in materiality of soul life even. For the soul lives on, and unless that which has been the trouble, the barrier, the dissenting influence in the experience is met in self's relationships to Creative Forces, it must gradually make for deteriorating experiences in the expression of such a spirit influence in matter—or materiality.

In this entity we find it coming under the influence of those things rather in the earth, that have made for that which in the flesh and in the mental forces makes for those expressions of conditions that must not only be met *by* self but in those who *have* been and are responsible for the entering of the soul into the experience. O that men (or man) would become cognizant of the necessity of preparations within themselves for being the channels for giving a soul the opportunity for expressions in the earth, or in matter! *This* soul, or this *body*, was not wanted; yet as it came with those surrounding environs, those attitudes and those wishes and those desires that made for the entrance, we have that which must be met. As we find, if those things are adhered to in a conscientious manner that we have indicated, much of that may be eradicated by the time there are those periods when the alterations or changes come in the activative influences within the body itself [adolescence]. If it is allowed to become a portion of the developing manhood and the expression of same into materiality, less and less will there be the opportunity for the eradicating of same entirely from the system. . . .

As to the expression of the entity in the earth, we find:

Before this it was in those environs in the land now known as Salem, and the experience about Providence Town when there were the expressions and activities that made for the suppression of individuals in meeting

51

those experiences that came as the expressions of spiritual manifestations in the experiences of others.

The entity was not only among those that made for the belittling of such but induced the material activity in the suppression, in the expression; and not only took advantage of those who were being oppressed but used some in such a manner as to gratify, satisfy, the passions of the body in associations with same. These made for the expressions that have brought in the experience of the entity in the present that which makes for the more often the attempt of expression of self during that sojourn, or during that experience; and almost a possession takes place within the body when there are those touchings upon those things when the *mind* of the body attempts to rest, such that others creep close to the border; making for those manifestations that bring into the experience the uncontrollableness within its own self. Yet much of that which may make for the corrections in same lies within those abilities of those that are responsible for its physical entrance in the present. (693-3)

A very severe case and a very sad one was 693. At first the boy seemed to improve, but later the condition returned in full severity. The treatment emphasized the need for prayer and spiritual attunement. The mother's description of the case was such that one wonders how it would be possible to reach the soul self.

This boy did not respond as one would hope and apparently was not cured or even helped permanently. There were, though, cases of karmic epilepsy which were reported cured. At least, there had been several years and no recurrence of the seizures. The treatment given in most cases was fairly simple but took a lot of time and had to be continued over a long period. It is possible that the tediousness caused some to neglect or not follow the prescribed treatment conscientiously. However, where the condition was karmic (no matter what the illness), the readings indicated that little help would be found unless there was spiritual growth and a change in attitudes.

Alcoholism frequently seems to be a karmic condition, though the Edgar Cayce readings gave no case where the condition was traced to any dramatic experience or incident. Rather, it was due to overindulgence in a previous life or lives. Several were warned of such overindulgence and told to beware of strong drink or alcohol in any form. Parents were sometimes warned to beware for their offspring.

A reading given for an eight-year-old boy warned that the influence from a Roman life could become a stumbling-stone "unless there are those constructive forces of those influences that are creative and manifestedly so."

> BEWARE, EVER, of two influences in the life from that experience—in this sojourn: Nicotine in any form, and alcohol in its hard forms. These will become stumbling experiences if there are indulgences in those directions such that they become habitual in the inclinations of the influences that arise not only as appetites but as the emotions or sensory forces of the body; for these will be easily influenced by such. (1417-1)

The previous experiences which give alcoholic tendencies are what we might call psychological karma, but these influences, if given in to, result in a physical condition. Case 1417 had emotional problems or attitudes which came from a still earlier life in Atlantis.

Another warning against strong drink was given in a reading for a girl fourteen years old. Not only did the reading warn her parents; it warned the young lady of future associations. It said:

> Here we find very unusual abilities and also some very unusual warnings to be given for such a lovely person.
> There will be these as warnings, these for those responsible for the entity: a tendency for the body to overeat or to be overindulgent in appetites. Be warned

for self, as well as associates of those who take wine or strong drink, for this may easily become a stumbling block to the entity.

Before this we find the entity was in the land during those reconstructions following the period called the American Revolution. Here we find the entity interested in building a home with the beautiful grounds about same.

In the name then Lila Chapman, the entity gained through the period, for the home to the entity and its family, and its children was that which took the greater portion of its time save the study of the Word which was given place in that home; and yet there came from same those who took too much of the cup as cheers. This brought disturbances, sorrows. Don't let it occur again. There will be the tendencies for attraction, not only for self, but for those about you. For that ye hate has come upon thee. Don't hate anything in the present. (5359-1)

A report from the mother confirmed this girl's tendency for overindulgence in food. Moreover, the reading was truly prophetic as to associations. She married a few years later into what her mother called a "drinky" family but said the husband was sensible, considering his upbringing. So it seems not only what we fear but what we hate may come upon us. Our attitudes and emotions thus bring certain experiences to us. Case 1106 appears to have become alcoholic due to his mental attitudes. These naturally result in a physical condition such as is described here:

As we find, while there are physical disturbances with this body, these arise as much from the mental attitudes—that were in the beginning taken as poses, and have grown to become rather conditions that are of the *self;* or as habits, as requirements, that have taken on those aspects from the *mental* standpoint that are almost—or at times, and under or in certain environments, become—*possessions!*

For in its final analysis, in the physical and mental activities of a body, it—the body—*mentally*—is continually meeting itself and that it (the body, mentally)

54

has done about *constructive* or creative forces within the body itself.

Then, as we find, to meet the needs of the conditions in this body, it must—or will—require that which will enable the body to either *become* determined within itself to *meet* its own self in *spiritual* reaction, or such a change of environment that will require the mental and physical reactions of the body to be such as to *enable* it (the body, mentally and physically) to *induce* that within the physical reactions to take possession in the place of, or to replace, those habit-forming conditions in the mental, as to rid the body of these conditions. (1106-1)

A second reading gave further insight as to how the appetite develops and weakens the will to the point that one is literally possessed by such.

Now as we find, all the circumstances and conditions that disturb the body—both from the physical and mental angle—should be taken into consideration; if there will be in the experience the help, the aid that is desirable.

We find that the appetites—or the habits AND appetites that have been created by the activities of the body—are of the nature of BOTH the physical and mental attitudes towards conditions and circumstances.

Through resentments from little things that have been said, the body has allowed itself to build that appetite which in destroying the will of the entity—through the activities of drink upon the system—has produced a weakness that will require a great deal of mental determination; that must be based upon the spiritual self from within. And there must be the application also of material things which will aid in creating a balance to the assimilating system—the liver, the spleen, the pancreas, the kidneys; so that the great desires from associations do not again OVERCOME the will-influence of the body.

These necessarily must be choices, or there must be a choice made by the mental body itself. First, that it would of its own accord submit to the treatments under such directions as may be had in the institution—such an one as in Nashville—for inebriates.

And with the submitting to the treatments the applications, the weights [waits?], the tests—if the body will then keep away from the associations that have caused much of the activities, and engage itself mentally and physically IN those activities that are the more constructive in their natures—then we may find not only material employment but an activity in the mental and physical life that will bring contentment and peace and harmony; and a life of a useful service to others.

And with prayer—determining in self, the aid and cooperation of those near and dear to the body in the mental and material ways—we may bring the better conditions for this body [1106].

Q. Is a cure within myself or is the treatment in an institution necessary?

A. To be sure, unless there is the determination within self to rid self of the appetites and desires builded in the will forces of the system, that have been to such extent as to produce physical reactions, then the cure may not be accomplished even in an institution—without the will in self of this to be so. But as we find, as we have indicated, the institutional treatments are necessary—with the determination within self. And it will be easier, more desirable for the body to go through the institutional treatments.

Do that, then: relying upon those things that have been pointed out: that the basis of all spiritual awakening, the promises of the better and closer associations with the Divine are within self. (1106-2)

Another case which gives further understanding as to how an appetite can develop to one's undoing is case 1439. His reading says that the physical disturbances, which "appear to be minor, are deep-seated and come from pressures between the coordinating of the sensory forces and the activities of the deeper organs."

Thus we have periods when there are greater disturbances that find their reaction in gratifying of appetites.

Thus we have the effect of that the body would do in reasoning becomes that the body does not really DESIRE to do in the physical, but the pressures are of such a nature that we have not a mental aberration or a mental disturbance, though the effects are in the physical that same character of reaction.

Thus we have the conditions such that there becomes the gratifying of appetites in the bodily system, or desires.

And we find the body then, rather than as planning for that which is destructive in the mental abilities and mental attitude of the body, becomes so overwrought by physical desires as to necessitate the gratifying of physical appetites.

Not a possession, save when there begins the gratifying of same; THEN there are the opportunities for those influences from without to possess the activities of the body in not only the cunningness of the activities but in that which to the BODY, under the influence, becomes as reasonableness to the influences and activities of that possession.

Q. Have my former activities been such as to make for development as looked on from the soul forces?

A. These have been rather a tendency toward retardments in some directions, developments in others.

The BODY, physically or soully, is not held for that which has become as appetites. Then to CONDEMN self, in the activity toward others, is to BUILD that which is destructive.

But with the attuning of the body physically and mentally, and CONSTRUCTIVE thoughts, putting that BEHIND that has made for those influences wherein the body became easily influenced, we will find constructive forces becoming more and more predominant in the physical activities.

Q. Is there any hereditary influence that has caused this moral letdown?

A. This is rather as that of possession through weaknesses created by appetites and physical conditions in the body. (1439-1)

It isn't the intention, it isn't the inclination of the body to give way to such influences! It is rather the INCREASING of the appetties by the directions of same through the physical body! (1439-2)

Now, to build that resistance required to bring normalcy for this body: And *we* find that this may build this resistance in nerve forces, that will aid in the nerve impulses in the ganglia that are so disordered here, as to reproduce nerve ends in the system and the *repulsion* by the strengthening of these will bring normalcy for this body. (606-1)

Gold chloride and bromide of soda were recommended.

Alcohol won't work with gold! This is the gold treatment, but it builds the resistance!
Massage and massage activity will be helpful; as well as keeping in the open all the time.
Do this, and we will bring normalcy for this body.

Q. In alcoholic cases, can a general outline of treatment be given?
A. No. Each individual has its own individual problems. Not all are *physical*. Hence there are those that are of the sympathetic nature, or where there has been the possession by the very activity of same; but gold will destroy desire in any of them! (606-1)

Alcoholism: Treatment

The ARE files contain several cases of alcoholism in which there is no definite indication that the condition is karmic. The condition, though physical, often seemed to develop as in case 1106. Furthermore, alcohol often appeared to aggravate another physical condition which had not been attributed to alcohol.
Case 391 asked:

What general rules and precautions should I take to keep in a healthy condition?

A. As has been indicated. Do not DRINK, but EAT PROPERLY! Do not ABUSE the body—either mentally OR physically, but MOST of all by alcohol; and especially hops or the products of same, or even the carbonated waters are harmful for THIS body—and, of course, the STRONG drinks are more harmful!

For, too much of anything as of hops or alcohol reaction with same—with the very nature of the disturbance—produces in the liver, in the kidneys, the disturbances that DESTROY the effect of that plasm in the blood which aids in the eliminations of used energies; and produces toxic forces in the body. (391-18)

Though the diagnosis was alcoholism, the physical symptoms or condition were usually different in each case, so the treatment recommended was not the same. Formulas were given which would discourage the use of alcohol, as it would produce nausea. Physical therapy and electrical treatments were also recommended to help the individual. A caution, though, was given that electricity and alcohol together produced an adverse effect. The readings emphasized the fact that the treatments to be effective depended upon the individual; he had to want to overcome the habit and must exert his own will, which had been weakened by alcohol.

Prayer to help strengthen was also frequently advised.

Q. Can those assisting do anything to prevent the body from indulging in stimulants?
A. They can pray like the devil!

And this is not a blasphemous statement, as it may appear—to some. For if there is any busier body, with those influences that have to do with the spirit of indulgence of any nature, than that ye call satan or the devil, who is it?

Then it behooves those who have the interest of such a body at heart to not only pray for him but WITH him; and in just as earnest, just as sincere, just as continuous a manner as the spirit of ANY indulgence works upon those who have become subject to such influences either through physical, mental or material conditions!

For the POWER of prayer is NOT met even by satan or the devil himself.

Hence with that attitude of being as persistent as the desire for indulgence, or as persistent as the devil, ye will find ye will bring a strength. But if ye do so doubting, ye are already half lost.

For the DESIRES of the body are to do RIGHT! Then aid those desires in the right direction; for the power of right EXCEEDS—ever and always.

Do that then.

Like the devil himself—PRAY!

Q. Is it believed that there is any inclination in the body here to cooperate and correct these conditions?

A. As just given, it is NOT the real DESIRE of the body to commit self to the inclination. There IS the desire, then, to cooperate.

Hence there has been given the way to overcome —through the PHYSICAL manner, the MENTAL manner, and the ATTITUDES.

Then let the body cooperate by putting behind self those things that easily beset. And look—LOOK—to the strength and the power of the Christ-Consciousness—the light WITHIN; and be able to say NO! and mean it! (1439-2)*

496 was another case where prayer was strongly recommended.

And, if the mental and spiritual forces are acted upon by those that have an interest in the welfare of the mental and spiritual reactions of this body [496], through the power of intercession by meditation and prayer, to counteract the forces from without that are working with this body, there may be brought an awakening within—in correcting these conditions—and awareness

* Mr. 1439 and his wife were divorced as a result of his alcoholism. Mr. 1439 never returned to his wife, Mrs. 845. We heard years later that he had gotten married to someone else and was doing all right, though we had no details as to whether or not he had conquered the drink habit.

that there is a worthwhile experience for self in the activities of the entity's manifestation of life, and will bring the abilities to be active in directions that would make for a change that will not only be helpful, hopeful, but worthwhile.

Who may make the intercession? They that have within their consciousness a channel to the Throne of Grace, that there may be given into the mind and activities of the soul of this entity those influences that may bring the changes in the experience of this body.

Q. In what manner may his sister [439] help him?
A. By making the stronger intercession in prayer, and in getting or asking others to aid in and with her in same. For where there is that intercession made through the combined efforts of many, the greater may be that directed influence towards the activity of any soul, any mental being. (496-1)

Another very impressive case of physical karma was that of a younger girl of seventeen, who was suffering from a painful hip condition—cancer of the bone. She was told:

During the period in Nero's reign in Rome, in the latter portion of same, the entity was then in the household of Parthesias—and one in whose company many became followers of, adherents to, those called Christians in the period, and during those persecutions in the arena when there were physical combats. The entity was as a spectator of such combats, and under the influence of those who made light of them; though the entity felt in self that there was more to that held by such individuals, as exhibited in the arena, but the entity—to carry that which was held as necessary with the companionship of those about same—laughed at the injury received by one of the girls [301] in the arena, and *suffered* in *mental anguish* when she later—or became cognizant of—the physical suffering brought to the body *of* that individual during the rest of the sojourn. The suffering that was brought was of a *mental* nature, and when music—especially of the lyre, harp, or of the zither—was played, the entity *suffered* most; for the song and the music that was played during that experience brought—as it were—the experience to the entity. Hence in meeting same in the present, there has been builded that which the entity passes through, or "under the rod"—as it were—of that as of being pitied, laughed at, scorned, for the inability of the personal body to partake of those in the material activities, which require the need of all of the physical body; yet in the music, in the acceptance, in the building of those forces through that which laughed at, which scorned—though knowing; now *knowing*, laugh to scorn those who would *doubt* the activities of the forces that build in a material body that activity in every cell, every force, to make a perfect body. (275-19)

Though Partheniasi (her Roman name) later suffered remorse and mental anguish because of her act and the Christian girl's agony, in this life her own hip bone was being gnawed by a disease diagnosed as incurable. The doctors had even suggested amputation to keep the cancer from spreading. She was paying in the same coin she had meted out.

This case had many interesting aspects. For this was a cancer case, pronounced incurable, which was cured. The young lady had a total of forty-five readings. Not all of these were physical readings; some were life readings which gave earlier development and former family relationships.

In her first physical reading the question was asked if her condition could be brought to normal and a perfect cure. The answer was: "Depends entirely upon the response of the body. The awakening of that within the forces of the body itself of the accumulated forces which may be brought by the mental forces applied with those of the material."

In other words, the cure would depend as much on the girl's mental attitude as on the physical applications.

A reading given a little later gave real hope and is in sharp contrast to the prognosis given in readings for some other cancer cases. It said: "Naturally, as given, the response would not be quick, but when once begun *properly*, will be sure and certain."

62

She came to realize that she was meeting herself and asked:

Q. How can I make good karma from this period?
A. As has been given as to what karmic influence is, and what one must do about same. Lose self in the consciousness of the *indwelling* of the Creative Force, in that channel which has been prepared for the escape of the sons *and* daughters of men, through the *Son* of man! This is the escape, and what to be done about it! Lose self; make His will one with *thy* will, or thy will be lost in *His* will, being a *channel* through which He may manifest in the associations of self with the sons and daughters of men! (275-23)

Some other interesting questions were asked in later readings. Why did the entity wait until this incarnation to make good karma from the Roman period?

A. Because it couldn't do it before!
Q. How many other lives have I had in between the ones you have mentioned through this source?
A. (After long pause). In earth's sphere, two. (Pause) *Life* has *continued!* (275-25)

When 275 asked who the martyred Christian girl of Roman times was today, she was told it was one near and dear to her, her brother's wife, her nurse, who was serving her in love and kindness.

One of the suggestions given to 275 was to study the harp. In an earlier life, in Egypt, she had been one of the first to use the harp, or lyre. This music would help her to meet the things she had to overcome and would be an outlet of her higher nature; for she developed spiritually and gained much in the life in Egypt. Some of the spiritual counsel which helped her was in reading 275-19:

Q. Give exact guidance how entity can best make good her karma during this life.
A. As has been outlined, now knowing what is to be met; not with scorn, not with sneers, but with patience, with fortitude, with praise, with the giving of pleasure in

63

music, in kindnesses, in gentle words, in bespeaking of that which may build for a perfect mind, a perfect soul, a perfect body; [by these] may the entity overcome those things that have beset—that not often understood, those things that so easily beset us; making the will the Creator and the Creative Forces. Be used by *them*, and the channel—the cup—will run over with blessings. Those things that easily beset bespeak not of those only that are weaknesses in the flesh; but the weaknesses in the *flesh* are the scars of the soul! And these, only in that of making the will one with His, being washed—as it were—in the blood of the lamb. We are through. (275-19)

This girl had been told in other readings that she had had two earth lives between the Roman one and her present life. She asked:

Q. What ideal from that time [Roman] prompted us to come together now in this present relationship?
A. . . . The ideals as set by those in their union, and each soul finding the channel, the opportunity for the expression in this experience for that needed in its own soul development as related to each of the others in this experience.

Not only what has been called karma, for these—as seen by that given—have to deal with and to do with what individuals have done with their knowledge of their opportunities in the experiences *to* the Creative Forces as manifested by the environ in that experience. It's well for you to analyze that! (275-38)

It may be well for the entity to know that each soul, each entity, each activity must be of the development within self that there may be through the actions in thought, in deed, in fact, those things that make for the continuity of that which may be spoken or acted in the associations with others. So does the impelling influence come into the experience of each soul in its journey through an experience. (275-35)

Today this person is normal and well, leading a very active, useful, and happy life. She achieved this by carefully following the counsel given in her readings. The treatment was effective because of her mental attitude and her effort to attune to Creative Forces.

The cruelty of the arena in Nero's reign evidently produced other similar karma; for according to the Cayce readings several cases of physical defects were incurred in this period.

In 1926 a young man twenty-four years of age asked for a reading saying he was paralyzed from the neck down as the result of a car wreck. He had had three operations but received no help. Apparently some of the difficulty could not be found.

Mr. Cayce gave this young man a physical reading which said:

> Now, the experience of this entity through this present physical plane, as a developing entity through earth's experiences would be more interesting than the physical conditions, for these are of the nature that, while assistance and relief may be brought, there is little to be done to bring the normal forces of the body, save through untiring energy, trouble, patience, and persistence, for in the cervical and the first dorsal we find there was in times back that condition existing in which a portion of the cartilaginous forces between the vertebrae was crushed. Not sufficient to injure the spinal cord direct, save as to cause that to bring about such conditions as to ward off, or prevent, the flow of energy. (33-1)

The treatment recommended was mainly massage and another operation. If the reading were followed exactly, he was told, he would eventually (though in a stooped position) have some locomotion in the body. The reading closed with this:

> Keep the whole mentality in that way as to build the best development, for, as has been seen, many of these conditions are merited through those actions of the mental forces and the spiritual forces of the body. Hence that as given in the first. See, this is Nero. (33-1)

This last sentence was given in an undertone which was hardly audible.

These last words were not included in the original reading sent to the young man. Mr. Cayce corresponded with him for a while, trying to persuade him to go to one of the big hospitals suggested, where portions of the spinal column could be removed, replaced, and rewired, so that eventually, even though the body would be stooped, there could be locomotion.

The young man was, no doubt looking for a miraculous "cure"; for in 1928 he wrote:

> I rec'd a letter telling me you have your hospital fixed ready . . . if you say you can cure me, I will give you $1,000, and if you don't you won't get anything. Isn't that fair? (33-1)

In 1940 a form letter came back to the ARE marked "DECEASED."

For eighteen years he was completely helpless and entirely dependent upon charitable Christians for his care. This experience probably enabled him to meet and overcome much of the karma from his reign as Nero. A report from 900-295, page 6, apparently referring to Mr. 33, said:

> We haven't been able to do any good, from the physical viewpoint, yet the information as was supplied to that man, illiterate as he may be considered by others, has been able to awaken in him something of a spiritual understanding, and though he—that entity—that subconscious self of his becomes aware of the destructive forces meted out to him through destruction he wrought on mankind at another period of his existence in the earth plane . . . he now finds himself face to face with himself, and with that he has created. . . . (900-295)

Thus we see the misery that can result from a life of destructive thought, emotion, and action.

Another case of physical karma was found in a woman fifty-three years of age, who had been a companion of

Nero. She had suffered from a serious back deformity since childhood, had always had a struggle even to live. At the age of four she had mangled a hand and lost part of one finger. Her life reading told her:

This entity was among those with that one who persecuted the church so thoroughly and fiddled while Rome burned. That's the reason this entity in body has been disfigured by structural conditions. Yet may this entity be set apart. For through its experiences in the earth, it has advanced from a low degree to that which may not even necessitate a reincarnation in the earth. Not that it has reached perfection but there are realms for instruction if the entity will hold to that ideal of those whom it once scoffed at because of the pleasure materially brought in associations with those who did the persecuting. (5366-1)

The next paragraph explained this entity's spiritual growth:

Thus may little or nothing be given that would deter the entity in any manner from holding fast to that purpose which has become that to which it may hold. For, as Joshua of old, the entity has determined, "Others may do as they may, but as for me, I will serve the living God!" (5366-1)

Another accident victim, a young man of seventeen, who had been a paraplegic for two years, was told that his condition was also karmic and had had its beginnings in the arena at the time of Nero. The accident had severed his spinal cord at the fifth vertebra.

His life reading advised him that he was to learn patience in this life. He had gained spiritually in his last life, which was during the American Revolution.

In the present there is that characteristic of orderliness, of cheeriness; and there are the abilities to make the best of bad situations, the abilities to use that in hand.

And would that every soul would learn that lesson,

even as well as this entity has gained in the present!

Before that we find the sojourn that is the more outstanding, as to the influences in the present.

It was during those periods when there were the persecutions of those who followed in the way of the teachings of the Nazarene.

The entity then was a Roman soldier, and one given rather to that of self-indulgence—and gloried rather in seeing the suffering of those who held to that principle.

And the entity fought in the arena and watched many that had met the entity fight again with the beasts and with those elements that made for the closer association with the elementals in the sojourn.

The entity saw suffering, and the entity made light of same.

Hence the entity sees suffering in self in the present, and must again make light of same—but for a different purpose, for a different desire, for a different cause.

For again the entity meets self in that wished, that desired on the part of those against whom the entity held grudges. (1215-4)

Not all karma from the Roman period, however, was what we might call bad karma.

We find in that period in the Roman rule when there were persecutions for the individuals who acclaimed the faith of the Nazarene. The entity then among those who were in power to administer the punishments meted out, and became a believer through the faith as shown by those persecuted. Then in the name Eldoirn, and in the employ of the persecutor Nero. In this experience the entity gained through that of the ability to change the mind, and to act as the change would indicate in the physical and mental experiences of the body, *developing* high in this experience; and in the present there may be seen that of one determined and one set; one not loathful [reluctant] in activity or in mind, but one that should be trained rather to play as well as labor physically. . . . One that may gain the inner knowledge of spiritual effects in the material plane and make physical application of same. (759-1)

A cursory study of the Edgar Cayce readings does not reveal a basic pattern or exact relationship between error and physical defect. Yet the aptness of the defect seems to reveal some sort of retributive justice. The emphasis in the readings is always on the mental and spiritual attitude of the error (sin), not on the act itself. The real problem was always a soul problem.

A similar case of this type of justice was that of a man who was suffering from congenital cataracts. His reading traced his eye condition back to a life in ancient Persia.

Before that we find the entity was in the Arabian or Persian land, as now known, in the "city in the hills and the plains."

There we find the entity came as a dweller from among the Persian peoples; given to what would be termed activities of a barbaric nature in its early experience. For the entity brought persecution to those of other tribes or other beliefs, by the blinding with hot irons.

Such activities the entity forsook in those experiences when there was the awareness of the activities of the teacher in the "city in the hills"—that teacher who gave those interpretations to the peoples as pertaining to that as would bring greater hope to those disappointed or discouraged, either in body or in mind.

And the entity became the leader in the musical instruments that were a part of the healing through those periods.

Hence, as indicated, those fields of activity in the present in which the entity may be the musician—especially of stringed instruments, or an individual applying the higher vibrations in electrical applications for healing, or the combinations of these—would be the fields of service in which the entity may find the greater contentment, and an outlet for the emotions, the longings within, as may be experienced by the entity in the present sojourn.

The name then was Ab-del-uha. (1861-2)

Here again we have music with its high vibrations recommended as an aid to healing. This man had blinded others, so in this present life he was blind.

By following the directions given in his Cayce readings, this entity regained partial vision and became an accomplished musician and teacher of music.

The illnesses which Edgar Cayce attributed to karma had a very wide range. For nearly every type of human illness can be found in the ARE files, and many were told the condition was the result of karma. Though the error was in the past, it was not always the same error which had produced, or resulted in, the identical disease. For example, a doctor who studied fifty-nine cases of arthritis found at least seven different things (causes) which had produced arthritis.

Such sins as hate, resentment, fear, or gluttony, over-indulgences, misuse of Creative Forces, or taking advantage in any way of others are bound to have a karmic effect.

These quotes from the readings show the relation of health to the emotions and what may result in the physical body.

Anger: Madness is certainly poison to the system. This should be a warning for every human. (2-14)

Hate: Do not belittle, do not hate. For hate *creates*, as does love—and brings turmoils and strifes. (1537-1)

And let not thine condemnation bring upon thee that ye hate. For that ye hate ye become. This is the law. (1261-1)

Hate brings that which is irritating, especially to those who are creative in other directions. (1727-2)

Self-Condemnation: In the mental forces, we find self-condemnation. The mental forces of the body must of its own accord lay aside those condemnations and be awakened to the elements within self of the divine. (5226-1)

Hives: Less animosities—holding grudges or thoughts which make the entity speak unkindly of others—these destructive attitudes bring on pent-up feeling and reflect or find expression in irritations. (5226-1)

Animosity: The attitudes, then, should be such that there is NO animosity, NO feeling of resentments—but a forgiving, loving expression towards ALL about the body—in EVERY form and manner (1196-12)

Ulcers: Be constructive mentally . . . don't build poisons as fast as you eliminate them. (348-19)

Prostatitis: Here we find hate, animosity, anxiety may be the poison that causes much of the disturbance. Live more in keeping with that which thou has professed. Did He justify Himself before His accusers? Did He attempt to even meet the words that were spoken condemning Him? (1196-11)

Arthritis: All illness comes from sin. This everyone must take whether they like it or not: whether body, mind or soul. For who healeth all thy diseases? Uncle John, or God the Father? (3174-1)

Case 1709, a young girl nineteen years old, was suffering both physically and mentally from a serious skin disorder. She had had this condition, diagnosed as acne, since she was twelve or thirteen years old. Though she had had various types of treatment and medication, she had received no help whatsoever. In fact, the condition seemed to grow worse instead of better. This plight had its origin, according to her reading, in a previous life in France when she was incarnated as a man. We would like a little more specific information, but it was apparently due to overindulgence during this French incarnation.

As we have indicated oft for others, we would again indicate for this entity; count it rather as an opportunity, a gift of a merciful Father, that there ARE the opportunities in the present for the sojourn in the material influences; that the advantages may be taken of opportunities that come into the experiences, even through the hardships and disappointments that have arisen.

Q. Is there a karmic reason for my present skin disturbance [acne] of the face? If so, what is it?
A. RATHER is it that of a glandular condition as combined with a karmic condition from the experiences in the periods of the reconstruction in France. (1709-3)

In a later reading she got some further information from this question:

Q. Do emotional disturbances affect the skin on my face?
A. To be sure, emotional disturbances affect the CIRCULATION: causing the flushes which leave drosses, and naturally affect the superficial circulation. (1709-5)

This imbalance was difficult to overcome, but the young lady did receive help, and her condition gradually improved.

It is interesting to note that another case of acne (5092) was also attritubed to overindulgence in a French period. Unfortunately, we do not have a follow-up report on this case. But the difficulty was definitely karmic.

This woman, 5092, was told:

Yes, we have the body and those conditions which are a part of the consciousness, aware and unaware, with the body-physical.

In giving the interpretation of the physical disturbances, many phases of this entity's experience should be taken into consideration. That there are physical disorders, and have been for some time, is self-evident. The sources of these are not so self-evident. For these are karmic conditions, and the entity is only meeting its own self. (5092-1)

She was given some encouragement, however, in the last paragraph.

Let that mind be in thee as was in Him, who is the way and the truth and the light, and we will make the light of love so shine through thy countenance that few, if any, will ever see the scars made by self-indulgence in other experiences. (5092-1)

Cancer

The writer found four cases of sarcoma (cancer) which were due to karma (there may be more) in the ARE files. Life readings on these entities would no doubt be of help to us in studying causes, but we have to content ourselves with the statements which refer to karmic consequences. Case 3387 was told:

Conditions here indicate sarcoma—that is a part of the karma of this body. These may be aided, but as to correcting entirely—the suggested applications will only be helpful for the conditions.

Q. What is the origin of these cancerous tumors?
A. Karma. We do something to start this and then we meet it in the circulation. (3387-1)

This gives us very little information. Readings for some other cases of cancer did not say they were of a karmic nature. The next case throws a little more light on karmic cancer. It evidently was a case of the way the condition manifested in the physical. Obviously this man was born with his condition, and it steadily worsened. For 3121 was born with a tumor on his left leg. This was removed by an operation. He then had ringworm in the tissue; and later moles, which were indicative of cancer, began to appear. There was an enlarged gland in the groin, which was treated with X-ray and radium. At thirty-nine the man was in a very serious condition of advanced cancer.

This disturbance is of a nature that by some would be called karmic. Hence it is something the body PHYSICALLY, mentally, must meet, in its spiritual attitude first; that is, as the body may dedicate its life and its abilities to a definite service, to the Creative Forces, or God, there will be healing forces brought to the body.

This requires, then, that the mental attitude be such as

to not only proclaim or announce a belief in the divine, and to promise to dedicate self to same, but the entity must CONSISTENTLY live such. And the test, the proof of same, is long-suffering. This does not mean suffering of self and not grumbling about it. Rather, though you be persecuted, unkindly spoken of, taken advantage of by others, you do not attempt to fight back or to do spiteful things; that you not only be passive in your relationships with others but active, being kindly, affectionate one to the other; remembering, as He has said, "Inasmuch as ye do it unto the least, ye do it unto me." As oft as you contribute, then, to the welfare of those less fortunate, visit the fatherless and the widows in their affliction, visit those imprisoned—rightly or wrongly—you do it to your Maker. For TRUTH shall indeed make you free, even though you be bound in the chains of those things that have brought errors, or the result of errors, in your own experience.

This, then, is the first spiritual approach—or the attitude with which the entity would seek to administer that which is helpful, that which will be met in nature.

For, as so oft has been indicated, each entity, each soul manifesting in the earth, is the result of what the entity has been, in its use of its opportunities, in its relationship to God the Father.

In the beginning let us consider that there is the body, the mind, the soul. The soul is spirit; the mind is as gas that may have its high or low pressure, and the body of its own; but the physical is of the earth—earthy. However, the body was made, was first created, of everything that was in the earth. Hence there are those influences that will meet these tendencies in the blood supply toward that called sarcoma in its nature.

This is a form, of course, of infectious disturbance of such natures as to fasten upon a body for its own destructive forces, and cells breaking have joined—as it were—one force against another. At times the destructive forces are in excess, and thus the injured portions of the body become more and more beset with these growths in the body, and they sap the vitality.

The organs, as organs, are very good. The body-mind is good; the tempering of same is within itself capable of being used towards being a helpful influence to someone, somewhere, sometime. And the time is ever now, when the opportunity presents itself. (3121-1)

The treatment was then given, but it was followed with this admonition:

Most of all, pray. Let the mental attitude be considered first and foremost. Do not promise thyself, nor thy God, nor thy neighbor, that you do not fulfill. (3121-1)

Case 3313-1 was not promised a cure but was given more encouragement that she could be helped.

Yes. As we find, conditions are such that there may be a staying of the disturbances, but these activities are of the consuming nature.

If there is the desire, there may be used the influences that we might suggest—though these will not heal or remove causes. For, as has been indicated oft, causes may be karma. Karma is cause oft of hereditary conditions so-called. Then indeed does the soul inherit that it has builded in its experience with its fellow man in material relationships.

The conditions here may be best retarded by the use at times, about once a week, of a magnet. . . .

Q. What is the cause of my condition and what treatment is recommended?
A. The basic cause is karmic. (3313-1)

Others—Parents

Sometimes the lesson to be learned included others, the persons responsible for the afflicted one. It could have been an error of neglect or something they (the parents) had inflicted on the entity. Several cases of helpless children indicated the parents, too, had a lesson to learn. Here is such a case, a boy eight years old.

As we find, there are disturbing conditions. The sources or beginnings of these are karmic. There were those disturbances at and just after birth which have produced plastic conditions in extremities.

As we find, there needs to be just the corrections which are being made, through the massage, through the treatments that will aid in breaking up gradually the lesions or the plastic conditions in muscles, in tendons, in joints, and sufficient of the massage that there is the ability of the systems to eliminate same. The karmic conditions are needed for the entity, or soul development of the entity, and those who have the responsibility of same, in that source from which all healing comes. For whether it be medicinal, mechanical, or what sources, healing can only come from the Divine. For as has been indicated, "Who healeth all thy diseases?" He in whom we live and move and have our being.

Thus we may through those administrations of that which is the spirit of truth made manifest, turn this karma, or law, to grace and mercy. For the pattern hath been given those who seek to know His face. (52091)

Treatment was directed, and then:

Keep the prayer; hope for, believe. For according to thy faith be it unto thee. (5209-1)

Another case where the parents, too, had a lesson to learn was that of a three-year-old boy, who had been spastic since birth. He also had a chronic ear infection and periodic fever but was blessed with a bright mind and winning manner.

As we find, there are such disturbances that are hard to cope with. These are conditions which are part of the karmic experience of the entity. . . . As to the administrations, with the care, patience that may be given, there may be brought help. This would require a great deal of care, yet this should not be given to someone else other than those responsible for this body's manifestation in the world of physical consciousness;

else those so responsible will lose their lesson to be gained.

Q. What conditions other than karmic caused this condition?
A. This is a prenatal condition. . . .
Q. How long will it take to effect a cure?
A. Not a cure is promised, unless there is the full trust in the source of healing, of health, of life itself. (5151-1)

A case of progressive muscular dystrophy in a nine-year-old boy was quite similar. Here is what his reading said:

Yes, we find the mother praying. We have those conditions which disturb the body.

In the present, while these are preventing the abilities of the body to walk, save that of pushing self through rolling chair, the worry is more with those responsible for the body than with the body itself. This is a condition of progressive disturbance, more of atrophy of the nerves which control the muscular forces of the body.

Here, as we would find, while the body is meeting itself, those responsible for the body had better be praying much more for themselves to be in attunement and to meet the conditions (not one, but both). (5078-1)

Treatment with massage, electricity, and diet was advised. Then the question was asked:

Q. What was the cause of this condition?
A. It's meeting its own self. This you won't accept or think, but pray about it and see the difference. This is karma for both the parents and the body. (5078-1)

Another type of karmic defect, which was also karma for the parents, was the deafness of a fifteen-year-old girl, who had been an invalid from birth. Her physical reading tells us a great deal, but a life reading would very probably have given more detailed information of what had occurred in the past to produce this result in her physical body.

We have the body [552]. As we find, much better information might be given for this body from the purposes for which this body, this soul, entered in this environ and in this experience. For, while there may be palliatives given, as for bringing normalcy to this body in this experience we find that no permanent relief—or little, at least—may be attained until there is a change in the purposes, the desires of the soul in its expression through the physical manifestations. A lesson indeed may be gained from those things that have brought about the physical experiences in this time!

While there is a course to be pursued from the material angles, much greater indeed is the attitude of those about the body; and with the approach they as individuals make as to the conditions and the purposes that they meet the requirements necessary for the care, the attention—yea, at times the very condition that impels them to minister to the needs of this soul at this time.

There has been a wasting away of not only structural forces but the inability of coordinations through the activities of the organs and the body-physical to perform those functions necessary to make for resuscitation of vital forces. And oft has been the wonderment by those that have ministered as to how that life in its manifestations continues to function through such as the conditions that exist here.

Little other than this care, than this attention, may be given. It is apparent that there may be given palliatives and aids in directions to keep the activities of the physical and mental body in its preparations for soul's development, most, through the experience. (552-1)

Here massage and use of the wet-cell battery were recommended. Then:

Q. What caused this physical condition?
A. Prenatal. Or, as has been indicated, that the soul must meet.
Q. Any further advice for those in charge of the body?
A. In that which has been indicated there is seen that there must ever be that prayerful attitude that at all times in

the ministering, in the care, there may be done that which will not only make for an attitude of helpful hopefulness for the body, for the mental attributes, for the physical forces, but that there may be gained patience, kindness, brotherly love, endurance, and—most of all—consistency in the attitude in the activities of those about the body.

During the periods when massage is being given, let *this* be as the prayer:

WE THANK THEE FOR THE OPPORTUNITY, O LORD, THAT WE MAY IN SOME MEASURE MEET THOSE THINGS THOU HAST GIVEN FOR THY CHILDREN IN THIS MATERIAL WORLD. LET THE POWER OF THE CHRIST SPIRIT, THROUGH THOSE PROMISES GIVEN, BE MADE MANIFEST IN MY LIFE AS I MINISTER NOW—AND IN THE LIFE OF THIS BODY [552] BE DONE THAT, O GOD, AS THOU SEEST IS BEST AT THIS TIME. (552-1)

Another reading given later for this child not only adds some further information as to her tragic physical condition but also gives us insight as to what may be accomplished.

Q. How may we gain entrance or understanding to this body when she cannot talk with us?
A. So often it is the lack of comprehension or understanding of individuals! Because the dog doesn't talk, people think he doesn't understand. Because those things in a different vibration are not normal to much that is reacting, it is felt there is not a response.

The *vibrations* that are to be set up by the application of the low electrical vibration will create more and more the ability for the *suggestive* forces to reach to the nerves of consciousness in the body itself, see?

As has been given, it will be long, it will be tedious but, as has been given, this is a duty from those to whom the body has come. If it is held by those who must minister as a cross, it will remain as one. If it is held as that which must be met, that they and the body itself may enjoy in material associations the pleasures of the activity of the spiritual forces, *well*.

The same with individuals where there is in their experience crosses to bear, hardships or surroundings that to them are overpowering, overwhelming, by slights, slurs, and fancies of the inactivity of a coordinating force. If these are held continually as crosses, or as things to be overcome, then they will remain as crosses. But if they are to be met with the spirit of truth and right in their own selves, they should create *joy;* for that is what will be built.

For, the Father of light has never failed man who has cried in earnestness unto Him. It is when individuals have desired their own way that the *souls* have suffered in the sons of men.

Follow those suggestions as we have given for this body.

Begin either with the battery activity and then the suggestions, or forget it! (552-2)

Obviously these parents were being told to get about learning their lesson.

A young man who was afflicted with multiple sclerosis was probably in a similar situation, as his reading said:

We have here an entity meeting its own self. The more gentle, the kinder others may be to this body, the greater help may come to the soul-entity to learn patience, to learn tolerance in physical for coordination of the mind or mental with the physical.

Deterioration is too far advanced for individual help other than may be administered to the body for its soul development. There may be only a few years, but don't make them harder, do be gentle. These will make the time longer, but do be patient, do show brotherly love. As ye would have kindness shown, show the kindness and gentleness. For this is the work of the Lord. (5268-1)

It is evident that the ones caring for this entity also had a lesson of patience, kindness, and brotherly love to learn. Even accidents may have karmic origins. A physical reading given for a young girl of seventeen was such a case. This girl had been thrown from a horse four years before, incurring a spinal cord injury. The doctors said she would never walk again, but the parents had not given up hope and asked Edgar Cayce for a reading. They were given some hope, but:

There are rather serious disturbances here. Portions of these, if the body will accept it, are karmic. Here we have a lovely body and yet hindered through an unseeming accident, brought to the inability of activity; incapacitating the body, as to prevent normal activities, by the crushing of the segments here in the lumbar and sacral areas, as well as producing a dislocation in the eighth dorsal.

As we find, this can be helped if there will be the use of the radioactive appliance for an hour each day. . . . (5191-1)

Massage was also recommended, then:

Do this, and use this period, when the appliance is attached each day, as the period for prayer and meditation; in the entity's own words, changed only to meet the awakenings as come to the entity, as this:

FATHER, GOD! IN THY MERCY AND LOVE BE THOU CLOSE TO ME DAY BY DAY, THAT IN MY WEAKNESS AND THROUGH MY STRENGTH I MAY BE A CHANNEL OF BLESSING TO SOMEONE! GIVE THOU, GOD, THAT STRENGTH —PHYSICAL, MENTAL AND SPIRITUAL—THOU SEEST I HAVE NEED OF AND MAY MY PRAYER EVER BE, "THY WILL, O GOD, BE DONE IN AND THROUGH ME EACH DAY." (5191-1)

Another accident case was also apparently karmic.

Q. Why this accident and for what purpose?
A. That there might be those influences in the experience that become as lessons. For those whom the Lord loveth He chasteneth and purgeth, every one. (1424-1)

We may think we are living a very exemplary life and not committing any sins, at least, no serious sins. Yet, as the Bible says, there are sins of omission as well as commission. The prayer group asked:

Q. Please explain why the Master in many cases forgave sins in healing individuals.
A. Sins are of commission and omission. Sins of commission were forgiven, while sins of omission were called to mind—even by the Master. (281-2)

One person's physical condition was apparently a sin of omission, for this entity, 843, was told he had lived when the Master walked in the earth and in this life was meeting self. He asked:

Q. Why have I been limited to a weak physical body in this appearance; what lesson will I gain by overcoming it?
A. As ye saw from whence health and strength and a perfect body came and needed little—it is that ye may know ye live and move and have your being in Him who IS strength, who is health, who is life. (843-9)

Sometimes the sin of omission is failing to help others. If the physical condition of 2319 is any indication, this sin of omission is the greater sin. Probably the entity pays in proportion to the error.

Number 2319 was a child who was both physically and mentally incapacitated.

Here we find a physical expression of wantonness and selfishness [in the past] manifested, in the present in the lack of the mental, spiritual and physical expression save through constant care upon the part of others.

WELL might many questions come to the mother, the parents, as to why and how this must be a part of their experience in this material sojourn.

Well that each remember, it is LAW; and that only in Him—who hath fulfilled the law, replacing it with mercy, love, hope and understanding—can such be wholly comprehended or understood.

It is not always the sin of the parents that such be their measure of responsibility, but oft it is as here—rather that the soul-consciousness of this entity may become aware of what true abiding love leads individuals to do concerning those who are wholly dependent upon others for every care; thus fulfilling, thus completing a full understanding of that law.

So easily is it misinterpreted, so oft passed over as being beautiful but not applicable in the own experience!

But to all here we see same manifested in a material way and manner, namely, "As ye do it unto the least of these, my brethren, ye do it unto me," saith the Lord.

So, with what measure ye mete—in body, in mind, in spirit—the same is measured to thee.

The fulfilling of such in the experience of the parents, of the entity itself, makes same null and void in the experience as sin. For the Lord loveth those who repent. For there is the more joy over the one that returns than the ninety and nine just that never strayed away.

So, it was for—it is through, it is by such love that has been manifested and is being manifested in experience of this entity, that he entered this particular environ.

As was manifested in the experience of Him, though He were without sin, He offered His body, His blood, His life, that we through Him might have the access to the Father of light, of love, of hope, of mercy.

Thus we find here an entity who in the appearances and experiences before this knew of—yea, in many of those sojourns was well acquainted with—those who did kindnesses, those who patiently and lovingly did minister to the need of those who were without hope, who were disturbed in body and in mind as to which way to turn and as to what course to pursue. Yet the entity turned away from same, that there might be the joys of the material nature, the enjoying of appetites in self for a season.

Yet here we find the entity is overtaken, and that what the entity has sown he is reaping.

These conditions, then, bring opportunities for those

who minister, those who care for such, to meet their own selves—in joy or in duty, obligation.

With love did the Father offer His Son. With love, patience and understanding did the Son give what will be the measure of faith of those who minister here to this soul, who is entering into an awakening through that being administered in the present. (2319-1)

Though 2319's sin is spoken of as selfishness, for he thought only of self, his error or sin was really one of omission. That is failure to help others. For he was in a position to really help his fellow man, yet he failed to do so.

The deafness of this entity (3526) was obviously retributive justice for his sin of omission.

The basic reactions here are somewhat of the karmic nature. These can be materially aided by meeting conditions in relationships to others in such manners as to be as the sacrifice, or as the recompense, in such disturbances.

Then, *do not close the ears,* the mind, or the heart again to those who plead for aid, or those whom by word or deed ye may aid in their comprehension of their relationships to Creative Forces.

For in the measures ye mete to others—in worshipfulness or in hate, in consideration or in disregard—ye actually mete thy material activities in relationship to Creative Forces, God. (3526-1)

Again the physical manifestation was preceded by wrong choices which came from the mental-spiritual. When an entity faces the fact that his physical body depends upon his mental and spiritual self, he is on the way to at-one-ment and health.

A rather similar case of deafness was 960. His reading indicated that his deafness was karmic in nature and came from the French Revolutionary period, in which he deafened his ears to the cry of the people. He also was told:

The mental attitude and the mental forces of this body need more attention than the purely physical conditions.

For the correct mental attitude towards self, and the duties that the body—physical and mental—owes and is due others, the physical conditions would near correct themselves. But without the awakening of the mental and physical responsibilities of this entity, those physical conditions which have brought about the weakening of the mental forces—through the strain produced on the nerve system—there will be no need of the correction in the physical, for this would only bring other conditions that would prove as detrimental to the physical being as the conditions which are produced. . . . (960-1)

It is evident that what we do not learn through wisdom, we learn through pain and suffering.

While suffering may bring understanding, causing others to suffer to satisfy one's own self brings reproach. (204-1)

So must there be, so are [there] those influences, those determining factors that have become—into man—as weaknesses of the flesh, ills in the physical being; bringing oft through some great suffering—as [it did] to Him. For though He were the Son, yet learned He obedience through the things which He suffered. (1527-1)

We simply have to face facts; we are responsible for our own health or physical condition. We cannot blame others or God; we must seek causes in our own inner selves.

Physical manifestations in a body are the result of the activity of the mind and the soul upon relationships which exist between individuals, conditions, or circumstances. Choices made by individuals in their relationships bring good or bad. Or there is each day set before us life and death, good and evil—we must choose. The constant thinking, the constant thought of hate, malice, jealousy brings physical conditions as a result in the physical body, as it does in a state or a nation. It is such results that produce warring conditions of nations, disturbances in a body. Change the thoughts and you will change the effect upon the body.

Remember the law—and the law of the Lord is perfect. As the mental, spiritual, and physical laws are kept more in a unison of purpose, a more perfect balance is kept in the whole body. (3246-2)

Karma is, then, that which has been builded in the past as indifference to that known to be right. (254-64)

It isn't a question of what sin, but a question of correcting the body-mind, purposes, and desires, letting sin be eliminated from the ideals and purposes of the body. (4009-1)

When you wonder why you have not been able to overcome certain conditions, remember that oft a thorn is left in the flesh to tempt, yes, to keep one aright. When one acquires the development to meet conditions, or when one raises self to meet all that arises, then self is set free. (281-16)

So it is possible to get off this wheel of return and end earth lives. We, however, continue our evolution in other and higher realms. But we can hope to free ourselves of karma, while here, and live under grace if we love and serve God and our fellow man.

Q. Why was it that [218-P-1-2] has been prevented from carrying out the readings given him through these sources [for his tubercular condition]?

A. That which has been builded must be met every whit, until there is the whole trust in that which makes the law of recompense, or the law of karma, of none effect. It's in him! (281-6)

Know that all the desires of the body have their rightful place in thy experience. They are to be used, not abused. All things given to man as appetites or physical desires are holy unto the Lord, yet they are to be used to the glory of God and not in the direction of selfishness. (3234-1)

Remember, the sources, as we have indicated, are the meeting of one's own self, thus are karmic. These can be met most in Him, who, taking away the law of cause and effect by fulfilling the law, establishes the law of Grace. Thus the need for the entity to lean upon the arm of Him who is the Law, and the Truth, and the Light. (2828-4)

This—find it in self. Know, so long as we feel there is karma, it is cause and effect. But in righteousness we may be justified before the Throne. Thus we may pass from cause and effect, or karma, to that of grace. (3177-1)

MEMORY: OUR GOOD KARMA—

TALENTS, CAREERS, VOCATIONAL

APTITUDES

CHAPTER FOUR

Each man reaps on his own farm.　　—PLAUTUS

Man plants a field of corn. God giveth the increase; the soil produces—but don't forget to plow it and hoe it. (165-B-24)

The foregoing chapters could be interpreted to indicate that there is only retributive or unpleasant karma. 'Tis not so! There are, though, various aspects to our karma. The readings make it clear that all karma is good karma; for ever is there the opportunity of making paths straight.

For one enters not by chance but by choice, that it may learn or meet its own self. And when there are those environs through which such material opportunities may present themselves, such a soul—seeking—finds expression. These become a part of the whole experience of an entity. (2990-2)

Since one aspect of karma is memory and is brought in with the entity, let us consider the skills and abilities which many were told they had brought with them from previous sojourns on the earth plane, having learned or acquired these abilities or vocational urges in previous lives.

Those who are trained in the former experiences in the earth, though they may not have applied the principles in the immediate present, may have the wisdom of the ages at their disposal, if there is the beginning and the application of self in those directions. (903-23)

The sleeping Edgar Cayce gave the following explanation of our memory of previous lives. What else but memory could explain the genius some individuals display from infancy? No doubt new skills quickly acquired are known skills.

In interpreting the application made by the entity in varied appearances, and the influence the same bears upon the abilities, the faults and the virtues of the entity in the present, it may be well for this entity that there be an interpretation of just how such experiences have an influence in the present.

This may be comparable to the experience of an entity as it undertakes its studies, its lessons in school. Not that there is in everyday life the remembering of daily experiences in school, yet these daily experiences create the background with which the entity, in its daily contact with problems, reviews in memory the problems that were part of the experience during such days of what is commonly called education, or unfoldment.

Just so in the daily experience of an individual entity through the various lessons learned, gained or lost in the earthly experiences, it builds a background to which the entity-mind responds as it applies itself in meeting the daily problems which arise.

One may ask, as this entity, WHY, then, does one not recall more often those experiences?

The same may be asked as to why there is not the remembering of the time when two and two to the entity became four, or when C-A-T spelled cat. It always did! You only became aware of this as it became necessary for you to make practical application in your experience!

So with the application of self's experience in material sojourns. When the necessity arises, the awareness as to how, where, and in what direction those opportunities were applied is brought to bear in the entity's relationships to daily problems. (2301-4)

The readings indicate we have some memory of previous experiences, whether they were in the earth or the interims between earth lives. These give us our abilities, and they also dictate our purpose for returning to earth life.

Each soul's entrance into material consciousness should represent to the entity the awareness that a universal consciousness, God, is aware of the entity's purpose, the entity's aims. And this consciousness represents an opportunity for the entity, in the material experience, to become a channel to glorify that purpose, that cause.

In each entity's experience, through various appearances and activities, there have been those awarenesses that fit that particular entity for this or that vocation, such an activity through which there may come the greater material benefit as well as the greater opportunity for mental and spiritual expression.

Each entity, then, has those urges arising either from the earthly sojourns or from those interims between the earthly appearances.

First, analyze self, as to self's ideals, self's principles. For know, the earth and all therein is the Lord's. All thine OWN is lent thee, not thine but LENT thee. Keep it inviolate. Knowing the rules as thou hast, disobey not. (2622-1)

Each soul has a definite job to do. But ye alone may find and do that job. (2823-1)

These quotations *could be construed* to mean an individual would be really suited to and successful in only one vocation or profession. This is not true, however, for several entities were told they could do well in two professions. For example, 853 was told his field should be writing or a datastician (statistician); and 415 was told he should be either a minister or a lawyer, for "in either that he goes into he will act in both capacities! But the greater would be the spiritual ministry, to be sure."

A few individuals were told they could be successful in almost any field or vocation they chose. This versatility, though, can be a problem. For example, 488 was told his abilities "are many, and unless applied in a specific channel or manner will make for rather that characterization of 'good for many things and not quite good for anything,' or the ability to become an 'almost,' or a ne'er-do-well, in a *material* manner; yet if centralized, specialized, with a *broad vision* as is experienced by those Jupiterian influences in the entity's makeup, will make for one of affluence, one who may build to high positions, not only of trust, not only of abilities to do things, but also to do things *well*." (488-5)

Others were told to go into a different type of work or business, and they became successful and happy when they made the change.

One of the first life readings was given for a young attorney, 5, who was seeking advice about his profession. He had apparently chosen the right profession according to his reading, for he had high mental ability and leadership qualities, with the ability to aid and counsel those seeking advice. His ability to counsel had been developed mainly in the life just previous to the present one, which was in this country, and in an earlier one which was in Greece. He was told that he had gained from the influence "in Jupiter, the broadness of vision, with the abilities to control, or be controlled, by others."

Nature has made of the entity a *leader*, yet the entity has allowed self to be rather *dominated* than being the leader as the entity may make of self, by first conquering self, self's own desires—and while not lauding it, or lauding the abilities, or lauding the knowledge, or lauding position, may use all to guide, guard, and direct many in such a way and manner as to *bring* for self that of its birthright, in the ability *to* lead, *to* guide, *to* aid those who *do* seek counsel, do seek advice, do seek that of the knowledge concerning the relationships of individuals with individuals, and individuals with groups.

In Venus is seen the love, and the counsel of others, that often overshadows that of self's own expression, felt as *duty*—rather than as sound counsel, or as proper for self's own development. *This* is that *again* wherein self may use self's abilities to self's undoing.

In that seen in influences in the Uranian brings for periods when there seems to be every condition imaginable awry—whether business relations, social relations, financial conditions—every condition seems to be awry. Again there are seasons of most things come too easy. These are to be met with that of that *builded* in self through the *mental* abilities, and the stableness of purpose which may be builded by self.

This man was a judge in his last earth appearance, which was in this country. He was among the first settlers and of the council which established same, in the name Doane.

The entity then became the judge of the peoples' differences which arose during those periods, and that influence, that ability, to see that which is *necessary* to bring about better relationships between individuals, rather than being a representative of corporations. *This* does not always appeal to the entity, for individuals, as individuals appeal the most. While the conditions which arise in the present experience of the entity make for varying conditions in these relations, yet will the entity ever find that the greatest *abilities,* the greatest satisfaction in the chosen profession, will be in that of *individual* counsel and *individual* advice—and the entity may go far in development of self, for many there be who trust in the abilities of the entity, even as during that experience.

In the appearance before this, he was in the Trojan land and was among those who counseled with Hector and with Achilles's forces, being a mediator *between* those foes of old, and bringing much to bear *on* the various forces which gradually drew the peoples together later in the experiences of that land.

Again the counsel of the entity may be found as records among those who wrote of the period, *called* that only in the minds; yet *real* in its actuality. In the influence felt is that halting between opinions of those that would act as the lording over others, or as the recognized leaders as varying with the abilities of self. Establish self rather as one that may be the leader in fact.

He was an Indian warrior in another life. From this sojourn he gained ability to counsel—especially in relation to do with lands, land grants, and the relationships of people in grants, whether as to groups, individuals, or associations.

His reading said: "Land grants are particularly interesting to the entity, and well to study same."

A still earlier life was in Egypt, where he was a teacher. He taught of the relationships of man to man and what is now called penal law. The codes of law which were established then are today prefaces to the knowledge pertaining to such codes.

The memory of these appearances gives the present ability in law; the ability in judgeship, and the ability to mediate between individuals, and between groups; but the greater ability lies in that of being the *individual* adviser, and for the judging of the rights of the individual according to the *written* law.

Q. Should entity resume the practice of law as partner?

A. (Interruption) Resume the practice of law for self, *separating* self—not as one that would be in the position of being divided, but rather of *finding* the *abilities* of self to meet the needs and to develop self. First find self. Then, when the physical body is in accord with that as will enable the self to establish the self, *do that*.

Q. Should entity resume the practice of law as partner with his father, or in separate office in Greensboro, or should entity practice law in an entirely different place from that in which entity has ever lived?

A. As given, separate self in a *different* office—but *not* in a different surrounding. The entity, in the *establishing* of self, will not be overshadowed—will the entity stand fast *to* that of the *abilities within self!*

Q. Should entity continue to specialize in penal law courtroom law work, which he loves, or try to make more money in other fields of law such as corporation law?

A. As has been given, the individual application appeals most—rather than the corporation. Would the entity desire to make the change, make the change in which he would become known as a giant *combatting* corporations, rather than fighting for them! For the man as a man, as an individual, as a *developing* one, is *individual* first and foremost. (5-2)

Another young man, 2340, was advised to go first into

the Navy and then to study law. An Edgar Cayce reading given for him when he was sixteen years old said that he had exceptional abilities, which were not yet localized.

We find that these may be localized either in water activities or as a lawyer or as a politician; yet most of these will require those periods of the changing scenes as will be the natural activities of the body.

Get most of these, then, out of the system! That is, know that you will pass through those, and go through those periods first.

Then, we would suggest first an active force in the Navy—or that the preparations be made in same for the life work as a lawyer; that is, while in the Navy, study law; and there will be the greater successes in the material as well as the fulfilling of many of those things that will be a part of the experience through such an application of self. (2340-1)

This young man was told that he had had many and quite varied appearances in the earth, which gave him many influences in this life. He had been with Cabot on his expeditions "and was a navigator, a seaman; not merely making voyages of discovery but as to making them a paying proposition, for those interested in the things in which the entity was interested."

These brought many varied experiences to the entity; and as the entity sails the seas, much of that which was the experience then will be a part of the entity's awakening to the needs for the purifying of mind and body for a greater spiritual service.

The interest in things of mystery, stories of the sea, things pertaining to the voyages of those who acted in the capacity of aides or as fences for the pirates; all of these become a part of the entity's vision or longing at times.

In the present we will find those latent urges may be manifested or submerged. Yet as we find, such a period of three to four years in the Navy would be MOST beneficial, most helpful for the entity; but study law when engaged in same! (2340-1)

Before this the entity had been a Roman centurion of no mean order and was stationed in Palestine. During this life he gained attitudes regarding religious tolerance, or the beliefs of various peoples and their effect.

Oft the entity acted as a counselor through the latter part of that sojourn, as there were the changes brought about. (2340-1)

He was a trader or a buyer or an adjudger of the values of the groups or the provisions or the commodities that were traded.

From that experience he developed an interest in things pertaining to the field, the stream, the farm—and also an interest in selling and city life.

Yet we find that waterway as a training rather than as a business would be to the entity the channels through which the greater activity may be brought.

As to the abilities of the entity in the present, that to which it may attain, and how:

First, analyze thyself, thy desires, thy hopes; and KNOW thy ideal—spiritual, mental, material; not as to what you would like to have GIVEN thee, but what ye would desire to attain to. Set thy goal high. Use and apply self in beneficial and in helpful experiences.

Never be a condemner at law, or in law. Rather be as a DEFENDER of that which is just and right; not a corporation lawyer, not a criminal lawyer, but rather one that would give advice and counsel as to how to keep FROM coming into or under the heavier forces of same—but DEFEND ever!

In self's study, self's analysis, keep the faith in thy Creator. Those of nature's laws—as has been indicated, of the sea, of the ocean—will be a teacher to thee.

Then let thy yeas be yea; never in partnership with others, for ye would be too light, too easy with them: but as an individual entity, seeking to fill that place in which ye may make manifest His love in the earth.

Q. In what section of the country will I eventually be able to make the greatest success?

A. In the western portion of the country will be the greater success, when eventually settling down; but make the voyages first.

Q. Through what particular channels should I begin to establish contacts in order to fit myself for the type of work suggested?

A. As outlined, join the Navy three years; but study law.

Q. Are there any particular subjects that I should take in my senior year of high school?

A. Anything pertaining to law and order. (2340-1)

We do not know how closely this young man followed his reading, but in February, 1968, he wrote requesting a copy of his life reading, and his letterhead indicated that he was vice-president and treasurer of Defender Life Insurance Company in North Carolina.

The Edgar Cayce readings revealed several potential geniuses. A reading given for an eleven-month-old baby boy said he had been Franz Lizt in his previous life. He would naturally show great musical ability in this life, and his parents were advised to begin his musical training early. The reading said:

Nickname the entity Franz, for it will be in keeping with the entity and is that it will be inclined to call itself when it begins to lisp or think ... much might be said of the entity's developments through the experiences in the earth and the UNUSUALNESS with which the entity will influence certain conditions in the present land if there is the training and development in those directions that are the natural talents of the entity.

Hence much might be indicated to those responsible for this entity's present entrance in the earth, in keeping the intents of the entity well balanced in the spiritual, material, and mental aspects of its activity.

It will be indicated as a natural tendency or trend for this entity throughout its experience to ingratiate self with others.

In the musical abilities should the entity be trained from the beginning. There is the natural intent and interest toward things of the artistic nature and temperament. There are the abilities to use the voice, as

99

well as the abilities in playing most ANY instrument—if the opportunity is given; especially in the composition, in the natures of composition as well as the playing itself. Symphonies, all forms of musical interludes and the like, should be the training to which the entity would be subjected—that it may be given the greater opportunities. And, as soon as he is capable of such, insist upon beginning with the piano—as a playing, as a means of entertaining. And the natural ear for harmony will soon be indicated in the activities of the entity. (2584-1)

This musical talent was not developed in one life only. Little Franz had done important musical work in two other earlier lives. One was in Palestine, where he helped in setting up the music in the temple; and the other was in ancient Egypt, where he set chants to music.

The entity was in the earth during those periods of the preparation and the accomplishing of the setting up of the music in the temple that was planned by David and completed by Solomon.

The entity was an associate then of both David and Solomon, being among the chief musicians for setting the psalms to the order of preparation for the various instruments upon which there would be the music for services in the temples. And the psalms of David as well as the songs of Solomon were a part of the entity's experience, in their preparation, as well as the psalms and the musical activities in which the entity engaged.

Before that the entity was in the Egyptian land, during those periods when there were those activities in the land to unify a troubled people, as well as those who had become as sojourners or dwellers in the land.

The entity was among the peoples from Atlantis, but was born and brought up in the environs of the Egyptian experience.

And with the establishings of the activities for correlating the ideas and ideals regarding the preparation of bodies for a material channel, for the service of betterment of the kind or class or manner of worship of the peoples, and the establishing of the physical activities in which individuals were engaged—the entity was among those who first set the chants of the various peoples to any form of music. This thus made for that establishing in the Temple of Sacrifice of the chants to which much of the activities were given; as well as, in the latter part of the entity's activity, that establishing of the chants that aided in HEALING—and in bringing the mental attributes of those who had determined to become as channels through which there might be the spiritual expression in the Temple Beautiful.

Thus we find again the music added to the abilities as a healer, the ability as one to direct.

Thus we will find those expressions in VARIED fields pertaining to all of the activities. (2584-1)

Further counsel or advice was given this child's (2584) parents for training little Franz.

As to the abilities, then:

First, to be sure, the developing years have much to do with the choices and the direction the entity may take in giving material expressions of the abilities innate and manifested as the body-mind develops.

Music, as it has been well said, is that expression that spans the distance between the sublime and the ridiculous, that which appeals to the physical, the spiritual, the mental emotions of individuals.

Then, whatever field of direction the entity may take depends much upon whether those emotions are awakened or aroused for the gratifying of material desires, or whether there is the spanning of that realm between the material and the sublime.

These should be kept in that direction, then, in which there may be a completion of that the entity has so oft set in motion in the affairs of men through the experiences or sojourns of the entity in the earth.

Then let those about the entity realize not only their opportunities but their responsibilities, as well as their privileges, in directing one who may play such an important part in the establishing of music in America. (2584-1)

The reading given for 3633, a twelve-year-old boy, labeled him a potential genius. The reading indicated the boy had great obstacles as well as great possibilities. His present difficulties stemmed from his last life, which was in this country, and from a life thousands of years ago in Atlantis, while his musical and artistic talents were developed in other lives.

In giving the interpretations of the records here of this entity, 3633, it would be very easy to interpret same either in a very optimistic or a very pessimistic vein. For there are great possibilities and great obstacles. But know, in either case, the real lesson is within self. For here is the opportunity for an entity (while comparisons are odious, these would be good comparisons) to be either a Beethoven or a Whittier or a Jesse James, or some such entity! For the entity is inclined to think more highly of himself than he ought to think, as would be indicated. That's what these three individuals did, in themselves. As to the application made of it, depends upon the individual self.

Here is an entity who has abilities and faculties latent within self which may be turned into music or poetry or writing in prose, which few would ever excel. Or there may be the desire to have its own way to such an extent that the entity will be in the position to disregard others altogether in every form, just so self has its own way.

In giving the astrological aspects, these are latent and manifested: Mercury, Venus, Jupiter, Saturn, and Mars. These are adverse in some respects one to another, yet are ever present and will be indicated in that in which the body will go to excess in many ways, unless there is the real training in the periods of unfoldment. And the entity is beginning to reach that period when, while the spirit must not be broken, everyone should be very firm and positive with the entity, inducing the entity through reason to analyze self and to form the proper concepts of ideals and purposes, and in doing this, we will not only give to the world a real individual with genius, but make for individual soul development. Otherwise, we will give to the world one of genius in making trouble for somebody. (3633-1)

Later reports on this boy confirmed the accuracy of this prophecy and of the boy's character. The reading continued:

As to the appearances in the earth, these naturally—as indicated from those tendencies—have been quite varied.

Before this the entity was in the land of the present sojourn during the French and Indian Wars.

The entity was among those of the French in the activities about Fort Dearborn; bringing those things into activity to have its own way, irrespective of the trouble or the great distresses to which others were put.

In the end the entity by sheer illness in self gained a great deal. For it may be said of this entity as of the Master, through suffering he learned the more.

The name then was John Angel.

Before that the entity was in the French and the Hun land when there were those disturbances in the establishing of the activities in what is now known as France.

Then the entity with certain groups made forays into the Hun land, and yet eventually escaped to the areas about the southern and western portion of Italy.

The entity then was in those activities in which the artist or the musician came into greater play, the ability to write verse and make music to it.

The abilities in the present as an orchestra leader or a writer of song or verse may be a part of the entity's experience, provided it doesn't have the "big head" or think more highly of himself than he ought; but having ideals and principles, having purposes and coordinating them, knowing that every other individual has as much right in the earth as you have yourself, even though he may not be in some respects as far advanced in his learning. For, remember, knowledge—or the seeking for the tree of knowledge—is the sin. It is the use of what you do know to the glory of God that is righteousness. God is not the respecter of persons because of one's

103

good looks nor of one's abilities. He respects the individual because of his purposes, his aims, his desires. Remember that.

Before that the entity was in the city of gold when there were those overtures and activities in the various lands, as in the land of Saad, the Gobi, and the Egyptian land.

The entity then was active in its abilities for entertaining, as in verse and in song; using these for purposes that added not only to the entertainment, but to the greater development and unfoldment of those peoples.

The name then was Scarpf.

Before that the entity was in Atlantis, during those periods just before the second breaking up of the land.

The entity was among the sons of Belial who used the divine forces for the gratifying of selfish appetites, and the formation of desires for the gratifying of self became the stumbling block for the entity.

As to the abilities of the entity in the present, that to which it may attain and how:

There are unlimited abilities. How will they be directed by the entity? How well may others cause the entity to be aware of such activities? These should be the questions in self.

Study to know first thy ideals, spiritual, mental, and material. Then apply self in such a manner towards those that there will never be a question mark after thine own conscience nor in the eyes even of others.

Remember that the Lord loveth the cheerful giver as well as those who seek His face.

Q. What should be his chief work?
A. This depends upon what he chooses—whether in music, directing of music, writing of music, or writing of verse. But in either of these channels, there may be the greater outlet. The voice of the wood, the voice of the air—any of those are the realms through which the entity may exceed, as well as succeed.
Q. Would all of his talents be developed?
A. All his talents will either be developed or run to seed and be drained off.

Q. Any other suggestions that may help his parents to guide him?

A. Let the parents study to show themselves approved unto God, workmen not ashamed, putting the stress where stress is due, keeping self unspotted from the world. (3633-1)

This reading is presented in its entirety, as it illustrates the complexity of individual development, the borderline between genius and disaster which is the consequence of previous lives. There is both good and bad; one life misused can be the source of difficulties thousands of years later. Misuse of Divine Forces inevitably takes its toll in dire consequences, in some painful experience.

Later reports told of the tragedy of this life. The parents realized their problem. They wrote that they had placed the boy, before this reading, in a very strict, very religious boarding school. They did not want him to be idle, as they felt idleness would destroy him.

As no follow-up reading was given, we do not know whether this was the best environment for the boy or not. The mother reported a very distressing mental and nervous upset a few years later. The reading was given in 1944. In 1951 the mother wrote: ". . . No doubt you have read of our tragedy. My son [3633], who has been emotionally unbalanced for three years, last Wednesday shot his father and grandmother. Hugh Lynn, your father was my friend and I brought [3633] to see him and also he gave a life reading for him which had plenty of warnings in it. I am writing to ask you to please get one of your prayer circles to work on us—and to pour spiritual power into my mother . . . and into my husband . . . and my son [3633]. We certainly need it."

The boy's trouble was later diagnosed as dementia praecox, schizophrenia. It seems obvious from his reading, however, that his real problem was a karmic condition which began in Atlantis, when he joined the sons of Belial. He was placed in a sanitarium and did make some improvement while there. His parents had hopes of his recovery. The mother later, in 1964, wrote to report his death.

The boy had lived to be thirty-two years old and

displayed great mental capabilities but did not make the artistic contribution he might have made because of his mental disturbance.

Another unusual boy was found in 2547. His spiritual development and memories are in sharp contrast to those of 3633; for 2547 had devoted himself to spiritual service in his previous life.

His reading by Edgar Cayce was given in 1941, when 2547 was only four years old. The greater part of the life reading was:

> As counsel to those responsible for the training, the developing of those abilities—spiritually, mentally—that are apparent in the activities of this entity; that it may better fulfill those purposes for which it entered this experience.
>
> Fortunate indeed may be those who have a part in the formulating of the ideals of this entity in the present. For he will formulate ideas for many, no matter in what turn the activities may be. But if these are guided in those channels through which the activities of this entity have been in the earth plane, we will find the GLORIFYING of the Christ-Consciousness in manifested manners of spiritual activity that has not been seen since the entity in its expression in the earth gave counsel to the many.
>
> Astrologically we find little influences in the experience of this entity. For the activities in the earth have so outweighed, outnumbered those. And no individual entity save the Master himself has given greater material demonstration of the activities of the spiritual forces in the earth of EVERY nature. (2547-1)

His reading said he had had only a few appearances in the earth and that his previous earth life had been in Scotland as a reformer.

> Before this the entity was in the Scotch land. The entity began its activity as a prodigy, as one already versed in its associations with the unseen—or the elemental forces; the fairies and those of every form that do not give expression in a material way and are only seen by those who are attuned to the infinite.

Then the entity in the developing was in the name Thomas Campbell, the reformer in the land of the present nativity; which, as combined later with Barton Stone, brought into activity that known as a denomination.

The intent and purpose was to UNIFY all Protestant thought, speaking where the Book spoke, keeping silent where it kept silent upon the activities or associations of individuals in relationships to groups or to masses.

Hence the entity throughout its experience was not disposed to be other than a speaker.

And the abilities as a speaker, as a minister, will be a part of those faculties, characteristics, that should be considered as the entity develops normally.

Do not allow the entity, in the first ten to twelve years, to get away from the spiritual truths in the Old and the New Testaments; not as an ism, not as a cult. For it will be easy for a cult, an ism, to be formed about the entity and its prognostications. But rather let it be as one glorifying the truths that are promised in the thirtieth of Deuteronomy, and in the fourteenth, fifteenth, sixteenth, and seventeenth chapters of John. These impress. Accredit the entity's abilities to these sources. When there are questions as to the sourse from which the entity obtains its information, agree that it comes from the infinite. For these are the developments.

For before that the entity was that one upon whom the mantle of Elijah fell, who in his material activity performed more unusual acts, or miracles, that are only comparable with the Master himself.

The entity then as Elisha brought into the experience much that was of the unusual in expression.

So in the present, in the experiences of this entity, there may be expected just as unusual expression; as those coming to the entity to receive the blessings from the handkerchief, the photograph even, or those things that the entity may touch or bless.

But let these be as NATURAL sources, NOT as something unusual. For, remember—those that have the training—those whom the Lord would honor He chasteneth.

These, then, are the manners: Let each day be an

opportunity—not in coddling, not drastic measures, but loving—as an honor, as a privilege to be appreciated and active, in that there may come those blessings to the entity.

Here we may see a demonstration and illustration of that which has been indicated or intimated through these channels, as of a PERFECT channel being formed for the advent of an entity-soul that would bring blessings to all—IF there is the directing of the developing years.

The responsibility then rests with the mother, the father, for the next eight years. There will then be given, here, those studies. For it will be easy to teach him Greek. It will be easy to teach him those things that were portion of the activity.

For before THAT the entity was that one to whom was entrusted man's advent into the world—Noah.

From this we find those weaknesses. Then, not as one refraining from these, but beware ever of any strong drink or fruit of the vine passing the lips of THIS entity—through these early periods, especially.

To these, and we will find blessings to man—through this entity. (2547-1)

Here we have a highly evolved soul whom we might expect to become a great spiritual leader, a minister or speaker. So far he has not indicated this potential. He is, though, only in his early thirties now, and his spiritual influence could yet become great.

He did seem to have the spiritual awareness as a child which his readings indicated. A friend who knew about his reading asked him for an object he had handled, thinking it would have healing vibrations. This boy gave her an object he had carved from wood, seemingly realizing its purpose and suitableness. He was, as his reading predicted, a very good student, but he missed school a lot due to bad weather and illness. He seemed to be especially sensitive to weather and on several occasions warned his parents of approaching storms long before anyone else saw any sign of a storm.

In 1957 a family friend reported that she had met 2547 and his young bride—that they were both very religious, in a Protestant (Baptist) faith, both teaching and working in religious education, though he had chosen the grocery business as his profession. She tried to talk to them about reincarnation and so on, but they seemed too orthodox to be much interested. The wife seemed more open than he did.

An up-to-date report (1968) on 2547 from his uncle, 416, states that this young man is the manager of a large chain supermarket in the small Southern town where he lives. He has a family and is a good solid citizen living a good Christian life but is not a minister or speaker, as his Cayce reading suggested.

A young woman (5241), when she was nineteen years of age, asked in an Edgar Cayce reading if she should attend college and was told:

> Enter rather nurse training or the psychological study as a technician, but college is not necessary. But better a premedical degree would be had, yes. (5241-1)

This advice was probably given because of natural healing ability. Her reading said:

> There will be found few individuals who have innately, though very probably not aware of it at all in the present, the abilities to heal with the hands as much, and they're not bad-looking hands! Look at them! These carry then, not necessarily in the hands themselves but in the individuality of the soul of the entity, real help that the entity may bring, may give to others. There would be very few instances where the entity would not or could not, if it would attempt it, heal a headache in a few moments and only by quieting.

> Thus those things of spiritual nature, or of divine science, and those things of spiritual as well as psychological nature should the entity study and apply in self's experience with others, though this may never be done save by and through the entity keeping itself in accord with divine purposes. Not that the entity is to be "goody-goody." Just be good for something and, as is and will be indicated, if the entity will apply itself in those directions, there has been the gift, as it were, of the

Maker, from the Maker, to the entity, the vainglory, but as an expression of the divine in and through the relationships with others.

Abuse it or reject it and we'll find hardships, confusions may come to the entity. But as a nurse, as a healer, itself, as in application along any of these lines where this may be applied, the entity may become, not merely well known, for it isn't to the glory of self, but the glory of the Maker, that these should be applied in the experiences of the entity.

From the astrological aspects we find Jupiter, Venus, Saturn are the latent urges. There is within the innate feeling, the personality, the individuality wanting to do something, not merely because it would be big, not merely to be well spoken of, but as the innate feeling of wanting to be worthwhile, wanting to be an expression of something out of the ordinary. Well, ye have it! Use it, don't abuse it, don't neglect it! (5241-1)

This young woman was given three lives to which her loving personality and healing ability were due.

She had lived in Philadelphia during the Revolutionary days and had helped in the cause for freedom. She had aided in instruction and carried messages to those in authority, even to Washington himself.

For the entity was even blessed by Washington. In the experience the entity gained, and hence that desire innately for helpful forces, for a universal consciousness of good, for freedom of activity, freedom of speech and those which are active in the entity's consciousness latent; and thus is the beauty, the loveliness of the character of the entity in the present. (5241-1)

Before that the entity was in Persia at the time of the rebuilding of the holy city with Zerubbabel. She was the companion of the priest Eleazer. She took from the records which were discovered there and brought to self, and to many, a greater knowledge of the closeness of the Father-God to man in this period.

Before that we find the entity was in the Egyptian land when there were the activities in the preparations for the exit from Egypt to the favored land, the people through whom was chosen the hope of the world.

The entity was then the close friend of Joshua. Yes, one of those to whom Joshua was engaged as would be called in the present, and of the daughters of Levi, not the same as Moses and Aaron but rather of Korah. There we find the entity beautiful, lovely, beloved of Joshua and yet weak in body, because of conditions under which the entity had in a portion of its experience labored, and thus weak-lunged, passing away during the period of the journey to the Holy Land. But to have been beloved of Joshua was sufficient to have builded into the personality that individuality of the entity, that which still makes the entity beloved of all who know the entity best, loved by all its companions, its associates, just as in those experiences with the great leader who was to carry the children of promise to the Holy Land. The name then was Abigal.

As to the abilities of the entity, then, that to which it may attain and how:

These are limited only to that which is the choice and application of the entity in those directions indicated. Not that a home should not be established, not that there won't be a beautiful home, but choose one in accord, not in discord with the abilities in self. (5241-1)

An interesting and unusual case, 3184, was a young woman of thirty when she applied for her reading. She listed her occupation as aviation and her religious preference as none. Her contact with ARE was through her mother, who wrote: "I think the book, *There Is a River,* came to me as an answer to prayer. I am a member of the Divine Science Church, 'The Church of the Healing Christ,' of which Dr. Emmet Fox is the pastor. . . . My daughter 3184, who at present lives in . . . Texas, is doing work which she does not like and yet fears to give it up, not knowing just where she can get a position doing the work she loves. . . . I can only tell her that if she can cast all fear and doubt out of her thoughts and really believe that God is guiding her to her true place where she will be happy and

111

most useful, that position will present itself, but it is difficult for a young person who was raised in the Catholic Church to do this."

The young woman asked: "Should or will I be able to make flying my life work?"

A. You can will to do whatever you like. Whether you want to or not, or whether others want you to or not, you will make it a life's work. It can be most worthwhile to self and to many others, if an association in the establishing of such communications; but let it be with those portions of the land indicated. (3184-1)

This desire and ability to fly stemmed mainly from her life in Atlantis.

The entity was in Atlantis during those periods when there were the separations, just before the breaking up of Poseidia.

The entity then controlled those activities where communications had been established with other lands, and the flying boats that moved through air or water were the means by which the entity carried many of those to the Iberian land, as well as later those groups in the Egyptian land . . . when there had been the determining that the records should be kept there.

Thus we find the entity in the capacity of the leader in making overtures in the Egyptian land. Finding the land in turmoil because of rebellions, the entity—with one Ax-Tell—undertook to set up their own activities. For the entity then was an associate of Ax-Tell, not a companion but a fellow worker with that leader Ax-Tell in Egypt.

With the return of the Priest, by the edicts, and then the establishing of the groups that controlled the religious and the political and the varied activities in that land with the return of the Priest, the entity first became sullen; then joined in with those movements for the preparation of people for the regeneration of bodies and THINGS in that period.

Again the entity was in communication activities. Those influences that prompted the entity's abilities in the present arise from that experience.

These [abilities] are limited only by the manner in which the entity approaches or uses its abilities, especially in the establishing of communications with other lands.

Languages that have been and are at times the disturbing element with individuals may easily be put aside . . . if there is the application of the special service in the lands or areas indicated.

Then, DO assist in establishing the airways with those peninsulas or lands of North Africa and the Iberian Peninsula.

Do keep self first in that attitude and purpose of a universal consciousness for the good of all. (3184-1)

The ability in communications originated in a later life in Greece and Persia. There she helped to develop steering for ships and the manner in which the compass was installed.

She had been a messenger during the Revolution in America and had also been a messenger in the Roman land during its period of expansion. This was a period when the thoughts of the leaders were for the good of all rather than the gratifying of personal desires. In this Roman period the entity was not in the present sex, but a man.

She was among those who planned the manner or means of communications with other lands, thus in what might be called today a diplomatic service.

Here, too, again may the entity in the present use those abilities in those directions of making connections and associations with those of various lands. For there will be the needs for the use of many in these directions in the reconstruction days to come. When communications with other lands are so established, by those means of activity, the entity may have an important place in some of these connections; especially with those such as the coast of the Mediterranean, the coast of the Iberian Peninsula. These especially will be fields, for to these—as we will see—the entity has come oft.

Hence, as has been seen, the communications of every

nature will be a part of the entity's consciousness; and it's in and through these that the entity may find the outlet for self and self's abilities. (3184-1)

This young woman had a check life reading seeking more information as to how she could get work as a pilot. Her reading told her she might get into British Air Transport as a ferry pilot by applying through Canada. She tried but did not succeed in getting a passport or getting into the Air Transport Service and was for some time thoroughly discouraged and unhappy.

A later report of May 8, 1956, from her mother says: "Yes, my daughter 3184 has made flying her life's work. As yet she has not flown out of this country but still hopes to some day. She has never married—says she finds planes more interesting than men. I say she has not met the right man yet—'there speaks the mother!' However, she seems quite happy and has an interesting life—is always studying and acquiring higher ratings. She now has her 'Air Transport Rating'—the same as the Transatlantic pilots—but I am afraid she is the wrong sex. She was the first *woman* Executive Pilot—now there are four others in the West—she flies for a corporation . . . she lives alone in an apt. and enjoys being alone."

In 1968 this young woman herself wrote to Hugh Lynn Cayce and reported:

As your Father so truly said—whether I will or no—I would make flying my life's work. Indeed I have, and while there have been times when I starved at it (because of my sex), there have been other times, as now, when it has been good to me—and never, starving or not, have I regretted the decision.

With respect to the Iberian Peninsula, except for a few stopovers in Lisbon or Madrid, enroute to somewhere else, I still have no connection with it, nor do I see yet how I ever will have.

Back in 1943, my greatest desire was to fly the ocean, and this desire never abated, even when I was enjoying other types of flying; the opportunity finally arose in 1962—after false starts, I started my own company for the delivery of light airplanes to foreign countries in

1965—to date have made 90 trips to Europe, South Africa and the Philippines, and love it as much now as I did the first time.

Her letterhead reads AIR FERRY ENTERPRISES . . . somewhere in Pennsylvania. Thus we can say this vocational advice and prediction came true, as well as the young woman's dream.

The home will become the really great adventure for the entity, that it may through its own close work with God bring into BEING those who will be emissaries—yea, be those who will rise in power in PRINCIPLE, in state and national associations and affairs.

This then is the glory, the crowning of thy patience, thy love, thy beauty of purpose, thy sincerity.

And above all, to self be true and—as has been given—ye will not be false to any. For thy body, thy mind is indeed the temple of the living God, and there He hath promised to meet thee consciously. And as ye become aware of His abiding presence, more of beauty and purpose and of harmony and of joy of life will indeed be thine. (1968-1)

This was the career and the prophecy given a young woman in her life reading. She was twenty-eight years old and working in an office when the reading was given, so was most anxious to be about this business of establishing a home and having the sons promised.

The last part of her reading emphasized and further explained the real reason for her purpose in this life.

The HOME is the real adventure, the real purpose of the entity's expression in the earth. For as seen, in Atlantis the desire for same brought disturbance [there she was a daughter of the children of the Law of One but in love with a son of Belial]; in Egypt it brought the better understanding; in the time when the Master taught thee, there was the perfect home with His presence abiding there AFTER the awakening; in the experience in the present land, it brought a helpful force.

Hence in the present, build thine own home upon the sure foundation. Thou hast met him—thou lovest him. He has disappointed thee, but bring that into thy heart and mind that—with the Christ-life and purpose—ye will bring into material experience a CHANNEL to be the blessings of the many.

Q. Should I marry?
A. You should—as just indicated.
Q. Whom?
A. As has been given, the entity knows him—she has been disappointed in him—but this can be amended.
Q. How long should I wait?
A. October. (1968-1)

This naturally was a very exciting and interesting reading for the young woman. She was still puzzled about the man to whom the reading alluded. She assumed he was the one who appeared to be interested in her and who was very attentive when she returned home. Something went awry, however, for she did not even see him in October and wrote that he was seeing another woman. So the young lady had a check reading on her Atlantean period and sought further information about marriage. The reading explained the turmoil of that life and assured her the man she was concerned about was the entity she had loved as a son of Belial.

Thus we find in the present, with the associations which have come about with an individual who represented that sojourn, or that one with whom the entity was associated in that experience, there have come disappointments, and the not being satisfied innately or manifestedly in self as to the perfect association, or as to there ever being a perfect cooperative influence.

Yet, as we find, and as has been indicated, IF there is the DETERMINING upon the part of each that they may in the present experience meet themselves, there may be the dedicating of their minds, their bodies, their purposes to meet and to fulfill within the present experience those things which would make for more harmony and more general peace of mind than can be done apart. Yet, if this is only the decision of the one, better that it NOT be undertaken.

Q. Since it is my desire to fulfill my destiny while in this experience, please suggest what I should do next.

A. As just indicated, let it be understood as to the self's purpose! This desire, this purpose, that it may be fulfilled in this association or companionship! But unless it is a cooperative undertaking, forget it—and find others!

Q. What prevented our marriage in October, in order that I might not let this happen again?

A. The lack of assurance as to the oneness of purpose on the part of each.

Q. How can I prepare myself to be a good mother?

A. Act in those ways and manners—in body, in mind, in purpose—to fulfill that within self that would be the IDEAL activity and relationships of a mother.

Q. Will my sons be influential in religious or political affairs, or both?

A. As has been indicated, we will find that the inclination will be to both fields; one possibly in one, one in the other.

Later advice was: "Do not allow a disappointment in a personality to hinder these from finding their greater fruition in this experience or sojourn." (1968-2)

This former son of Belial married the other woman. Case 1968 was then worried as to whether or not this was the end of her life purpose or if the sons would come to her if she married someone else. So she asked in a later reading:

Q. Will I eventually marry R . . . , or if I marry someone else, will those sons who will help to adjust the nation still come to me?

A. This is part of THY heritage, and that attraction should be from, and is of, the application of the principles of truth and spirit and of life, rather than the companion, see?

As to whether there will be that association with R . . .

will depend upon circumstance. As has been indicated for the entity, this should not be made as something that MUST be irrespective of conditions. But seek. There are those associations, there are those purposes. Then make way for them, among those who are of the sons of faith; and not as of old holding to the aggrandizement of self.

Q. Is it still possible for me to carry out my entire destiny as I planned when I came to this earth plane?

A. To be SURE!

Q. Have I met the one I should marry and how am I to know who he is?

A. That he is a child of FAITH, a SON of faith—as has just been indicated! (1968-4)

Still this young woman persisted and hoped, asking about the possibility of two other men as suitable husbands. She was told to prepare herself and to "think and realize within self that ye are not waiting on an individual, ye are waiting on the Lord. For ye have chosen and do choose correctly, ye will fill and fulfill that purpose the LORD hath with thee. And because this may be altered at some particular period of the experience it is not to be considered that self has failed." (1968-8)

Approximately five years after her first reading this young woman made a chance visit to a relative of her stepmother. Here she met again a childhood friend, and the association quickly grew into love and marriage. The two sons she was hoping for arrived in due time.

One young man, 2542, who is doing his best to follow his life reading especially as to profession, was told:

While many of those things and activities have changed, in which the entity attempted to apply itself through the sojourns in the earth, these may be those channels in the present in which greater expression may be seen for the entity's activity.

These might be indicated from the seal of the life experience of the entity through the sojourns in the earth:

A square, upon which there would be the circle—or the globe; indicating both the western and the eastern ships—especially of the air, and of all characters of communications to the varied centers. These, as a study for the entity, would bring much as may be indicated.

Upon and with a portion of this would be the activities in miniature of those centers that would not be considered as of the greater population, necessarily, but those that are the greater communicating centers—that bring the activities to both the commercial and the religious forces of the earth. Hence: Greenwich, Arlington, Frankfort on the Main, Moscow, Ankara, Bagdad, Buenos Aires, Lima, Auckland—these would be the centers which would indicate, in miniature, the activities in those portions of the globe. (2542-1)

This description of greater expression through a life seal is unusual, but it is very meaningful today, for this young man has studied electrical communications and is presently to go into communications work for the government. A later question, "What particular development is sought by the entity at this appearance?" was answered with, "Anything that would have to do with international law." Naturally anyone dealing with communications with other countries would be involved with international law, so it seems this, too, is being fulfilled.

The earth experiences which influenced this entity were of a diplomatic character and dealt with many peoples. In his last earth life he was active in the American Revolution, though his life began "in a foreign land, and the entity was trained as a lawyer—or a justice of the law; yet with the experiences brought about during the American Revolution and the activities there, the entity came with Kosciusko into this land."

The entity became closely associated with the leaders in the activities about Pennsylvania, Maryland, Michigan AND Virginia.

Hence, as has been indicated, during the latter portion of the entity's sojourn in the acquaintanceships were with those of the Lee home, those of Mount Vernon; for there the entity spent some time during the latter period of his sojourn in the earth, with the first President as well as the associates of those activities through that experience.

119

Thus Washington, Adams, Jefferson, Jay, and all of those were associates or friends and acquaintances of the entity.

The name then was Leonard Zolocoffa. In the experience the entity gained, though—as indicated —was hindered from carrying out its activities as a diplomatic agent. Yet the assistance given to the early activities of the various lands with the new land may be said to have come much because of the entity's counsel and suggestions during that experience.

Hence in the present, train the entity in law—diplomatic law; that will have to deal with many countries, many problems, not only political but social and religious. For eventually the entity will see a religious war.

Before that the entity was in the Roman land, during those periods when there were the expansions especially in North Africa, Asia, and portions of Palestine.

In the southern portion of Asia, or about what is now Turkey, were the activities of the entity, which extended into Syria and into Palestine.

For the entity then acted in the capacity of gathering data, and pointing out the needs for establishing rules that conformed to the needs of the people in the various sections to which the empire then extended.

Thus we find again the entity in the diplomatic activity, or that in which not only law and order but the social, political, economic and religious tendencies or trends of a people must be taken into consideration.

Hence we will find the entity interested in political, economic, social, AND religious activities in the present. These should be the channels or fields through which the greater development, the greater training, the activities as would lead to the use of the abilities. For these will offer the channels through which the entity may find the means of the greater expression of self.

Hence there will be the need for firmness, yet justice and mercy, and for the following out of a REASON for everything in which the entity may engage or be active. (2542-1)

A still earlier experience was in the Indian land.

Then the entity was a caravan keeper, or one who personally directed the means of exchange between India and Ceylon, Egypt and Persia and the Caspian activities, and those along the eastern Mediterranean. All of these were a portion of the entity's places of activity.

But with the acquaintance with those influences in the "city in the hills," the entity established that center there for its activities; thus aiding the founders there in making it a commercial center; yet never losing sight of the influences of the peoples in the political, economic, and religious tendencies in their activities.

Before that the entity was in the Egyptian land, during those periods when there were activities established for the propagation of truth and law and order; in which individuals were to be considered as a part of the welfare.

The entity was of the Atlanteans born in the land, being then part Egyptian and part Atlantean.

Thus we find the entity rising to authority in the tenets for the individuals that aided in establishing unity through the various groups, throughout then the active forces in the world.

The entity was associated with all forms of communications, that will again be a part of the entity's present experience—as indicated in its seal—and yet dealing with all types, all characters of conditions in the varied lands.

These will again be a part of the entity's associations through this experience, if there will be those trainings, those promptings, those directions in those channels that will fit the entity for that activity.

As to the abilities of the entity in the present, then, that to which it may attain, and how:

Much, as indicated, will depend upon the basis of the tenets that become a part of the policy, or the character as builded in the experience of the entity in the present.

But dealing with political, economic, and religious questions will be a part of the entity's experience.

As to how—this will depend upon the tendencies and trends. These we would give farther when the entity has reached the age of eleven to twelve. (2542-1)

It would be interesting to know what a later reading would have given, but Mr. Cayce's passing of course prevented this. The young man, now in his early thirties, is fulfilling the prediction on communications. It may be that his later years will see him as one of our country's diplomats.

The strange ability to control wild animals was a skill one young girl (276) was told she possessed. It was not suggested that she use this as a profession or make a career of it but "to show that close affection that may exist between the human mind, as controlling through the manners in which the entity is efficient, and to bring to the attention of others how animals—in their various spheres—are dependent upon their owners, or those who contact same, as to what *their* activities may be to the benefit of man; for, as was given in the beginning, 'Be ye fruitful; multiply, and *subdue* the earth.' Make all that was made, *making* that—then—as an example of, or *completing* as it were—the promise that is given to man, that he may be one with, one of, the Creative Forces in the universe, by the manner in which he may use those various abilities through his experiences in a material world; and as all of earth's creation is a form or manifestation of the love as is shown forth to those beings that may be one with the Creator, so may the love that may be seen between those of the lower order, or those in their development in a material plane, so may this entity show to others, to the animal kingdom, that which has been received, as may be given by self by the entity, in *their* behalf." (276-3)

This unique ability was acquired first in a very early life in Arabia.

That there are peculiarities to many in the experience of the entity is not to be wondered, when the sojourns are taken into *proper* association or correlations *with* these little peculiarities—as they may be termed; for in the experiences in the earth's plane, though few in

122

number, old indeed in earth's experience *is* the entity or *soul*.

In the one before this we find in that land now known as the Roman, and during that period when there were the ministering and teaching of those peoples that came up from Judea. The entity was among those who accepted those teachings, and coming in contact with those of that period, taught by the lessons of, the experiences of self and others in the contacts of this new peace, yet suffering in body, by privation—yet able in mind to control those beasts, both of the field and of the dens and lairs that the body was placed in; the body bore same, gaining—gaining—oft the liberation for the teachings again through these *strange* abilities in this particular period; being among those who journeyed again to the Grecian land for the teaching of the peoples, as the entity was carried away from same. In the body beautiful, in mind pleasant, in abilities surpassing many in that period; gaining through the experience, though suffering in *many* ways and manners. In the name Phoebia.

In the one before this we find in that land now known as the Arabian, and to that portion of the country where the banishment of those peoples sent from that known as the Egyptian land. The entity was among those peoples called the wild peoples or the barbarians. The entity then came under the influence of those so banished, and being awakened through those tenets that were held by those in the land the entity became one of the followers, and returning to the land gained in experience through the teachings; becoming an expert horseman of the plains, and carrying the messages to those peoples in the sand and waste places; returning to the land from which the teachings were gained in the latter days of the sojourn, the entity aided much in the building up of the hospital (that would be called in the present), ministering to the ills of those who suffered in body *and* in mind. In the present experience such may be that field, that ministry through which the entity may give into the lives of those contacted thóse deeper thoughts, that may find their expressions in *this* experience.

In the one before this we find again in this same land now called Egypt. . . . The entity was among those peoples who gathered in places to establish various groups, or families, or sects, to prevent the inroads upon the peoples from the beasts from without, and the entity aided through this experience in gathering together of various groups, various peoples, to join hands for the common interests of all. In the *name* Hein.

In the abilities of the entity, these—as seen—lie in that of ministering to others, and *in* the home. Will there be kept those ideals that have long been innate—though rebellious spirits rise within from *suppressions* that existed through the entity's experience—this may be curbed best through those of living gentleness, kindness, and pointing the way of keeping the body that temple *through* which He, the Father, may manifest. (276-2)

Nine months later this young lady had a reading on her life as Phoebia, in which she asked:

Q. Give date of incarnation as Phoebia and describe strange abilities of entity in that period, also as to control of those beasts of the field, dens, and lairs.
A. This, as we find, was during those periods when man was called upon oft to defend self against the beasts of the fields, in dens, in lairs, in arenas; and the entity through its own development—as had been attained or gained during that period—showed for the ability to walk in the denizens of the forest without being afraid, also to walk among those in the arena without fear; and no *harm came to* the entity through their activity, but from those that made themselves lower than the beasts; for, as has been given, all may be tamed, but the tongue hath no man tamed! In that day, then, during the first century, as is counted in the present. (276-3)

Today, 1970, as one might expect, this woman is surrounded by many and various kinds of pets. She has been raising dogs and training "companion dogs."

A man, 2030, who is now an executive in a large tobacco firm, had a life reading by Edgar Cayce in 1939. It said:

In the material activity, as a salesman, or as an organizer of groups for such, in the products that would have to do with the home or those associations of same, you may find the greater field of material security, as well as that of contentment.

Q. Through what contacts and connections should I seek to carry out the suggestions for life work?
A. In the first the training of self in that of salesmanship, in WHATEVER line of endeavor that may be chosen as an outlet for self. For the entity is a NATURAL salesman. (2030-1)

His abilities were brought from several former lives. He was in this country during the Civil War period and was engaged in activities related to the manufacture or the use of products of the soil, or the introducing of the uses of tobacco in the various lands or various ports.

Thus the entity, for the period, saw a great deal of opportunity to meet peoples and associations of peoples with activities in many lands.

And the ability for the presenting of convincing arguments for the use of this or that product is latent within the experience of the entity.

While the entity may at times appear to be argumentative over things of a trivial nature, or things lacking in importance, we find that deep within self (with the encouraging of same) there are the abilities to be active as a salesman in ANY FIELD that may be chosen by the entity, and especially in that in which there is the distributing of any character that is used in the home—whether of the electrical nature or of any nature pertaining to the betterment of the home—would make for the outlet in which the entity might find the greater contentment, as well as the opportunities for the entity to manifest its abilities in the spiritual and mental way also. (2030-1)

Tobacco does not (from this last statement) appear to be the best choice of product for this man to handle. Yet it seems to be a rather natural choice as the result of his Civil War life.

In another life in England, during the Crusade period, this man was "what would be termed in the present as the propagandist, or the one to SELL the idea to those who were in the rural districts, or those who were active in those influences in which groups of individuals worked during those periods only IN the ways of groups or sects of individuals for certain activities."

Thus we find that during that sojourn many of the leaders relied upon the activities of the entity, and never were any of those disappointed in the abilities of the entity.

From that we find the easiness with which the entity may meet individuals or peoples or groups, and to make friends with same, no matter what may be their stations, their associations or activities in the experience. (2030-1)

As a Roman soldier he was sent to Palestine during the reign of Herod Archelaus. Here he had sympathy for the persecuted, and he became inclined to be the peacemaker. "From the experience we will find the abilities of the entity to meet others, to determine the abilities of others, and thus adding to the characteristics necessary for a GOOD salesman." (2030-1)

We can thus see that many lives and many memories may contribute to one's present ability.

Practically every life reading gave some vocational advice; for the purpose deep within the soul had to include how it would manifest in a physical world. Some counsel such as this was given each entity.

Know that it is not all just to live—not all just to be good, but good FOR something; that ye may fulfill that purpose for which ye have entered this experience. (2030-1)

This counsel was naturally related to soul memory, the former experiences of the entity both in the earth and in the interims between earth lives. The will is free to choose—we may make wise or wrong choices. Moreover, these decisions may be influenced by the environment and the parents of the manifesting soul. Obviously the road is long and steep, but it must be climbed. Some apparently choose suitable vocations and means of supplying material needs; others are forced by circumstances or wrong decisions into unsuitable vocations. There were instances where individuals were advised to make changes, took the advice, and found the changes wise and happy ones. Older persons had made their decisions, and the reason for the choice could often be found in previous experiences.

The most revealing counsel was of course given to the young. Some of the foregoing cases reveal the results of the counsel or predictions. Sometimes the advice was followed closely, and at other times it was not heeded. We only give the reports.

Perhaps the two following quotations throw a little light on what causes a person of great ability to fail to live up to his expectations and to be retarded rather than to develop.

Obviously, it has to do with the entity's own decisions.

In entering the present experience we find, astrologically, the entity coming under the influence of Jupiter, Mercury, Venus, and Uranus. In the application of the entity and the experiences in the earth's plane, these would be found to mean little, were they judged astrologically alone; for often do the experiences in the various phases of development, through the experiences in the various spheres, bring the varied effect, as is applicable to an individual in the application of their own will. Not that will is ever taken from an individual entity, but that builded in each experience must be met by that entity, and only in making self's own will one *with* the divine Creative Energy, and becoming as one *with* same, may one develop in any experience; and in *this* many developments and many retards are seen. (288-1)

The shadows of those things from the sojourns of this entity in Mercury, Jupiter, Saturn, Venus, and the Moon have their portion in the very relationships and activity of the entity. These are but the mental urges that arise and become as the individuality of an entity in expression in the material world; while the appearances in the earth through the various sojourns that are become active in the experience of an entity at any one given place or position or appearance or period are as but the personality in the entity's experience . . . and are as the urges from the emotions that have been created.

Just as the entity's attending this or that university, this or that place of learning, would make a parlance peculiar to itself. Even though individuals may study the same line of thought, one attending Harvard, another Yale, another Oxford, another Stanford, another the University of Arizona, they each would carry with them the vibrations created by their activity in those environs.

In the same way emotions arise from individual activity in a particular sojourn and are called the *spirit* of the institution to which the entity may have carried itself in its activity.

So we find those astrological sojourns making these vibrations or impressions in the present entity.

Mercury brings the high mental abilities, the faculties that at times may become the developing for the soul or at others turned to the aggrandizement of selfish interests.

For the entity is among those who have entered the earth during those years when there was the great entrance of those who have risen high in their abilities and who are then passing through those periods when there must be the application of the will, else the very abilities that have been maintained in the Sun and Mercurian influences will become as stumbling blocks—and they become *extremists,* as the Uranian influences indicate.

So these influences find expression *innately* in the great store the entity itself places upon position, power, name, this or that degree, this or that social accomplishment, this or that activity.

These are the influences that innately arise from the sojourn in Uranus and a combination with Saturn and Mercurian forces: innately. (633-2)

This account would not give any semblance of a true report if it did not say that most life readings for women dealt more with homemaking and family relationships than with careers. Many young women were told they would or should make the home their life work. Counsel such as this was often given:

Do make the home the career, for this is the greatest career any soul may make in the earth. To a few it is given to have both a career and a home—but the greatest of all careers is the home, for this is nearer to the emblem of what each soul hopes eventually to gain. Then make thy home as a shadow of a heavenly home. (5070-1)

[For] the home is as a counterpart of that for which one longs, in the heavenly home or in the spiritual kingdom. Viewed from the spiritual, then, the home should be that which is the material and mental expression of an atonement with the Father.

This, then, is the ideal in such a place as may be called home. (538-6)

FAMILY RELATIONSHIPS

CHAPTER FIVE

Thus the whirligig of the time brings in his revenges.
—SHAKESPEARE, *Twelfth Night*

For the home is the *nearest* pattern in the earth (where there is unity of purpose in the companionship) to man's relationship with his maker. For it is ever-creative in purpose, from personalities and individualities coordinated in a cause. (3577-1)

Since karma is meeting self, we acquire karma as we meet self in our many attitudes and emotions, when we either serve in lovingkindness and patience or hold resentful, malicious thoughts. The counsel given in the readings makes it clear that what we do to our fellow man we do to our Maker; so our definition of karma is consistent. Our karma or problem is within self.

We are so absorbed with self that we fail to be considerate of others. We ignore the other person's need and comfort and are often highly critical of him; conflicts arise; so throughout the ages karma is acquired. We are attracted to the environment we need to learn our lessons. The closeness of the family relationships indicates we have problems to work out within them. Moreover, the fact that we do not consciously choose our family, other than the marital partner, probably means we face more "family" karma than anywhere else. Until the recent crime wave, more murders occurred in families or among friends * than elsewhere. We often see what the psychologists call sibling rivalry and youth is usually struggling to throw off parental authority. The very nature of the marital relationship makes it liable to problems and emotional disturbances. Conflicts often occur as a spouse struggles to be the dominant one. Instead of a loving partner, the married

* New York *Times:* MOST MURDERS FOUND COMMITTED IN FAMILIES OR AMONG FRIENDS. September 3, 1967, page 40.

person sometimes finds he is living with a domineering antagonist.

The life readings naturally dwelt on this facet of karma, for many people asked about their past associations with other people. As would be expected, the most frequently mentioned association and the one asked about most often was the marriage relationship. Very often husband and wife had been in this relationship in other lives, though the reading said he or she had been the companion then. Sometimes, however, there had been a family relationship, but not that of husband or wife.

Our likes and dislikes are no doubt frequently karmic in nature. We are immediately drawn to some people, while we withdraw from others. There is no apparent reason for these reactions, for we find later we can learn to like or even love some of these people to whom we react negatively.

We often wish the readings had given more detailed information about some former life associations; however, the answers to questions often said there had been an association and sometimes indicated the reason or the beginning of the present problem or relationship.

Reading number 903-23 gave an explanation as to how souls are drawn together in various appearances.

For a moment, let's turn to what is that termed as the Akashic Record, or that which may be said to be destiny in the entrance of a soul into materiality. For remember, matter moved upon—or matter in motion in materiality—*becomes* the motive force we know as the evolutionary influence in a material world. An entity or soul is a portion of the First Cause, or God, or Creative Energy; or the terms that may be had for the *movement* that brings matter into activity or being. Hence souls in their varied experiences—whether in the earth or materiality or the various spheres of activity about the earth (termed the astrological sojourns and their influences, where there have been the fruits of what? Spirit! As the motivative forces in a contact)—are again and again *drawn* together by the natural law of attractive forces for the activity towards what? The *development* of the soul to the *one* purpose, the one cause—to be companionate with the First Cause.

Then as the entity here contacts in materiality those of its own body, those of its own sympathetic condition, it is for the development of each in its associations one to another toward that First Cause.

As to each of the children, then, as we find these have been leading one another, leading self, the ego, to these varied activities. (903-23)

Apparently people are drawn together or attracted until they have a harmonious relationship. We are seeing ourselves in the other person if we harbor inner hurts, hates, or resentments toward the other person. Until we overcome ourselves and resolve the problem, we are bound to meet the condition or the person against whom this attitude is held. This karmic relationship then does not conflict with the statement that karma is only with Creative Forces. We do create the problem.

On the positive side great love also has tremendous attractive force. This is what we sometimes call "good" karma.

Edgar Cayce frequently gave counsel as to how better family relations could be achieved. It invariably advised the individual to begin with self. When we are really trying to serve God and do His Will, our associations with others become more harmonious.

Q. Is there anything I could do, or not do, to be of better service to my family?
A. When individuals apply themselves for the greater activity for self, in keeping with those things that bring only the activities of being true to self, it makes for the greater activities to the associations or family ties. For when one is true to self, one cannot be false to others—if the self is the spiritual self. (797-1)

No entity enters a material sojourn by chance, but from those realms of consciousness in which it has dwelt during the interims between earthly sojourns, the entity chooses that environ through which it may make manifest those corrections—or those choices it has made and does make in its real or in its inner self. (3027-2)

Here we get an inkling as to why these two were attracted to each other and why they became husband and wife in this experience.

Q. How was I associated with my present family in previous incarnations: first, my wife, 2175?
A. As the father of the present wife in the experience before this, and didn't always make it easy for any—owing to associations with others! Also in the Palestine activity ye were closely associated as the companion or husband of the one who is the present wife. Again in Atlantis, the associations were rather as acquaintances and helpful influences one to the other, yet questions oft as to one another.
Q. My daughter 2308?
A. In the period before this we find an association, as well as in the English land.
Q. My daughter 1566?
A. In the Egyptian period close associates, as well as in the experience just before this. (2301-1)

This couple, 578 and 1003, had been together in their last earth experience, which was in the Jamestown settlement.

In 1003's answer to his question we find some "good karma" from that association with his wife.

Q. How was I associated with my present wife, 578, in Palestine?
A. She was then the entity's daughter. Doesn't she try to boss him now? As the associations come as has been given, the entity has chosen well. We will find much help, mentally, materially, spiritually. (1003-2)

And this advice was given to a woman who asked about former association with her husband.

In Egypt and in the Persian and in others. In Egypt closely associated. In Persia ye warred one with another, for he then was among those activities which at times made questions. In the present in the use of these, how has it been given: patience, kindness, gentleness, long-suffering, brotherly love. These manifest in thy relationships with thy companion. (2982-4)

A widow of fifty-three who was supporting herself and daughter asked these questions:

Q. What have been my past associations with the following and how can I best help our relations in the present? First, my partner.
A. In the activities just before this there were the closer associations, among those whom the entity nursed back to health. Ye have had to help him this time. Don't fail him.
Q. My daughter.
A. In the Holy Land experience as well as in Egypt were the closer activities; as a friend in one and in the other just the reverse. Hence at times ye find the daughter as a companion and at times she wants to tell you what to do! (3615-1)

The answer to this person's questions definitely indicates it is always a matter of "meeting self."

Q. Please give as detailed an account as possible of former incarnations in which I have known the following people; the type of association I had with each of them; the purpose of our present relationship; and instruct me as to how we may be of the greatest service to each other now.
A. (Interrupting) Details of these, of such, would be as an interpreting of that in self at some given period of activity.
    The mother, the father, 1472, 2795, all were in that Palestine-Roman experience. As to the manner of associations, interpreting their reactions and thine own urges, ye may find these in the greater detail thyself.
Q. René . . . ?
A. He who persuaded thee in the Atlantean. Beware ye are not over persuaded again!
Q. Richard . . . ?
A. A helpful force in the Egyptian, as well as in the

137

Roman or Palestine. A coworker in Rome, and in the Egyptian a helper—working together.

Q. Marion . . . ?

A. An acquaintance, and one to whom much is due. (2850-1)

The reference to René with its warning is explained by the following quote.

Before that the entity was in the Atlantean land, during those periods of the early rise in that land of the sons of Belial as oppositions, that became more and more materialized as the powers were applied for self-aggrandizement.

The entity was among the children of the Law of One that succumbed to the wiles, and it may be WELL interpreted in that answer recorded in Holy Writ, "Ye shall not SURELY die, but it is pleasant for the moment, and for the satisfying of longings within."

Thus did the entity begin to use spiritual forces for the satisfying of material appetites.

Thus again, the needs for the interpreting in self of its ideal—spiritual, first; and know the author of same. And let that in the mental be held in abeyance to that spiritual ideal, as well as in the application of such in the material associations. (2850-1)

A man, 2460, who was told he was a grandson of Noah asked questions about his family relationships, which were causing difficulty in the present. His reading said his last earth experience was in this country, "and many of those about the entity in the present were among the associates or acquaintances of the entity during that period," but gave no details on the following questions:

Q. What associations in past incarnation cause the feeling of irritation toward my son—and how may I overcome this?

A. In the building of Babel, as well as in Laodicea.

Q. What were my past associations with my wife, 2330, that have created our present problems, and how may I meet these conditions for our mutual development?

A. Worshiped from afar in the past experience just before this [early America, Virginia]; as a companion or a relationship of those with whom the entity labored. And, so close—oft—not all that glitters seems bright.

Q. Give past associations with my sister, 1523—explain the urges that may be helpful to each other in the present.

A. The associations were as brother and sister, during the return of those to the land; being one among those whom the entity aided. They lose patience one with the other just as they did then.

These are to be turned, of course, into channels in which there will be "give and take." No one individual knows it all, though each of you feels you do at times! (2460-1)

Though very little information is given in the answers to these questions, we can see the source of the present problem and why it must be met.

Q. What was my relationship in the past incarnations with Robert Carey? Explain the present urges from these incarnations.

A. In the English experience, very unsatisfactory —because he left thee and ye never quite lost sight of the manner in which ye were treated. And doubts have arisen. Yet there are those obligations, those things to be worked out together yet.

As may be indicated from or by a little imagination of that as would arise from such experiences, these are the urges in the present.

Q. Should my present relationship with him remain closed?

A. It will be opened of itself, for it is not finished as yet.

Q. What attitude should I hold for our mutual development?

A. As ye would be forgiven, forgive. (2791-1)

The life in England was during the time of the early Crusades, "when there were those activities as to ideals that were rather ideas."

The manners in which individuals and groups were left, and the entity with its sex and with its activities, being left apparently with an unmindfulness of purposes, brought resentments. And yet the cowarding, by the force and power used in some portions of the land, brought determinations, not hates—these are far from the entity's experience. And count thyself blessed that hate is not a part of the experience, though the holding of grudges is sometimes too easily manifested. (2791-1)

Thus we can begin to understand that we are meeting ourselves and that "no association or experience is by chance, but is the outgrowth of a law, spiritual, mental, or material." (2753-2)

Here in 2030's questions are examples of past associations, both with members of the family and with others. It gives a good illustration of the way the relationship in former lives may vary within the family.

Q. Where have I been associated with the following in the past, and what were the relationships: my mother . . . ?
A. In the Egyptian, mother and son; in the Persian, the mother was then the one to whom the entity was wed, being of Jewish descent [the present mother]. In the experience just previous to the present, brother and sister.
Q. Billy . . . ?
A. We don't find Billy.
Q. 487?
A. Especially in the experience during the Egyptian influence or force, as we find, were their associations very close.
Q. 1983?
A. In the Palestine experience we find the associations, or the Roman.
Q. 341?
A. Almost as an adviser or counselor, or of an even greater influence to the young king during that experience—in the Egyptian sojourn. (2030-1)

Another example of a variation or change in family relationships was in 2340's family:

Q. Have I been associated with my parents before; if so, where and what were the relationships?
A. As we find, in the Roman experience the relationships were in a family manner, though not in the same relation as in the present. (2340-1)

Our little Franz Liszt's (2584) family relationships were given in the following questions:

Q. How has the entity been associated in the past with his present mother . . . ?
A. In the experience before this, it might be said that the mother was one who dwelt much upon the activities of the entity—though not materially associated. (2584-1)

This appears to be a case of one drawn to the entity because of his music but could refer to some other activity.

Q. His father . . . ?
A. Associations in the Jerusalem period, as well as in Egypt.
Q. His [paternal] grandfather . . . ?
A. In the activities of the experience before this, as well as in Egypt.
Q. His [paternal] grandmother . . . 1663?
A. In the experiences that are not indicated for the entity here, as well as in the Egyptian. (2584-1)

There had apparently been a former association with the brother, 2814, but no definite information about any former association with his brother was given in 2814's reading, as only one previous life was reported. This was his experience as Molière at the time of Louis XIII. 2814 was very close to his mother. His reading said: "One that will be found to be rather inclined to be moody, at times. It will cling to the mother, and the mother direction, as it did in the experience before this." An interest in music, however, was indicated. The questions regarding family relationships were:

Q. What connection with his talented brother, 2584?
A. This may be better indicated in other appearances; for there was not the association in the one indicated.
Q. Why has he come to his present parents?
A. It would be the natural attraction; for the mother, especially. (2814-1)

A pledge or oath of brotherhood resulted in a family tie in this life for 707. He had been born in this land in his last earth life and was an Indian medicine man, one of great influence not only in his own tribe but with other tribes. Again he is back in Alabama, born and living near the place he had lived before.

> Thou wert among the natives of the land that made for the first of the associations with thine white brethren that came into that portion of the land, thine own peoples in whose name thou hast come into the earth again. For with thine own present great-grandfather in the flesh didst thou then, as the medicine man of those people, make the first pact of brotherhood; for there the great camp of those people of the land was made—what is now about those little streams, thou in thine strength did set what was to those peoples—and as may be found intact in many places at present—the first conduits for the waters of that particular land, that brought *healings* to many that were afflicted with those things that made for warding off of what is known as *age* in the present. He was called Tecum Tec, or The Rock; and had the ability to call forth the understanding of the happy hunting grounds. (707-1)

The answer to this question seems to indicate that a past life association or tie of friend or family may result in a family tie later.

Q. What have been the associations with mother?
A. Mother in the Egyptian experience and a friend and associate in the one before this. (5241-1)

This next question makes us ask whether there had been

142

any prior association or not. Was it an unhappy association in the past, or is the brother a stranger to this entity?

Q. My brother?
A. We don't find the brother. That's why ye have these differences. (5241-1)

This next answer is interesting, as this woman's reading described a beautiful soul, interested in service and spiritual things. She was even told she had "healing hands."

Our attitudes or reaction to others, whether family or not, is very probably rooted in some past association. Number 2624 was told why she felt she did not belong in her family.

Q. Why have I always felt one apart from my family—brother and sisters?
A. Because ye were once cast out by some of those. (2624-1)

We can deduce from this answer that a feeling of not belonging does not necessarily mean there was no previous association. It could mean there was an unhappy one and something to be worked out in attitudes and family relationships.

Attraction of Souls

An answer in the healing group reading gave some explanation of the attraction of souls and why they sometimes stay for a very brief time.

Then, with the first breath of the infant there comes into being in the flesh a soul, that has been attracted, that has been called for, by all the influences and activities that have gone to make up the process throughout the period of gestation, see?
Many souls are seeking to enter, but not all are attracted. Some may be repelled. Some are attracted and then suddenly repelled, so that the life in the earth is

only a few days. Oft the passing of such a soul is accredited to and IS because of disease, neglect, or the like, but STILL there was the attraction, was there not?

Hence to say that the body is in any way builded by an entity from the other side is incorrect. BUT those mental and physical forces that ARE builded ARE those influences needed FOR that soul that does enter!

Q. The entity desiring to enter governs the change in sex, which may occur as late as the third month.

A. It may occur even nineteen years after the body is born! So, it doesn't change in that direction!

Q. The physical development of the child is wholly dependent upon the mother, from whom it draws physical sustenance, but its purpose, desire, and hope are built up or influenced by the minds of all concerned.

A. That's the first question you've asked correctly. CORRECT. (281-53)

Parents

We may wonder why we have the parents of the present and whether or not we chose them. These quotations throw a little light on that subject.

Q. Why did I choose to come to these particular parents in this plane, and for what purpose?

A. To learn many of those lessons that have troubled thee in thy doubtings in those experiences in the earth just before, and to learn to temper self as the lamb is tempered to the wind by Him that maketh both the lamb and the wind.

Q. In what previous appearances have I been associated with my present mother, and in what relationship?

A. Very close, in three of those relationships: in Egypt, in Persia, and in Virginia. (361-4)

These questions do not give the details one might wish, but they do show associations in other lives. Perhaps this young man would have asked about previous associations with his father, too, but the reading stopped.

Q. For what purpose did I choose my parents, and am I fulfilling that purpose?

A. These were as a channel only, for this particular entity. (3148-1)

Q. From which side of my family do I inherit most?

A. You inherit most from yourself, not from family! The family is only a river through which it [the entity soul] flows. (1233-1)

Q. Why was I separated from my parents at such an early age?

A. These are experiences that may best be known by the paralleling of some of the associations. For there are conditions, especially in the soul experience, not from the physical. For, remember it is the soul choice, the soul vision in which there are choices made for entrance into material experience, so that little of the channels, save as a channel, enters into the developing or retarding. For, as to soul—"Who is my mother, my brother, my sister? He that doeth the will of the Father!" (2301-1)

Q. In what period or periods was I associated with my mother, 1657, and what was the relationship?

A. Atlantis. She was your sweetheart then! (797-1)

This woman asked only about her mother. This was apparently due to the fact that she was living with her mother and was not closely associated with any other relatives at that time.

Q. How and where have I been associated in the past with my present mother . . . ? What are the present urges, and how may we use them for our mutual benefit?

A. These have been in more than one, and oft the conditions have been very much as they have arisen in the present. Before this, very closely associated; but ye mistrusted the entity who is now the mother, and in the present you find at times you wonder whether that's best or not.

In Atlantis you were in the same positions as in the present. The closer association brought the unfolding of the entity's abilities in Egypt after the disappointment.

Use the associations in the present—you can each

learn much from the other, but do not try to control either. Keep first those things that are first. Let the spirit and purpose guide. For, as indicated, the intenseness that is the natural heritage of Atlanteans that were thwarted in some period of activity is such that they will have their way. Do not do so to your own undoing. (3184-1)

Number 2148 had been previously associated with his parents, but his reading indicated that there was an even closer tie with his grandmother.

Q. What have been his former associations with the following: his mother, 2753?
A. As indicated, her son in the experience before this. Also in the Egyptian experience a close associate in activities in the latter part of that sojourn there.
Q. His father, 533?
A. In the experience before this an acquaintance, and related to but not in that same association as with the mother. Also in Egypt their activities were associated, as brothers then.
Q. His grandmother, 1409?
A. Oft has been the experience with this entity, but the closer association was in the Palestine experience. (2148-7)

Here we have another child who was close to the grandparents. Maybe he came to be with the grandparents rather than the parents, as there is no mention of the parents. His grandmother (3006) asked for the reading and was given directions as to his training, so she must have been the one with whom he was living.

Q. When, where, and how has the entity been associated in the past with his present grandmother 3006?
A. In the Holy Land we find there was an acquaintance, the entity receiving teaching from the one who is now the grandmother. And in the Egyptian land the entity was very close, being an offspring of the one who is the present grandmother.

146

Q. Why did this entity choose this body?

A. To meet the needs for the conditions in which there might be the unfolding for many of those things that were patterns of the experience through the varied activities in the earth.

Q. Has the entity been associated in the past with his paternal grandfather . . . ? If so, how?

A. In the experience before this. There the associations were as a helper and instructor one to the other.

Do prepare this body for the work, the opportunities it may have. (3202-1)

The questions below are from the reading given for a young girl of thirteen (2443-1). They explain somewhat why associations come into present lives and the reason for urges in the present which had their source in lives centuries before.

Astrologically, she had the love of home and the seeking of friendships. The friendships, however, would often appear to her just beyond reach. These characteristics came especially from two previous lives, one in this country and one in Rome.

Q. In previous experiences has the entity been associated with members of her present family? If so, were such associations amicable and pleasant?

A. Most of those in the family have been in one or the other period of the entity's previous sojourns, or some in most every one of them. For again, remember, as indicated, as ye sow, ye reap; and ye meet individuals in those activities.

We find that the present mother was also the mother in the Macedonian sojourn, and that the present father [1797] was also associated in that period—though far from being the father then, or even a companion, but rather the association was as of one being pitted against the other. Hence we find that tiffs arise at times in the present.

The brother [1817] was associated with the entity in Atlantis, as well as in the "city in the hills and the plains."

Q. How may the entity so conduct self as to live in the happiest and friendliest manner with members of her present family?

A. As indicated, the family—not merely by precept but by example—shall point out and direct the entity in those ways in which IDEALS are constantly—not by others so much, but by the entity—chosen and kept before self as something to be approached.

Q. How may this entity be helped so as to make friends and get along easily with others?

A. If one would have friends, one must show self friendly! This is not merely as an idiom, or as a saying, but truth! This should not be merely preached at the entity, but practiced WITH the entity!

Allow a great deal more of the visions to be expressed by the entity. And seek counsel from the entity as to the little things about the home—entertaining, friends, and the like. For, there ARE IDEAS! Hence give them the opportunity for expression, and not "preach at" the entity!

Q. Was the Atlantis experience the basis for the urges which make the entity high-strung and oversensitive?

A. Atlantis, as well as the Macedonian experience, when the entity was "sat upon." This makes the entity high-strung, or with the dislike of being "preached at." (2443-1)

Case 2390 gives some very interesting details, not only of parent relationships but of why an entity, having chosen its parents, elects to cut short its material sojourn. It also explains certain urges and emotions of the present experience, the influence of the former life upon those about the entity and upon the soul experience of the entity.

The [previous] sojourn of the entity in the material experience was short, as counted by material means or man's count of time; we find that the manners of activity about the entity during that period should be of interest, and their influence that prompted much in the experience, also the influence the entity had upon others. It should also be of a real study to those who analyze such as is CALLED the psychology of life.

148

We find many interesting facts in the experience that might be indicated. While not given here at first in chronological order, these should be put together in real outline.

For the entity's departure and entrance in the present covered an earthly cycle, according to that accounted by those of Holy Writ. The entity departed on the 24th of August, 1876. It entered again the 24th of August, 1910. Thus a cycle. . . .

Ye may ask what this has to do with the influences, the environs in which the entity sought entrance in this experience, as related to its experience when it departed—as it were—so early.

Something of the background of that environ may be given, then.

We find that the entity was born of a people and an environ created by a union of two very differently tempered individuals; and the entity seeking expression—as Leila—sought for that which was the greater hope and desire of the mother. Then an activity which caused the entity to seek deeper meditation—as indicated—or to realize the decision NOT to live.

For life itself—as has been given—is manifestation of God. Thus a soul, an entity, may hold on to life so long as it WILLS to obey that which is the consciousness as to the relationship OF the entity to life—or God.

Thus, as has been given and as is demonstrated or illustrated here.

Man may seek to give names to many of the conditions that arise in the experience of the young—or children. For, as is known, the greater numbers of the changes are during the first, second, and third year of experience upon an earthly plane, because of disobedience upon the part of one or the other, or both, such as to cause conditions that make the desire on the part OF such an entity NOT to maintain the consciousness in materiality. Thus it seeks ways, manners—as did this entity—to return to that effacement, and enfacement, which its conscience at that period becomes aware of.

This is demonstrated in this entity's experience in this particular sojourn in the present, that at the same age in years (earthly) there was that consideration for the same experience as HAD been gained or had before. For, as is and was understood by the preacher [Solomon—in Ecclesiastes], "What IS has been, and will be again."

As to that gained by the entity, then:

The material environ of affection, of association, of care, finds an expression in the present entity in a manner that at times it does not even acknowledge to self; yet it is latent.

The entity is affectionate to an exceptional degree, at times, yet with every man holds afar and seeks first to establish relationships as a friend, as a pal, though deep within self there is that affection as was so lavished upon the entity by the NUMBERS about the entity during that sojourn.

There is another latent experience which has come to the entity in vision, in dreams—a face in smiles, with a peculiar cut of beard upon same, oft associated with a lake—or water. This has come as flashes, as dream, and was a portion of an association, an affection the entity experienced through that sojourn, that caused the undeterminate manner—and thus the lolling away, the wasting as it were, not understood; holding as to what were the manners of expression between disappointment upon the one hand and that of affection from one to whom the entity was never so close and yet so, so very near in many ways or manners.

In the experience, it is given that the entity gained and created in the minds of those a tie that gave the expression to many, as to the love expressed in HIM.

To those about the entity, then, to know the entity was to love the entity—to see that expression in same that brought the expression oft, "A little angel!" This was oft the expression of those about the entity.

Hence the entity in the present oft cringes to those who would speak endearing words; and some words of endearment, of endearing terms, even cause the entity to shudder in the present.

Ye may ask—rightly—WHY such urges are in the experience so definitely as is indicated. Because, as given, of a one cycle. For remember, death in the material plane is birth in the spiritual plane. Birth in the material plane is death in the spiritual-mental plane.

Hence the reason that when those physical manifestations began to be impressed upon the brain centers—those portions of an individual entity that are a constant growth from first conception—there were the impressions to hinder rather than aid the memory of other experiences.

Yet here we find a manifestation where THIS entity, as indicated, should it choose or determine to do so, may see and experience (as it has in flashes) much of that experience now being interpreted here for the entity, as well as others. . . .

For, as ye gained from same, and as it made or builded that tie by the activity through the experience, that brought a spiritual attunement to those who had known the entity even for the span of the two years and eight months (to the day), there may come a usefulness in same, in moulding the ability to have—PHYSICALLY—what it longs for, hopes for—PEACE in Him. (2390-2)

Probably more details of family relationships down the ;es were given in 2753's reading than in any other.

In giving the interpretations of the records for this entity, these have in so many ways been associated with the entity through whom this information comes that these may be shaded; though these will be given with the desire and purpose that this be a helpful experience for the entity, enabling the entity to better fulfill those purposes for which it entered this present sojourn.

No association or experience is by chance, but is the outgrowth of a law, spiritual, mental, or material.

These will be found to be bound with this entity here, in each phase of their experiences. Thus this should be an interpretation that may enable those who would analyze or study same to see how, why, and where the various phases touch materiality at any given point.

Before this the entity was in the land of the present nativity, when the entity as Polly Moran, a cousin of Archibald Cayce (and the maternal activities through that experience), brought those abilities in the present for the greater relationships as to home building.

For the entity then, as related to this entity as indicated, was the mother of William Cayce, paternal father of Edgar Cayce!

Thus the close relationship. For again, as in that experience in Chesterfield County, Virginia, in 1692, the entity was a relative, and again in twenty-six [1826] the entity entered and was a relative—the paternal mother of its own children in some of its activities.

Through that experience the entity brought hope to many. While there were periods of unrest, periods of activity, periods of doubts and fears, much of those abilities as the home maker and home builder arise from that experience as Polly Cayce.

Before that the entity was in the Roman experience, when there were those activities so closely following the period of the Master.

Then in the name Erbert, the entity as the wife of Ersebus(?), a companion of Lucius in the activities in Laodicea and in Rome, was closely associated in those activities there and brought about in a strange land much that was of a practical nature in the application of the tenets of "Love thy neighbor as thyself."

There the entity Ersebus, as the entity's present companion or husband, was in that same relationship in that experience—and he was healed by Lucius, as there were those periods when there was that necessity for the entity Ersebus to fight with the beasts in the arena.

These bring at times in the experience of the entity the fear especially of wild animals, as well as the fear of open spaces alone, but companionships and the ability to give encouragement to others in groups is a part of the entity's experience in the present.

Before that the entity was in the "city in the hills and the plains." There the entity was an offspring of Uhjltd [E.C.] and his companion, who helped to establish and to build up the "city in the hills and the plains."

And the entity became the companion of one who attempted to override the activities of Uhjltd, causing some of those persecutions that brought about the division in the household later.

This brings those experiences of fear of clans, fear of groups, yet a particular experience as to blood relationships in the material world.

Abilities as a good nurse, abilities as one who may make for good companionships, are a part of the experience that may be manifested in the entity's present sojourn.

The name then was Isabel.

Before that the entity was in the Egyptian land, when there were those activities that established the periods of the regenerations of individuals.

There the entity was made as a priestess to the Priest, Ra-Ta, in that experience. While these were considered as the companions, yet in those experiences they were as the spiritual rather than the material relationships—as were the active forces through many of those that through that experience were purified or consecrated, by their activities either in the Temple of Sacrifice or in the Temple Beautiful.

From that experience there are the present abilities arising for straight thinking, that being offtimes —according to others—too easily persuaded by others, or the allowing of others to put burdens upon the entity. These are understandings to the entity, rather than as a fault.

These, of course, may be used as the developing force towards the learning not only of faith but patience. For in patience, as the entity learned then, ye become aware of your soul.

The close association with the Priest may bring the closer associations and activities through these material experiences; at least the acquaintanceships from other experiences have brought and do bring the closer activities and relationships.

The name then was It-Eb-El.

Before that the entity was in the Atlantean land, when there were those activities where there were the divisions of sexes.

This entity was in close relationships with those who were among the first offspring of such divisions, thus being among the first of the princesses of that particular period of activity.

The entity was raised to power, for the entity was blessed with that ability to hold to those things that had

153

been the practice of the father in that period or sojourn.

Thus the spiritual, mental, and material relationships to the entity are those channels through which growth comes.

The name then was Is-Es-So.

Q. When, where, and how have I been formerly associated with the following: First, my husband [533]?
A. He was Ersebus. Ye were the wife of Ersebus.
Q. My son [2148]?
A. These will be found better by paralleling the two life readings. These came in an experience before this, as well as in the Palestine period—when ye were his sister; but this was not of long duration in the material plane. And then in the Egyptian period, he was thy son then. (2753-2)

The answer regarding the relationship with her son was:

As indicated, her son in the experience before this. Also in the Egyptian experience a close associate in activities in the latter part of that sojourn there. (2148-7)

Q. My stepmother . . . ?
A. In the Roman land, the association then was as the daughter of the entity now known as ————.
Q. My father . . . ?
A. In the Egyptian as well as in the Atlantean.
Q. Edgar Cayce?
A. As has been indicated. These are as close relationships in both the material and the mental, and in the spiritual activities of a material world. (2753-2)

Home and Marriage

Karma is inextricably tied to attitudes and feelings; so references or questions on home and marriage are found in most life readings. The closeness of the marital relationship naturally produces problems which have to be met. Moreover, we take these problems with us until they are resolved. We will meet the person or the problem in some future sojourn unless we face self and resolve the problem.

Of course, the home and family present problems. The readings given by Edgar Cayce indicated that this is a vital part of our development; but both home and marriage should be part of what one seeks as his ideal. When asked if marriage as we have it is necessary and advisable, he answered simply: "It is!" (1641-1)

> For what is marriage? A man and a woman laboring toward an ideal set by God Himself—two souls manifesting as one in hope, in fear, in desire, in aspiration. (2072-15)

Q. Is marriage an aid or a detriment to man?
A. It is ever an advantage, ever a help. (257-6)

Before God and man there was the promise taken, "Until death do us part!" This is not idle; you were brought together because there are those conditions wherein each can be a complement to the other. Are these to be denied? (2811-3)

Q. Will I be much benefited by this experience, and how?
A. It depends upon the application. EVERYTHING in the experience depends upon the application. How will you use your opportunities? For weal or woe? These are NOT set! They do not happen irrespective or regardless! Life is earnest, life is work, life is doing; not having poured out, not having it given, but WORK! (1235-1)

> The home is the foundation of the ideals and purposes of the nation. Hence it should be and is sacred in the experience of those who would serve Him wholly and surely. (3241-1)

The home—the highest of man's achievements in the earth. But let each give and take, knowing that this is to be a fifty-fifty proposition. When necessities require waiting and patience even in those things that may at the time appear to be negligence on the part of one or the other, do not rail at such times or allow those things to become stumbling blocks, but always reason well together. In every association, whether with one another, with your own friends, or with strangers that enter, let your activities be more and more directed by the spirit of hopefulness and helpfulness in your attitudes with one another. And as these grow to the harvest in life, the Lord may give the increase. (480-3)

All entities—as these two entities—meet for a purpose. As to whether their ideals are the same in the meeting, does not depend upon the attraction they may have one for the other, rather upon what they have done about their ideal in their associations one with the other in varied experiences, or in some definite period of activity. Whether these have been for weal or woe does not prevent the attraction.

Thus, whether that attraction is to be for the advancement or the undoing of something in themselves depends, again, upon what is the ideal of each. (2533-7)

This couple (2390 and 2533) were attracted to each other from several former earth experiences. However, they had their differences. The wife asked why her husband could upset her so in little things and how she could overcome this. She was told:

Read what has just been given of thine own willfulness you are meeting. Many of these have been in various associations with this very same entity. Not in England as the one that caused those uprisings within self, but these are self—not 2533. Don't blame 2533! Don't blame self! But get out of it! Set it off, aside, and take a look at it! You will see in most instances he's right—you admit it, but you don't want to agree to it! (2390-9)

She was told that her willful ways came from an experience in England.

So seek that guidance—even as those urges arise of wanting to do and to have self's own way. These arise in the present experience from those willful ways, those willful experiences through the activities in England; for there may still be found about Salisbury those records of that wayward Oglethorpe gal. (2390-9)

These two have remained together and are working out a harmonious relationship.

Here a couple were told that they could aid each other in their development.

Q. What was the former relationship between myself and my present husband?

A. In the Palestine and Grecian land, when the entity—as Cleopiasis—acted in the land, the relationships were the same as exist in the present. For both were Grecians, beautiful of body, high of mind, and represented the Grecian activity in the Palestine land. They were in those of crosses oft in the land, owing to the turmoils in both the political and the religious activities, yet they learned much; and again they are together, that their lives may be more and more founded in that which was heard by the entity in the experience, "I am the resurrection; I am the life." Then, in thy relationships, let thy yeas be yea, thy nays be nay in the present; but ye become a tonic one for another if thy prayers are oft together, if thy purposes are as one.

Q. Will our love for each other endure through the years to come, so that we will live in harmony, or not?

A. If these are made more and more in accord with those of the spiritual imports, more and more harmony will be the outgrowth from this association. That each must bear and forbear one with another is true, for as ye were aliens or strangers in a strange land, under those of *unusual* experiences, so do ye find in the present associations thine minds and thine temperaments often as at war one with another, yet tempering these with patience, with mercy, with long-suffering one with another, ye may aid each one in the other's development.

Q. Would my present husband and myself each be happier living together or separated?

A. Living together. For that which has enjoined each in the associations in this material experience is founded, as indicated, in truth and light and love.

Q. Should I quit office work and keep house now, or wait until later?

A. Until later. Let that which is being purposed, which is being builded through the experience, that a sacrifice is being made in the present that those of thine own obligations may be met and thine own loved ones have the greater opportunity, not become as a burden or as a wonderment as to whether there is growing estrangements. For remember, *love* begets love! But when there begins the seeking for the data here and there, that thou hast experienced and may draw upon in thine inner self for the compilations of articles, books, manuscripts, or the like, then begin at home.

Q. How much longer should I continue my office work?
A. Through at least another year. (811-2)

Divorce

A couple on the verge of divorce, who had been separated for a year and a half, had a reading on their problem and relationship. They were unhappy, apparently somewhat in the position of not being able to live together, yet not being able to get along apart. Their relationship was karmic, and they were told they should and could work out a harmonious relationship. They had been together in ancient Egypt and had joined forces against the priest and the king of that period in a rebellion. At that time they had developed rebellious spirits and characters which were manifesting in this life. The wife, 263, had in many lives been in a position of power. In the life just before this one she had been socially prominent, associated with the civil and military groups in and about Charleston, S. C., and Fort Sumter.

Here is some of the advice given to them:

It would be well that each analyze the information that has been indicated for each, their faults and failures AND their virtues; and that each not attempt to find their differences but rather that upon which each CAN agree.

There ARE agreements in some directions. There are differences in many; yet, as is understood from the experiences of each, as well as the information indicated, it is NOT by chance that there is this union of activities in the present; but if each will accept same it is an opportunity through which each may be the gainer in the soul, mental, as well as material development.

If they each reject the opportunity . . . if they EACH reject the opportunity . . . it becomes sin and MUST eventually be met.

Then, there is EVERY reason for the ATTEMPT, at least, for each to meet these differences, and so little . . . save self, and selfishness, that prevents the attempt to at least meet the problems in the present. (263-18)

They were told to magnify virtues and minimize faults.

Study, then, to show thyself approved unto that ideal. Not merely because of what others may think, or because it is law, or because of that as may be said or thought, but because SELF desires to meet the problems . . . here . . . now!

And these will bring harmony, these will bring understanding, if there is the determination on the part of each to give and take.

It is not that either shall demand this or that of the other, but DEMAND OF SELF THAT YE MEASURE UP TO THAT THE OTHER WOULD HAVE YOU BE . . . IN THE CHRIST! (263-18)

Each was told to be more considerate of the other. It is difficult to say whether or not these two found real happiness together, but they did stay together and tried to work out a harmonious relationship.

Another couple considering a divorce had a joint reading seeking guidance on their problems. Though the couple were divorced later, the reading is of interest because of the karma involved. They had been associated in several previous lives and in the one just before the present one, which was an early American experience.

. . . Know that each enters with those activities in which each has lived and manifested, as a part of its natures, as a part of its MENTAL environs.

Also know that the meeting, the association, the activity in the material experience in the present is NOT of chance but a purposeful experience for each, and that each may be a helpmeet one to the other in attaining and gaining such an understanding of the purposes for that meeting, that association, as to ATTAIN the correct concept of the PURPOSE of their incoming or entrance into this material experience.

Know that this has not been completed in the present and thus is to be MET IN EACH!

Then why not now?

It is a practical, it is a purposeful experience—for each.

For the associations in the past experience in the lands about the present environs, or a portion of the same land and those environs about the Dearborn land, are those problems that form the present disturbance in the mental selves.

Do not then justify SELF by condemning one another! Justify self rather by living, being that which will be a constructive experience in the life of ONE ANOTHER!

For that is the INNATE, that is the real desire, that is the real purpose in each; else there would not have been that attraction one for the other.

For have ye either of you analyzed what real love is?

It vaunteth not itself; it thinketh no evil; it endureth.

And this IS the purpose, this IS the basis for that attraction one to another.

If material things then are allowed to become barriers, in the manners of expressing this influence, then the condemning of either by the other is condemnation upon SELF—and must be MET in self!

Study then to show thyself approved unto God! Be forgiving as ye would be forgiven. Remember that it is a partnership; not all to be given nor all to be taken by one. But do not CONDEMN either, ever!

Let thy ideals be rather as is shown in HIM, who patterned His experience in the earth among men in such a manner as to answer EVERY question of conduct, of mortality, of associations in ANY way and manner!

Then when ye are, either of thee, in turmoil—NOT one shall do ALL the praying, nor all the "cussing"; but TOGETHER—ASK! and He will give—as He has promised—that assurance of peace, of harmony, that can ONLY come from a coordinated, cooperative effort on the part of souls that seek to be the channels through which His love, His glory may be manifested in the earth!

Do not let aught separate thee! Else it will be the destruction of thine own selves through THIS experience! (1523-6)

This couple did not manage to resolve their differences and were later divorced.

The inability to attract a desired marriage, home, and family can be due to a former life. Miss 369 longed for a home and family. She especially yearned for a baby daughter but never had one.

[In a life, in Persia] . . . the nomads entered into the land of Croesus and took those of that land as hostage for the tribes. The entity [369], then the ruler's daughter, and in that school or that place so raided by the peoples, and the entity was taken as the hostage for Uhjltd, the leader in this raid, and held as same by this leader until taken from him by the next in charge [195] and there remained. In the experience of the entity then in the name Elia, that horror of being forced into any action, whether of mental, physical, political, or any condition of subject to another's will. The entity lost through this experience, to the detriment of self, to the low dreg that of taking life in the way to satisfy self; not in defense of principle or of self, country, or position, yet in the early portion of the life giving much to many in many ways. (369-3)

Not only did this Persian life leave its scars on this girl's soul (for she seemed often to consider suicide in this life, due to her unhappiness); a still earlier life in Egypt was casting its shadow. For many years she was involved in a love affair with a man who treated her unfairly. She asked:

Q. In which previous incarnations, and in what relationship, was the entity associated with the one who means so much to her in the present?
A. In Egypt; related as the husband after the exile, after the changes came about. To this entity the body turned,

leaned upon, meant much—yet destroyed much in the relationships with many during the experience. These should be builded and met in the present in much the relations as dependent one upon the other during that experience; yet those conditions as mean for the relationships should be, *will* be—if they will be followed—for the *developing* for each in the present relationships; for the dependence one upon the other is stayed. (369-7)

Her reading further said that the association was for the development of both in the mental and spiritual, or *soul,* development of each. It also said they should depend upon each other, and it could have meant that marriage would be beneficial to both. For some reason the man did not desire marriage, yet he seemed to love her; so the girl was literally eating her heart out. When she sought further explanation of his attitude, she was told: "As the body is being treated in the present, so the body treated the other in that experience."

Q. Before we entered the earth's plane this time, had we agreed to work out something together?
A. Rather the conditions existed, and the natural consequence was to be *drawn* together for the privilege, or opportunity, *of* working it out! Whether this is *done* or not is up to the individuals!
Q. Have I filled my part of the contract?
A. Thus far! What's to be done later now remains to be seen!
Q. Had he lived up to his end of it, how would this have turned out?
A. That's a question yet that may be! For these ever depend upon the wills, or the activities, of individuals as respecting their relationships. This *should* have made, however, had each remained faithful *to* that as in self, or as to what each means, does mean, *well* would have been the outcome! An advancement for each.
Q. Should he at some time desire to carry on the association again, has he not proven that I should not even consider it?
A. That depends!

Q. On what?

A. What is to be built by each, and *how* the relationship would be renewed! (369-9)

The man had become interested in another woman. This may have been due partly to the fact that this girl would break off their association. She would weaken then and renew the association. This entanglement so affected 369 emotionally and physically that she thought more and more of destroying herself. Apparently this thought pattern simply "took over," for she was found in her car in the garage, no gas, dead battery, ignition on, closed doors, indicating she had again taken her life. According to her friends, she had not been planning this. Her frequent thoughts simply manifested.

Some interesting comments were given to a young naval officer who had been divorced prior to his first life reading. He was told: "When ye leave the Navy, marry—but not IN the Navy." He asked about prior association and marriage with three girls in his first reading and about others in his second reading.

Q. What have been my past associations with Willetta . . . . And for our mutual mental and spiritual development what should be our present life association?

A. These have crossed thy past oft. In the experiences before this as a friend and associate who understood, yet not able to give that help either socially or materially as was desired.

In the experience through the Roman land, more closely associated.

But the closer still in the Atlantean experience.

As to what these should be, they should be natural growths and choices of each, rather than as a SET thing. For these, as they meet themselves, there is either the helpful or detrimental force wrought from the varied activities. These may all together become beautiful, if the purposes are one. If there are those things in common for creative forces, then beautiful—and close associations.

Q. With Lucille . . . ?

A. These as we find have crossed oft. Not very good at

163

any, too contentious one with another.

Q. With Betty . . . ?

A. These have met in the varied forms and manners. The BETTER may be determined by whatever the choice may be in the efforts in the present activities. For there is much in common, yet the desires and the motivating forces of the spirit of each are far, far afield!

Q. With which of the above would marriage be most advisable?

A. The first, provided the choices of each are as indicated. First know what is that ye desire—thy purpose. Is it creative or is it selfish?

The field of activity lies in harmony—that is, music and writing. Then prepare thyself, as ye have in the natural heritage of thy experience in the earth. (1776-1)

In a second life reading the young man asked about four other young ladies. There had been an association with two of them but none with the other two. He then asked:

Q. With which of these would marriage be successful?

A. This should be determined by the entity itself, in the studying, analyzing, of the purposes and ideals.

For in consideration of marriage—if it is to be a success—it must be considered not from merely the outward appearance, a physical attraction; for these soon fade. Rather it should be considered from the angle of spiritual ideals, mental aspirations, and physical agreements. These should be analyzed in the experience of the entity, as in the experience of the companion, in the choice of such relationships.

For these relationships are representative of the purpose of propagation of species, as well as those ideals that arise from spiritual and mental relationships—see? (1776-2)

The following question, which was added to the second reading, shows attraction from the experience just before this one. In that life Jean Cowper was the young man's wife. Strange to say, these two never met in this life.

Q. What have been, and what are likely to be, my

relationships with 951, who was Jean Cowper in her former incarnation?

A. If there was a meeting, it would be a sunburst for both at once! (1776-2)

1776 had been married and divorced prior to his original life reading. Some years later he eventually married the first girl he had asked about in his first life reading.

This question in 1222's reading shows an unusual source of possible trouble for a marriage:

Q. Have I ever contacted my husband [2493] in any other experience; if so, in what way?

A. He bought you. Doesn't he act like it at times? [She commented later: "He sure does."] (1222-1)

This reference was to the life just previous to this one. It was during colonial times, when many were brought to become companions to those who had settled in the land. This young woman came to Virginia as one of the bartered brides, or casket girls, and was traded for 2,000 pounds of tobacco. She gained throughout that life, though it brought turmoil to her at times; for she established a home and aided in teaching and training the young.

She also asked about her children:

Q. Have I contacted any of my children before in former experiences?

A. This requires a great deal of searching, as to some, where, how. These we do not see in the present. (1222-1)

A report later indicated that 1222 separated from her husband, 2493. It probably had something to do with his attitude toward her, but she did not definitely say so.

In 1942 a young attorney thirty-six years old asked Edgar Cayce to help solve his marital problem. His dilemma was really that of the age-old triangle: Should he divorce his wife and marry the other woman? He sought guidance in his decisions, as he had lost interest in his wife; yet he felt he loved both women but in different ways, and he did not want to injure either one. He did have to choose between them, however. The matter was further complicated by the fact that his wife was unable to have children, and he desired a family; furthermore, he knew she had been unfaithful to him.

His reading gave him very specific advice but also revealed that this triangle was a karmic situation which had to be met. Moreover, this problem was centuries old and stemmed from choices or errors he had made at the time the children of promise journeyed from Egypt to the promised land. His first reading told him the reason for his present problem.

The entity was a prince among his own people, but one whose activity was of such a nature as to cause Eleazar to act to stay the plague among those peoples, in the matter of the entity's associations with the Midianite woman.

In the experience we find that the entity in the early portion was so WELL thought of as to be called a prince among his peoples, a judge, a counselor to his brethren, among those who were chosen as leaders. Yet the entity allowed self-indulgence, self-gratification, to so overcome all of those purposes, all of those longings of so many, as for the entity to do that which brought (even for the moment's gratification) such disturbing conditions among those who sought the right way!

Then, in thy experiences of the present day, choose thou rather God's way. Take Him, His principles, His directing influence into account, as ye counsel with those of thy brethren, those of thy neighbors. And who is thy neighbor? He to whom ye may be an aid, a help today—whether he be in the chair beside thee or upon the other side of the globe—*He* is thy neighbor!

So live, then, as to present thy own body a living sacrifice, as ye did unknowingly in that experience; for ye stood BETWEEN destruction and life, and giving thy life, even in such an act, not purposefully. But NOW, in intent of mind and heart and soul, ye must do GOOD, and not "do others" in the way that brings discouragement, disheartening, discouraging forces, or disturbances. (2052-1)

This specific counsel was sought and given in a later reading:

In giving that as may be helpful for the entity at this time, many things—to be sure—are to be taken into consideration.

As the entity innately has experienced, these individuals represent a definite activity taken by the entity in its experience in which there was allowed self-indulgence, self-gratification, owing to the beauty physically of that individual who now would appear PHYSICALLY superior to that other duty and obligation which is a part of the entity's present experience.

And to allow such an influence in the present to cause the discarding, the irreparable activity, would bring not only degradation but a continued consciousness of wrong-doing, and fear would creep in. And, so far as the mental and spiritual life of the entity is concerned, it would prove degrading to the entity.

As regarding spiritual and MENTAL conditions, there is only ONE course for the entity, and that is to discard ANY relationship with [F] other than of a purely helpful nature from the social angle.

There needs to be the closer relationships with the entity whom THIS body, THIS entity so belittled in that experience in which there were the needs for the priest to disregard the laws and to stay the plague of self-indulgence among those peoples.

Thus, putting away that individual who caused these will be for the betterment of self, for the development of self and that individual, as well as building for those relationships which may bring spiritual, mental, AND material blessings to the entity—through the closer relationship with (S), who was the companion in that experience.

In analyzing these conditions, to be sure, entanglements have come about, but these must be settled within self. Just as the consciousness has caused uncertainty, so will the correct spiritual and mental decision bring harmony and peace—and give BETTER activities in the experience of this entity [2052].

Q. If I remain married to (S) how can I have children, in view of her condition?

A. By having those things corrected, that may bring about such—if this is the desire of each. There should be an agreement, a real desire between the two; not one but both must make for that desire—and live like it.

Q. What will be the effect of breaking away from [F] on the one hand and so far as her future life is concerned?

A. Be better for ALL concerned. Choose. For, as was given in days of old, there is today set before thee good and evil, life and death; choose thou. (2052-3)

Miss Gladys Davis, Mr. Cayce's secretary, felt impelled to write to Mr. 2052 to explain his reading further. She gave him counsel which we quote in part:

Your problem is a very interesting one from the standpoint of our research on the law of cause and effect, according to the laws governing reincarnation. I don't know how familiar you are with the Scripture. You may not have understood fully the significance of your incarnation when you were the husband of (S) and forsook her for (F). Please read the 25th chapter of Numbers and you will get the complete story. Of course, (S) is not mentioned; we only know from the Reading that she was your lawful wife at that time. It was against the law of Moses for the Israelites to associate with women outside of their group. You, with many others, broke the law. And, to stay the plague, the priest used you and (F) as an example, because you both were leading citizens in your own group. Just in the same manner today the court might electrocute the head of a gang of criminals as an example, to show that it means business, for the good of the whole.

Naturally, you cannot in the present be free from (S)—you have an obligation which dates back to that period when you not only thought so little of her that you belittled her in the eyes of all the people by turning to a heathen woman, but you thought so little of the laws given to Moses by God that you broke them in such a way as to become a curse to many. Even if you got a divorce in the present, you would still be tied to (S). When a spiritual law is broken, it must be met in the spiritual realm. When a material law is broken, it must be met in the material realm. In that sojourn you broke both the material and the spiritual law. Consequently, in the present you have the opportunity to meet it in both realms—by remaining true to your material vows not only in the flesh but in the spirit. No wonder your conscience hurt you when you got the Mexican divorce. Don't you see it would be the same always—until you have met and overcome your obligation to (S)? You asked if the Readings ever advise divorce. Yes, they do. In several instances a divorce has been advised, where the two people had either overcome what they had to work out together or else one had overcome and the other WOULD not. But first every means has to be used to make things work. I notice from your letter some years ago you spoke of (S) going through a period of seeing other men clandestinely. Can't you understand, from the above, how that would be her natural inclination—if you were becoming cold with her? Not having been able to depend on you in that long ago period, no doubt she has felt many times the urge to defy you or to do something to hurt you—innately she must have felt this, because of the hurt you did to her long ago. These thoughts and feelings do not die, but they live on and on within us, from age to age, until we have either become so degraded as to have no conscience or else so spiritual-minded as to become one in purpose with our Creator. The dependent love which (S) holds for you is exactly what you need—it is giving you the opportunity to make up for that other time. No matter how many virtues (F) now has, they would not long remain virtues if you were married to her; because to you both any relationship of a sexual nature would mean sin—regardless of whether you were legally married or not, because you were both put to death because of such relationship and used as an example to break up the spell of sin that was bringing plagues to the people. With (S), holding the proper attitude of love and protectiveness which you should have, you could be happy—because you would know innately that you were doing the right thing, and you could make her happy. With your attitude changed, I am sure that you can find such happiness with (S) that you have never dreamed of. I would suggest that you talk to her about the Physical Readings, and perhaps a little later she will be persuaded to get a Physical Reading to find out how she may correct the pelvic condition so as to bear children. We have had remarkable results through the Readings with such conditions.

I hope you will take this letter in the spirit with which it is sent. My desire was to clarify matters as I see them.

The young man made an abortive effort to follow the advice given in his readings. Maybe his attempt was only half-hearted. Perhaps he partially worked out some of his karma. At any rate, two years later he returned to (F), having divorced his wife. This also proved to be unsatisfactory. So he went back to his wife and attempted to work out a life together with her.

The following letter was received in January, 1946, as a result of a request from ARE for information as to how his reading was followed and was working out in his life. It gives the details and the results, so is quoted exactly.

Dear Miss Davis:
Your letter of Nov. 30, 1945, received but reply has been long delayed because of current emotional problems still besetting me.

In answer to the specific question you ask in your letter.

As to a clear cut choice between the 2 women in my life. I found that neither one was a "soul mate," so to speak. Both were far more interested in security of self and not truly companionable. However, I am glad to say that I took part of Mr. Cayce's advice and went back to the first one, my wife, for a while. However, I was not heedful of his advice concerning my relations with the second one, much to my regret, as I married her after receiving an invalid divorce [Mexican], and have one child, who is unhappy with his mother. I did leave this woman and go back to my first wife, but am ashamed and regretful at not taking Mr. Cayce's advice at once. I have now left my first wife as I discovered that I never truly loved her nor any other.

At last I may say that I am truly spiritually awakened to the true meaning of love. However, the experience I have had, probably part of the karmic pattern, has left me so lonely and emotionally devastated that I have lost interest in life. Last summer I met some one who was an "old soul" but only aged 21, as against my 39. She loved poetry and spiritual things and she idolized me as I did her from the very beginning. It was a case of soul mates and mutual worship. Perfect companionship was our mutual experience, and we became wholly lost in one another. In music, literature and art, we found the same emotional interests. Two people could not have loved each other more.

The difficulty in the situation was that this girl had the same unfortunate experience in marriage that I had had and had not agreed on final separation when she met me. On Xmas Day, she and her husband, who had recently returned from abroad, agreed to separate, and she called her mother to relay the message to me. On the same day, coincidentally, I had come to a final arrangement again with my wife upon the obtaining of a valid divorce. That night, my loved one got another painful attack of diabetes (she had it for 2 years) and had to go to the hospital. Telepathy between us continued (she was 150 miles away) and I suffered agony and prayed that God would send her to me. On Friday, Dec. 28th, she died, and my prayer was unexpectedly answered.

Perhaps we violated some Divine laws or were suffering from prior breach of Karmic laws. Today I have a wonderful opportunity in the legal profession but find I am unable to work. The world seems so empty. Perhaps you can interpret all this for me and tell me whether it is possible to find such happiness again.

I am unburdening my soul in this way to you, Miss Davis, as you have handwriting which is strikingly similar to that of my lost loved one. Therefore, I am curious to know what you are like and what your interests are.

Mr. Cayce said that I was a strongly emotional being.

I don't know whether Astrology has anything to do with it, but my loved one was a Scorpio with Sagittarius rising and Venus in Scorpio—and likewise deeply emotional. It is hopeless to look for anyone similar?

I can't tell you how much I miss Mr. Cayce's work in a time of need as in the present as my soul seems lost.

With Best Wishes, 2052

Another unusual karmic triangle is found in 2329's file. She was told that there had been great advancement in some of her earth sojourns and great retardments in others. This was apparent in the urges latent in the emotional influences of the entity:

However, there should not be judgments other than as of the spiritual nature or value; and not as to anyone's moral code, but as to purposes of same.

Know that the birthright of every soul is choice, or will.

Choosing then to do that which is to self an expression of a spiritual Law, a spiritual desire.

This may be hard for some to interpret, but it has become a natural thing for the entity because of its experiences not only in this sojourn but in others; yet the entity must adhere to that which is the ideal. For that is the way and the truth and the light. (2329-1)

This woman had had two former life experiences which would certainly be trying ones.

[She was] in the land of the present nativity during those early periods when there were the attempts of groups or individuals to bring into the land those who would aid the men to establish homes, and to bring into being those purposes that were of the nature as to be home building in its broader and greater and better sense.

The entity was among those who were brought to be bartered; and thus not well chosen as to one with whom the entity would keep the activities in relationships to such. Yet, because of those purposes in keeping with the better forces, it may be said that the entity gained throughout that sojourn . . . thus was not in that position of having the home that was kept as a faithful home, but it was not on the part of the entity that there were those associations kept with others.

This brought determinations, sorrow, and the eventual breaking of vows. These as we find brought to the entity the material gains, mental anguish, and spiritual confusion.

In the present we may find periods when much of self's confusion arises from the EMOTIONAL natures of the entity.

Before that the entity was among those who lived in the earth during the periods known as the Holy Wars; then the French and Spanish lands were under those aptitudes or activities in which many of the men were taken or left their homes.

The entity was among those doubted by the companion and was forced to wear a stay that prevented conception or liaison with others. This brought periods of disturbing forces of many natures; the determining to sometime, somewhere, be free, and to "get even." . . .

For the forcing to remain in a state of chastity brought detrimental determinations to the entity.

That these have and do become portions of the entity's experience, then, is only the meeting of self. (2329-1)

The answer to her question, "What are my obligations to my husband?" revealed that he was the one who, doubting her, left for the Holy Wars. She was told:

These have been as problems ye have worked out together before. It was this companion who forced thee to be in that relationship during those periods of his journeys in other lands, which has brought to thee the OPPORTUNITY for the meeting of same in the present. (2329-1)

Her letters disclosed the fact that her husband was impotent. Thus we again see the retributive justice of karmic law working in the present. She now had the opportunity to "get free and get even" as she had resolved in that long-ago time. They both had grown spiritually, though, meanwhile. She did not now wish to hurt or embarrass her husband. She said he was a fine man who was in the present kind and considerate. So she did not wish to leave him; however, another man had come into her life who was deeply in love with her. She, too, was attracted and felt she loved this other man. One cannot help wondering if he was the one who had bartered for her in her last earth life. We do not learn what the previous association with this other man was, for her reading did not give that information.

This woman probably paid off her karma, for she remained with her husband and eventually gave up the other man. She had, meanwhile, comforted the other man and alleviated his longing for her. Thus she had not injured or hurt either one.

Though the following advice was given for wives with alcoholic husbands, it would apply in most cases where two people fail to get along together harmoniously.

Q. Just what should I do about my husband and home?
A. As just indicated, live right yourself. Never so act, in any manner, in any inclination, that there may ever be an experience of regret within self. Let the moves and the discourteousness, the unkindness, all come from the other person. Better to be abased yourself and have the peace within.

For unless changes arise, some great disturbance will come.

But if ye so act that these appear to arise from thy neglect or from thy not caring, then the regret would always be with thee.

Then, act ever in the way ye would like to be acted toward. No matter what others say or even do. Do as ye would be done by; and then the peace that has been promised is indeed thine own.

Q. Is there any chance of him ever overcoming the drinking habit? *
A. Not if there's given the least excuse for his continuation

* *Alcoholism*, Chapter III.

174

in same! But kindness, gentleness, and prayer have saved many a soul! (1183-2)

The attraction of this next couple came from a former life in ancient Persia. It seemed to be love at first sight, for after their first meeting the young woman went home and told her sister that she had met the man she was going to marry. They were soon engaged, and the marriage took place two years later. The marriage, however, was soon in trouble, for the man gambled and drank, and she had to support the home.

Q. What can I do other than have patience to bring about harmony between my husband [1439] and me?
A. Live thy life in such a manner that those who see thee, thy husband, thy companion (for ye have much to work out together!) will see that thou hast taken onto the words of truth and life.
Q. Is my husband's apparent weakness caused by any organic disturbance, or is he at times possessed?
A. This we would have from the experience of the husband. But as we find, the companion or the husband was thy weakness in the sojourns in the Grecian land and activities. *Thou* must be his strength in the present.
Q. Name the periods and relationship in which I have been associated with my husband and give a reason for the present association.
A. As indicated, in the Grecian—and the husband was the weakness. *Now* the entity, for the lost experiences there, must be the *strength* to him in the present.
Q. Is it for the best interests of all concerned to try to continue living at my present residence?
A. There apparently must come a change there. But let this come of the *natural* sources or natural conditions, and not of thine *own deliberate* making. (845-1)

In the physical forces of the body there needs be *rest*, there needs be relief from *physical, mental* anxieties. For these continue in the present to make for that influence wherein the very vitality, the very life existence is being put into that position of where there is the rebellion between the spiritual, the mental, and the material; and these make for such physical anxieties between the material forces and the soul forces that they rebel one with another.

Hence there come those injunctions as of old: "There is today set before thee good and evil, life and death—choose thou."

For He, thy example, thy mediator—yea, thy mentor—is life, the father of life, the giver of peace, the giver of harmony.

These then are as conditions in all the relationships, in the home, in the associations, in the domestic relations, in the activities. Whatever thy choice is, let these be ever with an eye to service to that living influence of being a better, a greater channel of blessings to someone.

Not of self-choosing an easier way; not of self attempting to escape that as is necessary for thine own understanding, thine own soul development; but rather ever, "Thy will, O Lord, be done in and through me—use me as Thou seest I have need of, that I may be a *living* example of thy love, of thy guidance in this material experience."

Q. Am I making any progress in working out the conditions which were caused between my husband and me in the Persian-Arabian period?

A. These have been helpful in self and in making for the greater opportunities for the greater service, that the changes as come may be of such natures that what thou chooseth to do may make for those periods of expression in a manner that will make for those forces that will bring development for both.

Q. Is he making any progress?

A. As man seeth, no. As looked on from the experience from soul forces, yes.

Q. Would a separation of any sort be of help?

A. This must be a choice within self. Self's own development is in jeopardy. Choose thou. As *we* would find, it would be helpful for a separation.

Q. Am I being someone's strength?

A. A strength to his development, and the realization may come the greater by the separation.

Q. Is there any way whereby he can be made to realize the harm he has caused by his activities?

A. As has been indicated, as has been given oft, this may

only come from within. And the *desire* for help, the *desire* for aid, must be within self.

The body upon the own resources, upon its own undertakings, though it may suddenly bring the separation from the experience yet in the main, in the *real* forces—and undertaking.

Q. Was anything wrong with the prescription to prevent his appetite for alcohol, or did his will force overcome the effect of same?

A. Will power overcame. For this only sets at naught the desire; and these associations, influences of "What will people say?" produced the activity to disregard those influences created by same.

If there is the desire, there may be added those properties again that are known as the gold cure. This will aid, but it will *not* prevent from the breaking through. That is, taking chloride of gold; one minim the first two days, two minims for two days, three minims for two days; then discontinue for two days and begin again. And by the end of the second round it will make him very sick; but it still may be overcome by will—but very ill to undertake for the first one or two periods.

Q. Should I try the prescription again?

A. Try this.

Q. How may I get him to stop long enough to get it in him?

A. Just give this in water when this is asked for; if this is desired to be undertaken.

Q. For the best interests of all concerned, would it be wise to commit my husband to an institution for correction?

A. This is the same as may be given in any of the better institutions. This may only be done through persuasion, but make the choice rather that this is as a last attempt to aid. Give those as just indicated. In the quieter moments make this rather as the last stand.

Q. What kind of work of activity could I get him interested in that would help him?

A. There must be some changes from within for the desire to be not only good—at *any* of those problems or those activities that he is well fitted for—but to be good for something for *others* rather than his own appetites. These must be created first.

Q. Has the change already taken place in my residence as

177

referred to in my life reading, or is it yet to come?

A. Will be yet to come, and depends—to be sure—as has been indicated—upon the changes.

Q. Is the craving for alcohol by [1439] an organic condition, or is he possessed?

A. An organic disturbance is merely a possession when it has reached the nth degree as to be possession. And hence, as has been indicated, oft such—when there is the understanding that the reliance can be only in truth and life—will either break or separate. (845-4)

The foregoing quotation shows the seriousness of the home conditions. Mrs. 845 made a real attempt to help her husband and resolve their problems, but it is evident that her husband did not want to overcome his alcoholism and that no one could help him unless he desired help. She had reached the place where her own spiritual development was in jeopardy, so was advised to leave her husband. The home conditions were further complicated, as this woman's niece had come to live with them. Mrs. 845 was assured that this was a karmic involvement which came from her Persian life, "where so many rejections and so much of self and so much of activity there is to be met. For each soul, each entity, *constantly* meets self. And if each soul would but understand, those hardships which are accredited much to others are caused most by self. *Know* that in those you are meeting thyself!"

In the Persian experience Mrs. 845 had been among the people who went from Greece to the city in the hills and the plains for understanding and aid. Yet later with others from the Grecian land she renounced "much of that which had been accepted by many from those teachers in the land, bringing into the experience those fears and doubts. And in that experience the entity lost as a whole, gained and lost; and in the present we find from that sojourn the fears and doubts arising from the activity in their relationships with individuals, with groups or the promptings in the experience of others. This, if the entity will look from within, is that which must be overcome in the present experience. Not that there is the trusting in others for their activity, but as for the needs that they, too, may be strengthened by the very *strength* of self as in Him who *is* the Giver, the Author of life, light, and immortality to the souls of men." (845-1)

So in the present life she had to choose. She was told:

> Remember, you are meeting self. In whatever choice is made, face the issues in thine own life, in those with whom you may be associated. For these problems that are thy problems are others' problems. Meet them as is befitting that as is *shown* thee in thine inner self. Loneliness is destructive, yet in *Him* ye may find companionship. (845-4)
>
> Hence there come those injunctions as of old, "There is today set before thee good and evil, life and death—choose thou." For He, thy example, thy mediator—yea, thy mentor—is life, the father of life, the giver of peace, the giver of harmony.
>
> These then are as conditions in all the relationships, in the home, in the associations, in the domestic relations in the activities. Whatever thy choice is, let these be ever with an eye single to service to that living influence of being a better, a greater channel of blessing to someone. (845-4)

The marriage did end in divorce, and Mrs. 845 did not remarry. A later reading said it would be better if she did not do so. It also assured her that while she had not sprouted wings, she had made great spiritual development. She helped many people and was of great service to ARE.

We have no later report on the husband.

The advice given this next couple indicates clearly that divorce is no simple matter; each case is individual, and generalizations are difficult.

Though these two were counseled that they should not separate but should try to work out their difficulties, they separated and were divorced shortly afterward.

Mrs. 2811 was again married in 1945, but it was a very brief affair. Her first husband also remarried as soon as their divorce was final. It seemed that he had been interested in the other woman for some time, and she (the other woman) also broke up her long-standing marriage to marry him.

179

In 1953 Mrs. 2811 married again, and that marriage lasted until the husband's death seven years later.

We won't separate here yet; there is a lot for them to do together: We won't answer questions yet. . . .

In considering activities between individuals in this material plane, there are many conditions to be considered. This relationship, which is the experience of each as a responsibility of one for the other, as one to the other, not something about which to find fault with each.

There has been a pattern indicated in the experience of man, to whom each should go. These are not old women's tales. These are men's, these are women's souls.

There should be, then, a seeking together; not finding fault with what has been done or what may be done, not spying on one or spying on the other. Each can think for self, but before God and man there was the promise taken "until death do us part!" This is not idle; these were brought together because there are those conditions wherein each can be a complement to the other. Are these to be denied?

These have not been fulfilled. These have not been completed. For there is the love, the hope, the desire that each be in harmony and peace. But the harmony and peace must be within SELF first, if it is to be between one another. This ye know, ye will never find harmony by finding fault with what the other does. Neither will the other find harmony without considering what the other will think, or be, or care for.

Know ye this, each of you: The law of the Lord is perfect, ye cannot get around it. Ye may for the moment submerge it, but thy conscience will smite thee. Try it! For a period of six months, never leave the home, either of you, without offering a prayer together: "Thy will, O God, be done in me this day." This is not sissy, else ye would not be conscious of thyself as being a living human being this day.

Then quit yourselves like children of God, appreciating that privilege. Speak to Him as to thy

Father; He will answer thee as thy Father who loves thee. (2811—3)

Karma, manifesting through its attractive force and memory, can precipitate some real problems which we have to face. Most of us have either seen or experienced a situation similar to this next case. It is, of course, something from the past, another karmic triangle, where the involved parties came to Edgar Cayce for advice. Mrs. 413 came with her husband, 289, her sister 845, and "the other woman," whom the reading refers to as R, saying that 289 and R were so much in love they didn't know what to do! Mrs. 413 told G.D. (Mr. Cayce's secretary) that she knew it was not a purely physical "sex" attraction, since 289 had been impotent for some time. Mrs. 413 and her sister, Mrs. 845, were both in tears and at their wits' end to understand or cope with the situation. The reading follows.

Mrs. C: You will have before you the relationship and the situation which exists with and between 289, 413, and R, present in this room. As I call the name of each, you will go over this situation carefully and analyze it in relation to that individual; giving the causes, whether physical, mental, or karmic, and advise the best course to follow considering that necessary for the best development of the individual. Then you will answer the questions submitted by each individual; first 289.

Mr. C: Yes, we have those conditions and circumstances, those personalities, the individualities of each here. These are conditions that are arising in the experiences of each meeting themselves from those experiences in the earth's plane and thus become what are commonly called karmic conditions.

If they each allow themselves to become involved in such a manner as to belittle, belie, their own conscience, their own concept of an ideal, then it becomes to each sin.

If there is the application of that which has been given by Him as the manner in which such relationships, such conditions may be met, then they become as stepping-stones for the experience of each.

These then under the circumstance, under the conditions which exist, become not as mere trite sayings, but as that which must be experienced and lived in the life of each—"As ye would that men should do to you, do ye even so to them."

That there is the recognizing of conditions that are in part an answer to those experiences in the existence of the entity in the material experience, then becomes hopeful in the experience of each.

Yet if there is self and self alone considered, these become as merely the egoism of each in such measures or manners as to become something that would debase all instead of that which should be beautiful.

Let love be without dissimulation, that is, without POSSESSION, but as in that manner as He gave. "Love one another, even as I have loved you"; willing to give the life, the self, for the purpose, for an ideal. Other than this, these become as that which will bring in the experience that in which each will hate self and blame the other.

Ready for questions.

Q. Was companionship lacking at home the reason for this situation?

A. Rather, as has been indicated, the answering of that in which the self finds rather the answer within self of former relationships.

Q. How can relationship between R and myself be suddenly stopped, when it has been going on several months?

A. Why should it be stopped? Why should it not be made beautiful, rather than that which becomes a thing ugly?

Q. How can this be done?

A. Make it so! So live in the lives, in the relationships, as to the duties and to the obligations! What must be to each the heritage it would give its children, its grandchildren, its third and fourth and fifth generations "to those that hate me or love self better than the love as shown in the grace and mercy which has been given each."

Q. Would a physical reading be helpful in overcoming this?

A. This depends upon whether there would be the practical application of same. The reading, or the information or knowledge as to the sources or the causes, is only making for each individual CHOICES to be made—and that must be within self, or else ye will hate thine own self!

Q. [R]: Why did this situation arise in my experience, and how may it be overcome?

A. Study to show thyself approved unto thy Maker, a workman not ashamed, but rightly dividing the words of truth. It arose from those experiences and relationships which formerly existed. Then make it a beautiful thing, and not something ugly!

Q. [413]: What have I done or failed to do which has resulted in this?

A. Condemn not thyself, as neither of the three should do; but quit yourselves rather as true children of a loving Father, so living toward each, not regretting, not rueing, not condemning because that which is natural in its nature arises in thine experience.

Thinkest thou that thou art the only one that has met or meets such in thy daily life?

This is not an excuse, then, but live, act towards each in the same manner as ye would that each would act towards thee if conditions were reversed.

For all stand as ONE before Him. Keep thy conscience, thy mind PURE before Him, knowing that no power arises save from Him, no emotion that arises in the experience of individuals can do so save through Him.

If such emotions are kept pure, they are as blossoms in the garden of God. If they are destroyed, they become stepping-stones to hell.

Q. Why is it necessary for me to have this experience, and what am I to gain from it?

A. Patience—and love. Why necessary? Meeting thine own self—as each is doing. In determining the activity that each should take, separate selves from the actual emotions that arise—pro or con—and look at thine own self. What would ye have thy God say? What would ye have thy children say? What would ye have thy neighbor say?

These, then, are not merely thoughts, but thy thoughts become deeds in meeting thine own self. Then, quit ye like true children of a loving Father. Be patient, be kind, be longsuffering—and above all, patient! But DO NOT break nor leave the ideal as is set in Him. "I condemn thee not," said He. Then neither condemn one another, but be ye like Him.

We are through. (413-11)

G. D.'s note: For a year or so longer Mrs. 413 "suffered" through the triangle when all were advising her to get a divorce, but it finally dissolved. See 413-13, A-4. See subsequent notations under 413-1 and 413-3 reports; also see subsequent Ck. Physical Rdgs.

January 26, 1942, letter to E. C. signed by Mrs. 413 and Mr. 289: After reading your message of Jan. 8th over and over many times [see under 2678-1, page 9], it seems so much like a divine message that I feel like just bowing my head and saying "Amen." I am very grateful for an invitation to join such a group, and may God hear and answer the prayers of every one. Sincerely, [289 and 413].

February 3, 1967, G. D.'s note: Mrs. 413 has given practically her entire home for the last 20 yrs. "taking care" of her invalid husband, Mr. 289.

5/20/68 her husband died, after suffering terribly for the last few years from emphysema. Mrs. [413] plans to live now with her daughter [578] and son-in-law [1003], to whom she is very close. (413-11)

GROUP KARMA

CHAPTER SIX

> There is a destiny
> That makes us brothers:
> None goes his way alone:
> All that we send into the lives of others
> Comes back into our own.

> —EDWIN MARKHAM, *The Creed*

Many philosophies teach that we reincarnate in cycles or at rather regular periods. Certainly souls and groups of souls must be incarnated at the same time, if they have things to work out together. The readings stress that souls do have the opportunity to meet again and again in earth lives until they have dissolved their differences and worked out any problems they may have. Some law of attraction draws these entities together. Chapter Five presented many cases of souls being together to work out mutual problems. The Edgar Cayce readings, however, show there is no regular or definite time between earth lives.

Miss 275's * family gives us as complete a picture of former relationships and karma within a family group as can be found in the Edgar Cayce readings. Every member of the family had at least one life reading, and details of previous associations were obtained in check readings. All members of the family were in Egypt during the Ra-Ta period; so a check reading was sought which would give more details on their association and/or relationship then. The interrelations and karma incurred can hardly be understood, though, without some knowledge of the history of the Ra-Ta period.

The priest Ra-Ta led the ruler Arart from Arabia into Egypt. Egypt was a land of plenty ruled by an elderly, weak king, Raai. The king did not defend his country, so the invaders took control. Things were fairly amicable for a while. But when Arart began to impose laws and taxes, dissension arose. A native Egyptian leader was influential

---

* See Chapter Three, case 275—cancer of the hip.

and powerful enough to incite rebellion. So the ruler Arart placed his son Araaraart [341] on the throne to deal with the natives. Araaraart was only sixteen years old when he undertook to rule the land. He managed to stay in power for ninety-eight years, through the various dissensions, revolutions, and rebellions. The native Egyptian who was the leader of the rebellion against King Arart was adopted into the ruling family as Aarat. This pacified the Egyptians, and Aarat became a valued aide to the young king Araaraart and worked with him for the good of all factions. The young king chose twelve men as counselors to help rule. The twelve were chosen from the various factions and represented the conquerors, the native Egyptians, and the Atlanteans. Many Atlanteans had been migrating to Egypt, as they feared another deluge would engulf their land. The Atlanteans, being a strong and capable people, more advanced than the Egyptians, also sought to take control of the land. Peace reigned for a little while. The king and his counselors administered civil affairs, and the priest Ra-Ta tried to influence the king to rule wisely for the good of all. Ra-Ta taught divine law and attempted to awaken the people spiritually and speed up their evolution. To do this Ra-Ta decreed the people should establish families, and the priests were to accept monogamy. Those who sought to discredit Ra-Ta persuaded him to take a second wife for eugenic reasons. When a child was born to these two most highly developed mental and physical beings, the plotters demanded that Ra-Ta be banished for breaking the monogamy law. The king was loath to do this and was really in a dilemma, for he depended upon Ra-Ta for guidance. Moreover, he doubted that this was the best solution for all. Araaraart finally yielded to pressure and banished the priest to the Nubian land, though the wise Atlantean Hept-supht had advised against the banishment. Since Hept-supht supported the priest, he, too, was exiled.

Iso, the priest's child, was kept by the king as a hostage. Later the king's brother Ralif led a rebellion (the Ibex rebellion) against the king. One of 275's brothers was involved in this rebellion.

The various groups or factions are represented in the present family. As they were in this Egyptian period of turmoil, strife, and rebellion, which naturally produced animosity and conflict, we can understand why they would have karma in the present. We can almost classify them as those who shared the priest's exile or followed his teachings and those who supported the king. The Atlantean Hept-supht, the father of the family today, apparently worked constructively for the good of all, often acting as mediator between the groups. He "went native" and married a native Egyptian daughter of one of the political leaders, so he was acceptable to all factions. His wife of that period is his present wife and the mother of this family group.

Since much of this karma began in ancient Egypt during the Ra-Ta era, check reading 275-38 is included here. It gives some idea of the turmoil, rebellions, and revolutions of the period.

In order that their association can be more easily understood, a list of Miss 275's family with individual case numbers is given, too.

> Miss 275—Ai-Si, seventeen-year-old daughter who had cancer of the hip.
> Her Father, 378—Hept-supht
> Her Mother, 255—Iszeiu
> Her twenty-seven-year-old brother, 452—Hi-La-Pti
> Her twenty-five-year-old brother, 282—Ra-La-Ral
> Her twenty-three year-old sister, 457—Issiun
> Her nineteen-year-old brother, 488—El-Tpan
> Her thirteen-year-old sister, 276—Valtui
> Her twenty-three-year-old sister-in-law, 301—Isibio; wife of 282, and 275's nurse.
> Her thirty-year-old brother-in-law, 412—Ariecel; husband of 457
> A friend, 288—Iso
> A friend, 341—Araaraart

Three nieces of Miss 275 had life readings also and were told they were in Egypt during the Ra-Ta period. For some reason, perhaps because they were not of the immediate family, they were not mentioned in the check reading on the period. It could be that their life readings gave sufficient detail of their lives then.

Her niece, 299—Del-lli; daughter of 282 and 301

Her niece, 314—Apt-Sio; daughter of 282 and 301

Her niece, 3172—El-Ex-Ea; daughter of 457 and 412

Her aunt, 1742—Lei-Diie (378's sister), though not in the family group, is included, as she was also in Egypt and Rome at the same time. She was of the opposite sex in the Egyptian period.

HLC: Give in great detail the history of the period of the priest Ra-Ta in Egypt, bringing in the actions and incidents of the following characters, bringing in the time and age of each when they entered the scene, and giving all the connecting links so that a story may be written: Hept-supht—now [378]; Iszeiu—now [255]; Hi-La-Pti—now [452]; Ra-La-Ral—now [282]; Issiun—now [457]; El-Tpan—now [488]; Ai-Si—now [275]; Valtui—now [276]; Isibio—now [301]; Ariecel—now [412]; Araaraart—now [341]; Iso—now [288].

Mr. C: Yes, we have the periods here, as in each. That this may be translated into the experience that makes for the cause of the associations of each individual in the present, it may be given in the manner as to how they each in the present find not only their associations but their own name and activity. For, as given in that respecting the influencé, the teaching of the priest, there was left with each entity a mark, either in body as expressed physically or in the name, that they each are called in their experiences. So, in the present we will give an outline showing what took place, if it were translated into the present view of experience of individuals. All of these are the modern names, you see.

The king or leader of the peoples in Arabia [165] led the whole of his land into Egypt. Among this group we find [452] (oldest brother), who was of those peoples, and one in purpose with that to be accomplished by the entering into the land. There was found the declining years of a very weak ruler in the land that had turned the greater portion into the hands of the peoples to do as they chose, so long as they did not bother him.

With the entering of the group, or of this clan, little or no resistance was made by the natives as to the establishing of order until there began to be set up the laws as to what was the contribution or tax on peoples in the native land. And some native, and natives, raised questions—which made for first the political positions of groups in the land. Among the daughters of the political leaders was [255, mother].

In the establishing by the priest that of moral law, and the beginning of the undertakings of the establishing of what we term in the present as religious activities or as service in rote by individuals that join themselves to such activities—at this time there was the coming into the land the Atlantean peoples. These were going back and forth for the periods of the rebellious influences; the activities of varied individuals in the Atlantean land were active in this period. Among those that came in and became native, we find [378, father]. He, with the modern ideas among a peoples that were attempting to adjust themselves to the varying conditions, joined with the priest in bringing something of order in the laws and in the direction of conditions in the period.

With the rebellion of the natives, the elder king [165] put the son [341, friend] on the throne to match wits politically with the native [900] in the establishing of the political powers and rule in the land. And with this establishing came that period when the priest [294] broke the law that was set by him concerning the number of wives accorded or given to the priest. And this brought first the political uprising. Then the religious war. And the priest with the princess [538] was banished, with all those that adhered to the priest's activity, including the aide to the priest—[378, father]—to the Libyan land. There we find the first establishings of the land as a place for carrying on that the priest had given in the way of man's knowing his relationships to the Creative Forces. In this activity [275] and [488, youngest brother], natives of the Libyan land, became followers of the priest. The children of the priest, [282, brother], [288, friend], were left in the land of Egypt as political hostages and religious hostages. The activities of the native [255, mother], in gathering much from that which had been given by the Atlanteans, estab-

191

lished what would be termed today a school and an
orphanage for the children of the land, hence applying
much that had been given as the relationships between the
Creator and the creature in material manifestations. Hence
these were under the care of this director in the land.

After the turmoils, the return first of the Atlantean
through the political influences brought to bear by the
numbers of Atlanteans that were sojourning and entering
into the land, as there were evidences and prophecies of
Atlantis being broken up, and Egypt was chosen as one of
those places where the records of that activity or peoples
were to be established. Hence the Atlantean, or [378,
father], returned after only three years in banishment. And
the union with the instructor and teacher, as man and wife,
began much of that which has been given of the messages
sent to and from Egypt and Abyssinia during the exile of
the priest.

Conditions settling somewhat, after political rebellions
and native rebellions and in the rebellions in those of the
family by the peoples that were both native and of the heart
or [165] clan, and among them [457, older sister], and these
acted in Ibex with the king's brother, who became a
stumbling block to many.

When the recall of the priest came, the preparations and
the return, including not only the household of the
priest—wherein was the wife with the children born to
them in exile, among—or the older of which was that one
who became the wife of the son of the priest, as they came
back into activity in Egypt—[301]. This occurring, however, many years later.

The return brought for all a new era of associations and
activities.

[452, oldest brother], becoming associated in the priest
activities—that during the years of decline, before
regeneration—acted in the capacity of making the lessons
or tenets applicable in the experiences of other peoples, as
demonstrated by the activity in the Arabian land
where [276, younger sister] was the ruler that came into the
land of Egypt to be initiated into the activities through the
temple, through the various associations of the necessary
activities of the groups that were taught by the priest, by
[275], [488, brother], [378, father] in their varied

positions have been indicated in that given.

As to the lives or the family associations, which, as we shall see, led to those activities, those marks as indicated, as set by the adherents to the principles of that taught by the priest, as making for marks that in body-physical or soul or both drew them together.

In the household of the Atlantean, or [378, father], [255, mother], were few of those of bodily drawing, save of others. Hence there and then, in their desire, those in their varied activities in themselves asked for, desired, sought that they might influence those in their expression or opportunity for their activities in a material world. Hence we find those in the present of their own household, their own activity, to mete to them in the present experience that which may furnish each with their own experience that of establishing that tenet as found to be the answer for an ideal in their experience in that association.

With those we find in each activity [452, brother] as the priest, only one as a companion or wife, that if sought and found in the present may make for a true union in this material world. And such as have in an experience found an ideal may be said to be soul mates, and no marriages made in heaven nor by the Father save as each do His biddings. For His sons, His daughters, His mothers, His fathers are they that do His will in the earth.

In this union there came only three, as to make for activities in their associations in the home life, acting as the emissary, much activity that has been indicated or may be given specifically was in the affairs of that entity in the experience, which may be likened unto the evangelist in the present.

In the home of [457, sister], as indicated, in the rebellious forces of the Ibex, yet coming under the influence with the establishing of the schools, the hospital activities (of which the entity that had been of the natives, or [255, mother], might be said to have supervised), she came to know [412, brother-in-law] in relationships in that association, yet each wending its own way without either ever being wed in the experience—and may be called, as in the present, each ever mindful, but never physically completed in their relationships.

In the life or home life of [488, brother], acting as one

that aided or came with—or among the 167 souls that returned with the priest from Abyssinia, being of powerful physique, what would be called copper-colored in the present, yet coming under the influence—with his abilities, with his activities in the land, both with the sister [275] in the experience, brought such of an activity as related to the athletics in the action of those that were developed by all the associations from the state, from the religious forces, or from the activities in all the relationships, made for a strong influence upon this phase of the development in the experience. But going as an emissary, under the influence then of the one acting as the evangelist—or [378, father], as has been given—lost in self when making relationships with those in the land that has since disappeared, that brought family troubles. And the pity, the love as expressed by those in power, drew him as among the fold in the present.

The sister [275] in the temple service as the one that not only aided in the sacrificial temple, where the initiations through fire in the cleansing of the body of desires for carnal influences, as well as the activities and services in the Temple Beautiful that made for the setting in order in the plaques that as would demonstrate or illustrate to the entity or individual that necessary for the purifying or keeping before them for the purification and in keeping same in their experience; joined with one in wedded life in the temple service, and when these relationships—are they established from that as was set before the entity in the activities of those that have become the father, the mother, in the present experience—may make for the home life in the present that will bring a blessing to self and the activities with and among others, joys and understandings.

In the life as in the relationships of [282, brother], [301, sister-in-law], as established in that experience, makes for what may be looked upon by many in the present as the ideal relationships when viewed from that as of man and wife in the present. Let each hold more to that as may come to them in those experiences of knowing that the counsel to those that are given activity in their care, that the words and directions in each counsel may be in keeping with Him who loved little children, who blessed them and said, "Of such is the kingdom of heaven," and there may

194

be builded in the experience of those that again come to their protection that which will make for the greater development in those souls that again seek through *this* channel for a manifestation in a material world.

In that in [276, sister], as given in that as was given by the entity in its application of unconsciously applying spiritual law in material world to the things that became much of a blessing to mankind in the application of the spiritual laws as gained under the supervisions in the Egyptian land of those that are as companions in the present, that as aided in giving to a people the blessings of the consciousness of their souls in themselves, and a duty and an obligation and a service that needs be rendered to the Giver of life, or the Giver of expression in consciousness, in life, in its relationships to its fellow creatures and to its Maker. The life in the experience separated, yet a household that grew too large—for only twenty souls entered in the experience through the entity-body in its relationships to its peoples.

In that as brought then these in their relationships in the present, as has been indicated, first the desire upon the part of souls that had consecrated themselves in body, in mind, to be a channel of blessings to souls that they had through experience, in manifested form, seen struggling in their own various spheres.

As to the relationship of the king [341, friend] to this whole group, that as one that may in the present *view* that of an ideal set in many, that will self be cleansed and kept in that as has been the experience of self in its sojourns, that as it chose to enter in the present for the experience, may look, may listen, and by meditation with its ideal forces as set in Him make for an application in self as to the use of the knowledge as respecting their relationships in a material world.

In that as of the abandoned child of the priest [288, friend], may in its association, in its relations in the present, find that as may make for that in material forces set as an example for the clean, the moral, the Christian principles and ideals in a material life.

Ready for questions.

Q. Exactly to whom was [275] wedded?
A. When she finds him she will know!

Q. What was meant by marks being placed upon the body, in those ways and manners that may only be known to those who are in that physical and spiritual attunement with Ra-Ta as they pass through the material or earth's spheres together?

A. As has been indicated, their names, as set, their titles as given to each.

Q. Exactly to whom was [276] wed?

A. One of her own peoples, an Arabian—and you will find him, but don't catch him wild!

Q. What ideals from that time prompted us to come together now in this present relationship?

A. As has been indicated. The ideals as set by those in their union, and each soul finding the channel, the opportunity for the expression in this experience for that needed in its own soul development as related to each of the others in this experience.

Not only that as has been called karma, for these—as seen by that given—have to deal with and to do with what individuals have done with their knowledge of their opportunities in experiences *to* the Creative forces as manifested by the environ in that experience. It's well for you all to analyze that! (275-38)

The life reading of this group do not report all of them together again until the present time. Several of them, though, have been associated in incarnations between these two lives.

PERSIAN: Four of this family group, [301], [282], [452], and [378], were associated with Uhjltd (a reincarnation of Ra-Ta) in Persia, where Uhjltd was a healer-teacher. [282] had been a son of Ra-Ta, and [301] was his Egyptian wife. Both of their present daughters were also in this Persian period. [299] was a sister then of her present mother [301], and [314] came from India suffering in body and was healed. [452] and [378] we find again among the followers of the teacher Uhjltd (Ra-ta).

GREECE: We next find three of these entities in Greece. [275], [255], and [488]. There is nothing in their readings to suggest that they knew each other or were associated there in any way. [488] was associated with Herodotus, while the other two were interested in art, particularly sculpture. [275] was told she had been a model for some of the sculpture of the period, so it is possible the two knew each other.

HOLY LAND: Two of them, [452] and [457], were in the Holy Land, but were not in the same period; for [457] returned to the Holy City under the leadership of Nehemiah, while [452] was John Mark, therefore a relative of Mary and Jesus. As a child he was lame but was partially healed by John the Baptist and later entirely healed by the Master.

The niece [3172] also had a life in the Holy Land. The exact time is not given, but she was told it was a period of persecutions. And "the entity added much to the helpful welfare of individuals through those periods of persecution, as well as in periods of activity in the many varied lands." (3172-1)

ROME: Most of this family had a Roman incarnation during Nero's reign. These entities were told about their Roman life: [275], [301], [378], [412], the nieces [299], [314], and also [1742] (378's sister).

[378] was told:

Before this we find the entity was in that land known as the Roman, during those periods when there was the accepting and presenting of those tenets to those peoples of the land, from that land which had been attempted to be subdued in the period.

The entity then was among those that were in secondary power when Nero ruled in the land, and the entity—in the name Pomllomo—had charge of those records that were kept as reports from the varied tetrarchs throughout the lands that were subdued or put under service—or surveillance—by the Caesars of the period.

The entity lost and gained, through the attempt to be impartial, undesirous of working against the activities of the ruler; yet the inner sympathies were with that experienced by the entity through the various travels that were necessary to make the closer associations with the representatives in the varied lands.

Then the entity became associated with many of those that are in the entity's own household in the present, and their contacts, their aids, their fallings away, are necessary for the developments of all so associated in the present. (378-12)

This could mean that others of this group were in earthly sojourn but not in the city of Rome during this period.

Again we have the two factions or attitudes. [301], [1742] (378's sister), and [299] were among the Christians. [1742] was a sister of Peter's wife and a follower of Paul, while [299] was a child of one of the persecuted.

[412] and [314] were of the ruling class but did not join in the persecutions. On the contrary, [314] tried to have things changed and "kept self *above* those even of its surroundings, and *never* submitted of self to those indulgences as did many of the associates through the period." She was forced into a marriage which she abhorred and "*rebelling* in same, brought destructive forces to her *own* being [suicide], through the manner of *leaving* the earth in that experience." [412] was among those who were in authority and power but not as a ruler.

In this experience the entity gained throughout; for entering as one with a purpose, not only as of that for the relationships of self to the country and to the peoples whom the entity served, but also in the filial and in the relationships which made for the closer understanding. . . . Though oft in duty in the *physical* sense, there were done deeds that were abhorrent to the entity, yet duty remained—and to Caesar there were rendered the things that were Caesar's, and to God the things that were God's. (412-5)

The karma between [275] and [301] discussed in Chapter Three was incurred in Rome at this time.

GERMANY: The father [378] was in Germany during the crusade era and went on a crusade to the Holy Land. He was told this was really a period of retrogression because

198

of the attitudes and disillusion he developed. For he returned from the crusade broken in body, disappointed in people, and full of doubt and fear.

ALSACE-LORRAINE: Three of the family, [452], [457], and [282], had a life in Alsace-Lorraine—the area between France and Germany. This area has been an uneasy one overrun by the Germans and the French, conquered by one and then retaken by the other; so these entities were involved in the political and religious turmoil of the time and area. Probably their paths did cross, but we do not know whether or not [452], [457], and [282] were associated in any way during their lives here. The mother [255] also had a German life which could have been in this same area; for it "was during those periods when turmoils were in the land, and in that region where those people were in war against one another." (255-5)

[1742] (378's sister) had an incarnation in Alsace-Lorraine. She was "among those that suffered much, and much was there of the attitude of vengeance, of strife, of contention, experienced by the entity; yet the entity gained much and lost much *through* the experience. In the *name* Hertziel. In the experience in the present there is seen those many contentions arising over the various fields of endeavors through which most contentions arise in this material plane—the home, the conduct as to the religious life, and the conduct as to the political life. In those things has the entity had *definite* ideas, *definite* stands taken, as from those influences innately carried over." (1742-2)

Again, we find one of this group in another period of turmoil, for [301] was in France during the French revolution.

AMERICA: Five of this group had their last earth experience in this country, the United States. [275], [378], and the niece [314] were here during colonial times. [378] was in lower Manhattan but not among the Dutch of the area, and [412] came in as a hired soldier, probably Hessian. [412]'s life was cut short when he turned to secular things because of a lack of consideration for all concerned. Much of his business acumen came from this life. The niece [3172] was in the United States later at the time of the Civil War—again a period of internal strife and turmoil.

Here we have the members of a family group and some of their past lives which are affecting them today. The turmoil and rebellion which started in ancient Egypt seems to follow them; they seem to be involved in the earth during times of strife and turmoil. But then when has there been real peace and harmony in this earth?

We naturally ask, as [275] did, about her Roman karma: Why did they have to wait so long to work this out? The answer would very probably be the same: Simply, "Because you could not do it before."

It is interesting to note that several of the family had a great interest and ability in music, which many displayed in other lives. Some seem to have other artistic skills also. The youngest niece was even told she could have a career in music. All of them appear to be people with ability.

The various tendencies and personalities of these entities also seems to manifest down through the ages. The oldest brother of [275], whom we first saw among the invaders of Egypt, "has innately and actively ever been the messenger to many!" He became a priest and served with Ra-Ta in the temple. We find him again with Uhjltd, where he was active in exchanging ideas with peoples in other lands. As John Mark he gained more understanding of Truth from his discipleship with Peter.

In this experience the entity suffered much in many ways, being afflicted in body and being questioned oft by superiors as one not well grounded in faith; yet the entity gained throughout the experience in the service rendered to many. Then as a missionary. Then in the present and ever, must come the experience of seeking to give that as is *innate* principles in the activities of the entity in material, physical, and the spiritual life. (452-1)

His reading reported him next as being born in Alsace-Lorraine and coming to the United States as a missionary. Today he is again a missionary and a student of Truth.

The father [378], the Atlantean, displayed leadership and ability in his various earth experiences. Moreover, his efforts seemed to be of a constructive nature and for the good of all.

The mother, as one would expect, was reported as a homemaker in her other lives.

We would expect [301] and [282], who were again husband and wife in this life, to have an ideal marriage, but this has not been the case. For some reason the marriage was dissolved, but [282] became successful as an accountant and was happily associated with his daughters.

The youngest brother, [488], who had many abilities,* did have trouble, as his reading warned, in finding his vocation. He finally settled on chemistry as a profession, married, and raised a family. He is now deceased.

[457] and [412] have had a happy, successful marriage and raised two children. [412] with his business acumen has established a large and prosperous business.

The Healing Group

Another example of group karma can be found in the healing group. The story and beginning of the group healing is given here.

*The Formation of the Healing Group**:* One night in September, 1931, Edgar Cayce went to sleep not knowing that a dream he would have in the next few hours would influence the lives, the health, and the spiritual purpose of many thousands of people in the years to come. In fact, today we cannot even begin to speculate on the eventual results of that dream, as its influence is spreading in ever widening circles and is touching more and more lives.

At that time, he had recently organized the study group which became ARE Study Group No. 1 in Norfolk, Virginia. In his dream he saw the members of this group gathered together for the reading, previously given, on their first lesson. One of them, No. 295, laid her hand on Edgar Cayce's and said that with his permission and that of the

* See Chapter Four, page 102.
** Guidance For Healing, by Juliet Brooke Ballard.

others present she would tell them what the reading was going to tell each to do. She then proceeded to explain that they were to have a healing circle and choose six other persons besides herself to constitute it. One was to be the leader, one the interpreter of "what each wants and how the circle is to pray for the individual." "Spiritual healing" would result. Prayer was to be twice a day, at seven in the morning and six in the evening. Breathing exercises and "the manner in which they were to act" were then prepared according to the instructions of the interpreter whom No. 295 had chosen.

This was the gist of Edgar Cayce's dream.

Naturally, after a vision of such seeming importance, Edgar Cayce immediately sought information on it. In the reading from which we have drawn the above details, No. 294-127, he was told:

A. This, as has been seen, is as the promise that was given [in No. 262-1, the reading on the study group's first lesson] that each in his or her individual way and manner would be given a vision, a message, as to his or her part or portion in the undertaking to which the group as a group, individuals as individuals had pledged themselves.

As indicated, there had been left a most important part of a program that should be begun [along] with the studies undertaken from time to time. In not seeing what each was to give to the particular lesson, they were each to determine and ask in their own way, for their own enlightenment.

As seen, the body could lead in that portion or part of the work, aided and abetted by those who were seen in the vision as it happened.

Well, then, that this group—when others have given, or sought to know their part—that this group as seen, the seven, be given that as an additional portion of their part in the work.

To be sure, this will be altered as to meeting, as to times, yet eventually this group may hold—with even thousands of others—such a prayer for those who are sick or afflicted in any manner that they to whom the will is given will receive what they seek through the efforts of these who were with Him. (294-127)

After such a complete endorsement of his dream, Edgar Cayce had only one other important question to ask, and it was included in the second reading for the study group as a whole.

Q. Are the seven presented to me to be the healing group, or was this emblematical?
A. This is both *emblematical* and is, in fact, the portion of the group that should begin their activities in this definite line *and* manner, *aided* by all who may seek or desire to be a portion of same. *These*, as given, leading in their respective places and times, for as each of these gather as a body for aid to another, there will be from time to time a message from one to another. This is not only a promise, it's a threat! Be mindful of it, but be faithful to each as they are received. (262-2)

After this we find a special reading being given for the seven individuals indicated. This was the first in a series (the 281 series) that was to be given for the Healing Prayer Group, of which some dealt directly with its work and others later ranged into the deep and mystical subject matter of the Book of the Revelation.

Why Were the Seven Called?: Those directed to this additional service came to the unique venture, questioning why they had been chosen. The answer was conclusive.

Each as are gathered here are fitted in their own particular way for a portion of that work designated by the group as the healing group. (281-1)

It was later, only after the group had been obtaining its readings regularly, that information was sought as to *who* had called it together.

Q. Was our group called directly by the Master or simply through a dream of Edgar Cayce?

A. Each will determine that by that they have received from the Master. (281-8)

From inferences in Reading 281-10 (A-18 through A-23) and others from time to time, it seemed to be implied that Jesus had had an incarnation in Egypt under the name of Hermes. At that time Edgar Cayce, then Ra-Ta the priest, had been seeking to rebuild the spiritual life of that country. One member of the Healing Group, No. 69, was told that she had been associated with "the Master of Men" *then* (281-10, A-21) and that this association was one "that made for the building up of that consciousness of the laying aside of the various forces, or sources, that in the present find themselves as attributes of the mental, or the sensations or imaginative forces of the body" (281-10, A-23). It was also brought out that members of this group had worked together before for just such a purpose (281-1). Also, we recall that in Reading 294-127 these individuals were characterized as "these who were with Him." So it seems possible that the Master (then Hermes, later Jesus) was guiding these persons in healing work some twelve thousand years ago. Again they had been called to this vitally important service—at a time when such ministrations could be of supreme importance.

Q. What is meant by *the day of the Lord is near at hand?*
A. That—as has been promised through the prophets and the sages of old—the time, and half-time, has been and is being fulfilled in this day and generation; and that soon there will again appear in the earth that one *through whom many will be called* to meet those who are preparing the way for His day in the earth. The Lord then will come, even as ye have seen Him go . . . when those who are His have made the way clear and *passable* for Him to come. (262-49)

Early Directions and Advice: The Healing Prayer Group, thus selected and given a designated task of healing, was naturally a little unprepared and uneasy as to how its mission was to be performed to bring about the most beneficial results. The members felt uncertain as to their own worthiness to participate and were anxious to know to which portion of the work each was best fitted. They also wanted to know how to go about doing this while working well together. In the readings the group received, numerous questions were asked by individuals.

In the very first reading, 281-1, Edgar Cayce in a preliminary explanation seemed to imply that different members had had close association with other members, which brought karmic situations to be worked out together, especially if these associations had been "the last experience." He added, however, that there had been "those experiences with the group as a whole where the greater portion have worked together for the common good of all." These had resulted in "contacts where there was healing brought in their individual experience with the divine forces manifested in a material world." The group "as a whole" was to be assisted in its "dispensing of an ideal" by being able to call on the services of Edgar Cayce, through whom "sources of information" could be given each to "assist and aid in all phases of their experience." The individual members fitting themselves "to be a manifestation of His love in this particular experience" would "lose self in love and service to others."

Judging from this explanation and the preceding references, it would seem to us that there is a striking parallel between the age of Ra-Ta and the present. Just as Hermes had had a spiritual climate provided by Ra-Ta, the priest, from which to draw individuals to work with him in the old Egyptian era, again some of those interested in Edgar Cayce's work today would be used by the Master to serve their fellows. Surely the Master thus uses sincere seekers in any group which tries to alleviate the ills of mankind. The psychic ability of Edgar Cayce was to be utilized in bringing to these individuals helpful information and advice.

Following this general background, answers were given to the queries of various members of the group as to how through meditation they could better fit themselves for this work.

Perhaps the members of this first ARE Healing Prayer Group were a little oppressed by an awesome sense of responsibility. At any rate, in their next reading (281-2) they were given a message from the Master asking them to "lift up" their hearts so He might enter. They were told that just as they had chosen to follow Him, so had He chosen them to be a blessing to others who sought His help in their lives. The members' faith and trust would be the measure of the "grace, mercy, and peace" that would come to those they sought to help. An explanation was given as to why there is more power for healing in a group than in individuals. "These bring the strength of union in group, rather than individuals—who may in *self* find turmoil, when 'I would do good, but evil is present.'" The one who was designated as the channel for the healing would be aided by the consecrated effort on the part of others. Those to be helped were to seek, themselves; and when they came to individual members, these in turn were to seek the assistance of the group. Once the group achieved union of purpose, those who needed help would be attracted to it.

ARE

The Association for Research and Enlightenment itself is also an excellent example of group karma. The work readings given to direct the work of the association tells us:

> The Egyptian history, especially, should be correlated for the benefit of those attempting to carry on the work at the present time. For much is being attempted at this time which was tried during that experience.
> Again the cycle has rolled to that period when the individual entities are once more gathered together in the earth for a definite work. These various experiences react as to cause and effect, through the various forms, upon the environmental and hereditary conditions. When these are studied aright, any given fact may be worked out, even mathematically, as to what will be the response of an individual towards any portion of it. Hence this should be particularly interesting to those desiring to make a success of this at this period. (254-47)
> None are being drawn into the purpose of establishing this closer relation of God's Truth in the earth, through spiritual things, mental application of mental things, or

the material through which both manifest, other than those who first established the same in Egypt.

In that beginning there were those gathered in various offices and positions. As each bore his relation to the people of that period, each in the present relation to the people, according to individual development plus the desire to manifest that which was built in that momentous period in man's understanding. . . .

In choosing the ones to lead, counselors were chosen among the people of the land, both from the native and from those who came in from the north. . . . In choosing the leader who would become priest, this became a momentous question as to whom should be chosen. And when this office was first set up, there arose many dissensions. In the division which afterward arose, they became like minor or major rebellions during a physical existence.

When the priest, Ra-Ta, was again established after his return from banishment, there arose that which became the study which is being founded this day in a distant land. . . .

The work is to be first of all an educational factor in the lives of those who are contacted through the efforts of the association. This pertains to the physical, mental, and spiritual, for these and their relations to one another are the primary forces in the physical or material life. The greater understanding of the relationship of these factors and that the Whole is One, must be studied in their individual, collective, and coordinating influences in the lives of individuals. Then, first, it should be given to the individual, then to the groups, then to the classes, and then to the masses. . . .

First there must be wholehearted cooperation. All should be of one mind. And that mind should be to serve in the fullest sense in the dissemination of that which is gained through the sources of the association work and its application in the physical, mental, and spiritual life of its members. Without the wholehearted cooperation and oneness of mind and purpose, irrespective of position, condition, or relation with one another, there may not be expected the result desired. This could not any more be than a misdirected mind could understand a spiritual law through a purely physical application, or a physical law by spiritual application. For the spiritual is the life; the mental is the builder; and the physical is the result. . . .

There must stand first and foremost that the directing of yourself in the inner man must be made in oneness of purpose, in accord with the truth set forth in the purpose and aim of the Association. For when they all labored with one accord and were of one mind, there was added daily such as would receive the word of truth that made men free. (254-42)

Another reading given on September 2, 1941, implies that the association is working out some group karma in carrying on the work of the association. As has been indicated through these channels, the period at present is a representation or a reenactment in a manner of the Egyptian experience, when there were those periods of dissension, discussions arising from the positions of each of the entities and THEIR relationships to the tenets and teachings as of that represented here in the purposes and ideals of the Association for Research and Enlightenment.

Differences and disturbances that arose through those periods brought much that necessitated (for more perfect spiritual and mental understanding) the opportunities for each meeting self in relationships to the other in this present sojourn.

This, as may be interpreted by each, has come to pass. (254-111)

Aims, Purposes, and Ideals: The members were told in another reading:

All with one purpose, one aim, one desire, yet in their own *way* and manner, should present that which they have received. And though someone may laugh or scoff at what ye say, *be* not dismayed; for so did they at thy Lord.

As to manners or ways as a collective group: What ye *find* to do, with willing hands DO ye. This may to thine own mind, then, appear to be very indefinite, intangible.

208

Yet is there not set in the experience of each that through some specific office, through some specific group as a part of a working unit, there is specific work set for that unit?

As an individual, then, do thy part, *realizing* that each and every chain is only as strong as the weakest link. Thou art a portion. Hast thou fulfilled, *wilt* thou fulfill, that as is shown thee by thine own experience with same?

Q. What should be the central purpose, the central ideal, in presenting the work?

A. The Truth that shall make you free in body, in mind, and one with the living force that may express itself in individual lives.

Where there is illness of body, then give that which may make it free from those adaptings of itself to that which has bound it in this material expression.

Where there are those troubled in mind, with many cares, if they are seeking for the spiritual way, they, too, may find how in their own experience they may give the greater expression in their application of that they have in hand.

Where there are those who seek for the channel in which they may be the greater expression in this material plane in the present experience, they, too, may find their own selves and their relationships to the holy within.

These should be the central themes. As to the choice of this or that manner to be used, follow the manners which have been set through which individual groups here and there may receive enlightenment or aid in a better understanding or concept of what such information is that may be supplied through such a channel, and how it is of help. These are being opened.

Those that are seeking for channels to aid those who in the body have become under the bond of this or that affliction, this or that ill or ailment, may stress this particular line of endeavor in their activity. And some who are already aiding in such directions will seek the concept of some that are here. Give expression in mind. As ye have received, give out.

You who feel that you are of little help here or there,

or in manner of giving expression in thy words of mouth, then so live that ye have received that Spirit of Truth—not of any body but of Truth, or Christ—may be manifested. And those seeking—though ye struggle with the cares of earth, the cares of life—will, too, take hope and find in thine effort, in thine endeavor—though stumbling it may be—HOPE, and find the face of Him who has set a way for all who will enter in, who will sit at last upon that judgment within thine self. For, "As ye have done it unto the least of these, ye have done it unto me." (254-87)

These directions were given later for handling the material in the readings:

Hence the preparation and handling, then, must be from the material angle, and presented from the material as well as the spiritual angle—and that the organization is an ecclesiastical research, as well as a scientific research organization not of a sect or set—but as the Law of One! (254-89)

A reading given for the 1936 congress dealt with the purposes and work of the group.

Yes, we have the purposes of the Association for Research and Enlightenment, the members that are present; as a group or a membership and as individuals.

In considering the work of such an organization and its standards, that as composed of individuals of all character of experience, all influences that are of a nature that has brought about the interest in a work of that purposed by the activity of such an association, we find it is—as has been given oft—first to the individual, then to the groups, then to classes and masses.

As to the activities that are before this organization, first—as we find—there is a period just ahead in which there will be given the greater opportunities for service by each and every member. This is not only owing to the general conditions of an unsettled nature but to the termination of a period and the beginning of a period when there is to be the *living* by individuals of that which has prompted them. Not as ones seeking for self-exaltation, not as individuals seeking for an easy way, not as individuals seeking for a manner or a means of escaping their own selves; but rather as in using their understanding, their comprehension, their knowledge, their love, their patience, their long-suffering, in such ways and manners that there may not indeed be the perishing of hope and faith in the earth.

Such opportunities are before all those who have purposed in their heart to *do* good unto those not only of the household of faith in their individual tenets or beliefs but unto *all*, because each soul that manifests itself in human form *is* thy brother—and the spirit and soul of same is in the form of thy Maker. For the Lord's sake, then, the opportunities are not to be used to self's own glory but that the glory of the Father may be made manifest in the earth.

These be the opportunities, *these* be the experiences through which each and every soul will pass within the next year.

For there is set before thee those choices to be made, as to *whom* ye will serve.

As to *manners*, then, in which each soul shall conduct self as respecting this as an individual organization, it has oft been given that this is not under any schism or ism or any individual tenet other than that which has been of old, "I AM MY BROTHER'S KEEPER!" That should be the cry that should be in the heart of every member, every individual. "I AM MY BROTHER'S KEEPER!" (254-91)

Yet through all,
We know this tangled skein
Is in the hands of one
Who sees the end
From the beginning:
He shall unravel all.

—ALEXANDER SMITH

THE RETURN

CHAPTER SEVEN

Yesterday is but a memory
Tomorrow an uncharted course
So live today so it will be
A memory without remorse.

—ANONYMOUS

If thou hadst walked in the way of God, thou hadst
surely dwelt in peace forever.   *Baruch 3:1*

To be free is to gain the knowledge necessary to loose
the bonds that bind one, whether they be mental,
physical, or spiritual. (1215-8)

The foregoing chapters are based upon the fundamental
building blocks of the wisdom expressed in the Edgar
Cayce readings. A clear understanding of these major
tenets clarifies and expands an understanding of karma in
our lives.

The primary premises are presented here under the
following headings.

We must conclude, that our one and only problem is
SELF. Since our karma is only with Creative Forces, we
must learn to attune to Creative Force and make our will
one with the Father's.

Life IS! Each soul is an offspring of the Creative
Force called God, and is innately—and manifestedly by
application—the result in the experience of how or the
manner it has manifested that prerogative of WILL.

The soul IS, and lives on, making its record in the
building influence, or the stream in the experience of the
body, the mind, the soul, called the mental life of an
entity. (954-L-1)

There is no urge in the astrological, in the vocational,
in the hereditary, or in the environmental which

surpasses the will or determination of the entity. For the entity finds it is true, there is nothing in heaven or hell that can separate the entity from the knowledge or from the love of Creative Force, called God, but self. And that the entity should determine in self to apply, rather than mere knowledge or surmise, but apply and listen to the still, small voice within, and the entity will find that the promises are true which have been made. . . . (5023-2)

True knowledge is therefore the correct interpretation of experience and an application of this throughout one's dealings with one's fellow man, day by day. The standard then is not whether it has brought riches and fame, nor events that are well spoken of by worldly men; but rather has it made the individual a better neighbor, a kindlier friend—one more longsuffering toward those who would hinder? Does it bring patience? Does it bring love in any manifested form? All these show whether the True Knowledge is being manifested in the experience of any individual. (262-23)

Remember, in the analysis of the urges which are latent and manifested, which arise from activities in the earth or the realms through which the entity passed, none of these urges surpasses the will of the individual entity; that which is the gift of the Creator, that ye may make yourself one with the Creative Forces, and thus indeed a child of the living God.

The abuse of the abilities separates self from the Creative Force. (5254-1)

That force, known upon this plane as WILL, is given to man over and above all creation; THAT force which may separate itself from its Maker, for with WILL man may either adhere to or contradict the DIVINE LAW—those immutable laws which are set between the Creator and the created. (3744-41)

Man alone is given that birthright of free will. He alone may defy his God!

So soon as man contemplates his free will he thinks of it as a means of doing the opposite of God's will, though he finds that only by doing God's will does he find happiness. Yet the notion of serving God sits ill with

216

him, for he sees it as a sacrifice of his will. Only in disillusion and suffering, in time, space, and patience, does he come to the wisdom that his real will is the will of God, and in its practice is happiness and heaven. (2537-L-1)

The entity [must] come to the realization that life is continuous, and because of its change in manifestations it does not stop, but in the varied conscious experiences of the soul, its purposes, its desires are continuous—unless they are acted upon by the will of the entity in regards to the relationships to self (the I am) to the GREAT I AM, the Giver, the Maker of all good and perfect gifts.

So ever is it in the experience of the soul-entity that *changes only come by the activity of the will;* that which is the birthright to each soul from an All-Wise Creator whose desire and will is that no soul shall be separated from Him, but that all shall find their place in His oneness. (1129-2)

It would appear from the readings that man is receiving emotional vibration not only from this life, but from all previous lives wherein the negative emotions have not been met and changed by his own WILL. The readings tell us that a way of escape from the tangled web we weave has been and always is open to use if we will to change and make our will one with the Father's.

Each soul is accountable unto its Maker for what it does with its opportunities at each and every turn of its experiences in that we call life in the earth's plane. (335-B-1)

There must be the ability within the heart and soul to look squarely at self, to look self in the face, and know whether or not it is failing in its attempt to be nearer to God. If we live truly with ourselves, we never fool ourselves.

We have made our present, and we are constantly making our future. Today is the result of yesterday; and tomorrow is the result of today. It is a continuous process as life itself is continuous. A great Candid Camera is always taking pictures of our every thought and act. The record is being made, though we may be unaware of it.

The record

The record that is builded by an entity in the Akashic Record is to the mental world as the cinema is to the material or physical world, as pictured in its activity.

So, in the direction to an entity and its entrance into the material plane in a given period, time, place—which indicate the relative position of the entity as related to the universe or to the universal sources—one only turns, as it were, to those records in the Akashian forms to read that period of what was built or lost during that experience. (275-L-2)

The records [of each individual] are upon the skein of time and space. Oh, that all would realize this and come to the consciousness that *what* we are—in any given experience or time—is the combined result of what we have done about ideals we have set. (1549-L)

A study of such things (this aside, to be sure) will give many an individual an insight as to what is meant by reincarnated influences or karmic influences builded; for karmic influences are more of the spiritual than of an earth's experience, for what we create in the earth we meet in the earth—and what we create in the realm through spiritual forces we meet there! And getting outside of the realm of the material does not mean necessarily angelic, or angelic influence! (314-1)

In giving the interpretations of the records that are written upon the skein of time and space, these are the forces and influences that each soul builds in its passing through time and space. Thus they become a part of that which the entity must meet in all phases of its activity.

That which is in keeping with the law of *Creative Forces,* or energies, is developing. That which is of self, self-aggrandizement, self-indulgence alone, is retarding.

These then are the lines that create what some call karma. Hence meeting them is the law. For what ye sow, so shall ye reap. But as has been interpreted by the entity in much of its study, its analysis of the atonement, or atonement with the *Creative Forces*—being the law, one

218

meets or overcomes. But such overcoming must be a continuous practice in the daily experiences with others. (2329-1)

For each entity in the earth is what it is because of what it has been! And each moment is dependent upon another moment. So a sojourn in the earth, as indicated, is a lesson in the school of life experience. Just as it may be illustrated in that each entity, each soul-entity, is as a corpuscle in the body of God—if such an entity has applied itself in such a manner as to be a helpful force and not a rebellious force. (2823-3)

Good lives on. Only evil dies and withers, as it is left uncultivated. Good that is uncultivated grows and yields some thirty, some sixty, some an hundredfold. For it is ever that to which each soul would attain. (3268-1)

Each entity is a part of the universal whole. All knowledge, all understanding that has been a part of the entity's consciousness, then, is a part of the entity's experience. (2823-1)

Lessons

We are here to learn and earn.

This is left to the individual. The Lord can only offer. Man, as His child, as a cocreator with the Creative Forces, accepts or rejects. There's no halfway. You are or you are not. To be sure, there are various stages of unfoldment, of development, but use that which thou knowest to do and the Lord will give thee the next step. He doesn't fail in His promises, even though ye may be far, far away. (3654-1)

While we all are at different stages of development and may be working on different lessons, we do not make much progress until we can recognize our problems as opportunities. We begin to grow when we face up to the fact that we are responsible for our trials and misery. We are only meeting self. Our present circumstances are the result of previous actions whether long removed or in the recent past. So if we are beset with problems, blame not God, for they are of our own making.

Our miseries are the result of destructive or negative thoughts, emotions, and actions. We can avoid trouble and misery if we live lives of noble thought and action.

Oft may the body ask self, "If the Creative Forces, or God, is mindful of man, why does He allow me to suffer so?"

Know that though He were the Son, yet learned He obedience through the things suffered in body, in mind, in the material earthly plane. (1445-P)

Opportunities

Actually, we have no problems; we have opportunities for which we should give thanks.

For the destiny of an entity's experience in any particular sojourn depends upon what the entity has done and will do with the opportunities of every nature that are presented to him, in the material world, in the mental expression, in the spiritual imports that prompt him. (66-L-1)

There is no standing still. Either one progresses or retards; one who does not use every means for development and for gaining the better understanding of how to use what is at hand is retarding. (900-309)

An error we refuse to correct has many lives.

It requires courage to face one's own shortcomings and wisdom to do something about them.

Development

Then, as to whether there is the development or retarding of the soul-entity is dependent upon the manner in which the abilities of the entity are exercised or used.

Not all that is considered by some as material success is soul success.

Not all that is soul development—as considered in other spheres—is considered material success.

For each soul enters the material experience with

opportunities in the abilities that have been attained or acquired as a part of the individuality and personality of the entity.

Each soul-entity enters with that hope of preparing itself for closer or greater communion with its first cause or first purpose. For each soul is in the image of the Creator.

And as it is in purpose, in spirit, it seeks to magnify or manifest the spirit of the Creator. Hence, as implied, God is spirit and seeks such to worship Him. (3420-L-1)

The purpose of all should be that they may be a channel through which there may be a manifestation of the Father's love, the Father's mercy, the Father's longsuffering, the Father's patience with a stiff-necked people. (262-58)

Purpose

The soul comes into each experience for the express purpose of manifesting in materiality under the environs of those things builded in the past, or the hereditary influence of the entity. Whether the meeting of any experience makes for development or retardment depends upon what the entity does with the knowledge pertaining to the Creative Forces in all the activity—what the soul, the body, does about what it knows, in manifesting what the soul worships as its ideal. If that ideal is the Christ-Consciousness, well. If that ideal is selfish developments, or the aggrandizing of activities in the carnal forces, then these must bring rather the fruits of such into the experience of the soul. As the warning has been given, there is today set before us good and evil, life and death. The growth of the soul depends upon what the will chooses.

Stumbling blocks or retardments arising in the experience of each soul are evidence of the mental and soul environmental-hereditary influences. What is accomplished by the soul in each day of activity depends upon whether the ideal is high or low, or whether the belief or faith is such as to make for *selflessness* in the experience. For the assurance has been given from the Father-Creator of life, light, hope, and immortality in the earth, that through the Son and the belief in Him, He is able and willing to supply that necessary strength in the experience of each soul to meet those emergencies, to meet those vicissitudes in life, to meet the needs in every way and manner. This is constantly shown in the soul of every entity in the material life. Yet many find that self-expression and the personalities of individuals appear to be such as to make for stumbling rather than aid, even when by the word of mouth those individuals profess with their tongues their hope, their faith, in that same light.

These become the stumbling blocks to many. Hence impersonality becomes the watchword for all under such experience. *Selflessness is that to which each must attain, in Him.* In love, faith, hope, charity, there are those activities and reflexes which show that the spirit of the Master aids in all such expression in the manifested life of an individual.

When there is giving away to fear, to doubt, to avarice, to greed, to all those things that are the fruits of darkness, such souls banish from themselves the spirit of truth and life in every activity.

There is in each experience that which is both good and bad, yet the Christ stands in self's stead in the abilities to meet each of those conditions which have been builded as but a portion of the structural body of the soul, if the faith, the hope of the promise in Him, is held first and foremost. As said of old by all who proclaimed a name, "Thou shalt love the Lord thy God with all thy heart, thy might, thy mind, thy soul." And He gave that likened unto it in a manifested form. Before His entrance finally into the earth it was rather as a tenet, yet He fulfilling the law then proclaimed, "and thy neighbor as thyself." This He did in the body. Would we be like Him? Then let us not only proclaim but act and think those proclaiming influences that we have walked and talked with Him in the inner conscience; not so much by speech but rather in the loving activities of mind, of body; and the result is the development of the soul. (288-L-7)

It is not what one knows that counts, but what one does about what one knows!

Then, it is application to which each soul must adhere to prevent confusion and bring about harmony. (1182-L-1)

Constructive experience

This then becomes the question—what is a constructive experience?

Is it one wherein there is the necessity of toil or labor? Or is it one wherein there is the satisfying or gratifying of the mental and spiritual body?

The answer is: If it is to be glorification or justification of the bodily emotions or forces ALONE, it is NOT constructive. If it is to the glory of God, of the fruits of the spirit of truth and good, it is constructive, whether through hardships or through gratifying of what may appear to others to be only bodily forces or emotions. (1522-1)

Rather is it what ye PURPOSE! For the try, the purpose of thine inner self, to Him is the rightness. For He has known all the vicissitudes of the earthly experience. He hath walked through the valley of the shadow of death. He hath seen the temptations of man from every phase that may come into thine own experience; and, yea, He hath given thee, "If ye will love me, believing I am able, I will deliver thee from that which so easily besets thee at any experience." (987-4)

Selflessness

The spiritual journey is not an easy one but must be made. We may take a long or a short time. God cares not how long we take; we choose the way. If it is filled with obstacles, we have only ourselves to blame.

That which is so hard to be understood in the minds or the experiences of many is that the activities of a soul are for self-development, yet must be *selfless* in its activity for it, the soul, to develop. (275-39)

"For those who would study respecting self and self's

223

development, yet being selfless in their development," this was given:

As has been given by Him as the teacher, as the minister, as the savior to all men: "I of myself can do nothing. The Father that worketh *in* me, He does the works that you see." When the body is using of itself that which is the Creative Force in itself, we see—as in this body—it uses its very own self; hence is selfishness, or the aggrandizing of the qualities in the mental forces of the body-physical or in the mental intelligentsia of the body itself, and has forgotten or neglects that which is creative or constructive in itself. Yet when the body—physical and mental and spiritual—uses itself in giving to another that which is helpful, hopeful *to* that soul, it draws from that source in the spiritual influences, or God, to give to the other. Hence the illustration that has been thus drawn.

Then, to awaken that within self that may be the more helpful, that will make self the greater channel, for others . . . there needs be only that the trust remain in Him and there be the arousing to those consciousnesses of His presence dwelling in thine own experience and in thine own heart and soul, that every atom, every cell within the whole physical body, mind, and soul becomes attuned to those spheres of activity that are aroused by the consciousness of His presence being with thee. For there are the abilities to give out to others. (275-39, page 3)

Ideals

It is necessary, to be sure, that there be coordinating of ideals and ideal relationships with those whom the body may contact day by day. But to let little differences, little animosities, little hurts interfere with the real ideal and purpose of an entity or soul is to go backward rather than onward with those abilities which the entity possesses to create for others what will be helpful and hopeful in their experience. (815-B-1)

We must reach the perfection that Christ did. It may take a long time and many earth lives, but sometime, in some life, we must reach our goal.

He that came into the earth as an example, as a way, is an ideal—is THE ideal. They that climb up some other way become robbers of that peace, that harmony, which may be theirs—by being at one with that He manifested in the earth. (2537-1)

The counsel Edgar Cayce gave made it very clear that this selflessness was gained through service and helping others. This help must be given in love and willingly, not for personal gain.

For it has been given that in service to others, in and through that done for others, more may be gained for yourself. (900-280)

And give service, not as eye-service, but as service of the heart to the maker. (641-L-1)

Then make the paths straight—just being kind, just showing brotherly love. Thus may the entity find in its very self its relationship to others. (3508-MS-1)

Law of grace

You may ask: What about Grace? Doesn't Grace help us? It does, of course, and we have alluded to it. Grace is really God's love. It helps and protects us if we are attuned to it. If we do not accept His love, He can only wait for us to accept and seek Him. When we attain that state of Christ-Consciousness and make His will our will, we live and operate under Grace. We are then free of karma, or self. The extent to which we attain this selflessness is the extent to which we live under Grace. It is a matter of our own choice and must begin with our will.

These bits of counsel explain more the relation of karma and grace.

Karma can be met in the ideal, and, as a law, changed from law as penal law to grace, mercy. But this you show, this you manifest not by bragging, not by applauding, but by daily living. (5224-1)

. . . over-indulgence. This, of course, makes for conditions which are to be met. For what one sows, that one must also reap. This is unchangeable law. Know that this law may be turned into the law of grace and mercy by the individual, through living and acting in their lives in relationship to others. (5233-1)

Thus we may through those administrations of that which is the spirit of truth made manifest, turn this karma (palsy) or law to grace and mercy. For the pattern hath been given those who seek to know His face. (5209-1)

We may choose which law we wish to operate under.

Are thy choices according to thy ideal? This ye alone may answer, ye MUST answer. For, as He hath given, ye must pay for EVERY whit! For the law of the Lord is perfect; it may so convert the soul. But the law is not taken away—it must be fulfilled every whit, every jot and tittle. Under what law choosest thou to be aware, or to work? These are the choices of men, as they are choices by man according to the concept of thy spiritual law of the adherence to moral standards. (2650-1)

And again, 5001 was told in a little different way that he must choose:

These will make for activities, but in what manner? For the law of the Lord is perfect, and whatsoever an entity, an individual, sows, that must he also reap. That as law cannot be changed. As to whether one meets it in the letter of the law or in mercy, in grace, becomes the choice of the entity. If one would have mercy, grace, love, friend, one must show self in such a manner to those with whom one becomes associated. For like begets like. (5001-1)

As long as we are in the physical body we will have problems; they may be only urges but must be dealt with in some way. What do you choose?

. . . meeting those things which have been called karmic, yet remembering that under the law of grace this may not be other than an urge, and that making the will of self one with the WAY may prevent, may overcome, may take the choice that makes for life, love, joy, happiness—rather than the law that makes, causing the meeting of everything the hard way. For self is constantly meeting self. (1771-2)

Much might be said respecting karmic conditions. These are builded more in the mental self than in the spiritual self. For changes—IDEALS, not ideas but IDEALS—are of spiritual concepts. If the entity rejects such, as it sometimes does in self, these naturally build barriers. But these are as we have just indicated—have ye chosen what you desire to be? Or is there such of self that it desires to accomplish its ideals with its own freedom of activity? Then, in such choices that which has been of the karmic nature becomes the activative principle in the experience. But if there is the choice that this or that, whatever may be the choice, will be met in HIM, then the karmic force is not necessarily something that you meet irrespective. For a way is opened through HIM. (2487-2)

Yet it is a fact that a life experience is a manifestation of divinity. And the mind of an entity is the builder. Then as the entity sets itself to do or to accomplish that which is of a creative influence or force it comes under the interpretation of the law between karma and grace. No longer is the entity under the law of cause and effect, or karma, but rather in grace it may go on to the higher calling set in HIM. (2800-2)

In complying with the laws of the giver of all good and perfect gifts, grace is commuted to those who would seek to do His bidding, who place themselves in the hands of God, who gives life abundant. (900-193)

Overcoming

We gain the consciousness of Creative Forces through prayer and meditation. This is not the end, however. Our knowledge and understanding must be applied in our daily life. Our spiritual life and growth unfolds gradually as we live TRUTH and serve our fellow man. The readings said over and over again that we serve God only as we serve our fellow man.

For each soul is in that process of development to become fully aware of its relationships to its Maker. And in the manifesting of the fruits of the spirit you find these are attitudes and activities towards your fellow man, those you meet day by day. And as the Lord gave, "In the manner ye do it unto the least of these ye meet day by day, so ye do it unto thy God." (1650-1)

All who seek knowledge are seeking the greatest gifts of the Universe. Then using such knowledge to worship God is rendering a service to one's fellow man. For as given: The greatest service to God is service to His creatures. (254-16)

For until ye have in thine own material associations known thyself to be the saving grace to someone, ye may not even know the whole mercy of the Father with the children of men. (987-4)

The law of the Lord is such that he who runs may read. Even the fool may be taught in the way if he himself seeks, but none are so blind as those who *will* not see. Open thy heart, thy mind, thy purpose, so that ye may say, "LORD, HERE AM I, THY SERVANT. USE ME IN SUCH A WAY THAT I MAY BE A CHANNEL OF BLESSING TO SOMEONE TODAY." Such principles, such purposes—not merely by the statement, but by the desire to apply self—will open up . . . greater possibilities than the entity has been conscious of yet in this experience. (3654-L-1)

Daily—yes, three times each day—repeat to self this, and then *live* it! "LORD, WHAT WOULDST THOU HAVE ME DO?" Put that in thine heart. Let it be manifested in thy dealings with others, in thy labor as a secretary, in thy activities in the home, in thy meetings with friends, in *any* phase of thine experience .(2995-L-1)

The weakness of the man is the wisdom of God. The knowledge of God, the wisdom of God applied in the daily experience of individuals, becomes strength, power, beauty, love, harmony, grace, patience, and those things that, in the lives of those who are applying them, make for a life experience that is worthwhile, even in the turmoils of the earth and in those activities of sin and sorrow and shame and want and degradation. These are worthwhile experiences, that the glory of the Father and the Son may become known and read and seen and understood by others who would take counsel from daily activity in the earth.

Then as ye go about to apply this thou hast gained, this understanding, this concept of thy relationships with thy fellow man, thy relationships with thy Maker, ye seek, ye pray, ye meditate upon Him who directs thee. For as ye meditate ye feel, ye see, yea, ye hear the voice, the spirit, the moving influence in thy life. And yet when ye go to apply same in thy conversation with thy brother, thy friend, thy neighbor, ye forget what manner of voice ye heard, what vision ye have seen. What is the prompting? The things of the moment crowd in to such an extent that indeed ye find the spirit willing but the flesh weak. Then the wisdom is ever that as He hath given: "Not my will but Thine, O God, be done in and through me." Let thy conversation ever be, "If the Lord is willing, if the Spirit of the Christ directeth. . . ."

Ye say ye believe, but do ye show wisdom in acting that way? "I, thy brother, thy Christ, will stand in thy stead." Wisdom is divine love made manifest in thy daily conversation, thy daily avocation, thy daily acts as one to another. This is wisdom, and as ye apply it, as ye make known in thy conversation, in thy acts, it will become more and more part and parcel of thy very self. (262-97)

This does not bespeak that self becomes the "Goody-goody," or as one afraid to do this or that! All force, all power that is manifested in the earth emanates from a spiritual or God-Force. Man in his madness, or in his SELFISHNESS, turns it into that which becomes either miracles in the experiences of man or crimes that cry out to the people, who heed not. Know that the Lord is GOOD! And to do good, to be kind, to be gentle, to smile even when in pain, to look up when others are even tramping upon thy feet and give praise to Him in the inner self, is what He seeks for, and He has promised glory and honor to those who do it. The mysteries of His love? Man makes these. For He is not afar off, but within thine own heart. For the body is indeed the temple of the living God. Dost thou keep it, and the mind, in the condition in which ye may entertain Him there? For as ye do it unto the least or the greatest, ye do it unto Him. For he that would be the greater among men is the servant of all!

There never has been one that loved the Lord and had to beg bread; nor one that lived the life of love and failed to find harmony and peace in the inner self. Then, do that which thou knowest how to do today! Tomorrow will be given thee the next step to take. . . .

Ye cannot buy thy way into the grace of thy Lord, nor into those purposes in thine inner self—for they cannot be satisfied by self-indulgence nor self-gratification.

In what ye would purpose to do, use not others for stepping-stones because others may have used thee. Bear ye up under it, knowing: The Lord is the avenger of those who misuse His love in their relationships with their fellow man. And He, the Lord—the life that is within thee, that is thinking, moving; the being within self—is the avenger, not self! (815-B-1)

Will

Remember there is no shortcut to a consciousness of the God-Force. It is part of your own consciousness, but it cannot be realized by the simple desire to do so. Too often there is a tendency to want it and expect it without applying spiritual truth through the medium of mental processes. This is the only way to reach the gate. There are no shortcuts in metaphysics, no matter what is said by those who see visions, interpret numbers, or read the stars. These may find urges, but they do not rule the will. Life is learned within self. You don't profess it; you learn it. (5392-1)

Overcoming self and release from the "wheel of return" is gained only by doing HIS WILL.

The will is the factor that, in choice, is the birthright; and that is only sold for appetites that gratify for the moment the self—desires or self-indulgences.

And what the entity does about that free will is the heritage of each soul, as its birthright—the WILL—makes for development or retardment; and nothing may separate thee from the knowledge of the Father but thyself. (1219-1)

When there has been and is made the best possible effort that you may give to do that which is in keeping with His will—as is understood by self—leave the results in His hands. . . . (243-B-3)

For when troubles, distresses, heartaches, and disappointments come, to whom may ye turn? Not to thyself! For this has been expended in the gratifying of thy desire—if ye have made these things that are temporal thy God!

Only when love, patience, perseverance, long-suffering, and brotherly love are shown, may ye know indeed upon whom to rely.

For of such is the law of creation, of hope, of faith, of patience. And in PATIENCE ye possess the knowledge of thy soul. Then how gave He? "Agree with thine adversary quickly!"

Then through the coming year have this as thy meditation. (254-101)

God, in Thee do I put my trust! Thou knowest my heart, my mind, my purposes, my desires! Make them, oh God, Thine!

May I choose to do that Thou wouldst have me do . . . for I would be one with Thee!

And even as Thou hast promised, as Thou has shown us the pattern in the mount of our own conscious may we walk with the Son of light and mercy and grace, even as shown to us in Jesus—the Lowly One!

And may our will be with Thee, that Ye may come and abide with us day by day.

Not my will but Thine, oh God, be done in me! (254-101)

Ever keep the mental and spiritual in that direct accord with the higher forces innate in the entity, not warring against that known and felt within self as the correct thing to do. (341-P-6)

Then, let all so examine their hearts and minds as to put away doubt and fear; putting away hate and malice, jealousy and those things that cause men to err. Replace these with the desire to help; with hope, with the willingness to divide self and self's surroundings with those who are less fortunate; putting on the whole armor of God . . . in righteousness.

Magnify in the daily life the fruit of the spirit of truth, that all may take hold and make for that activity in their lives; knowing that if ye do it unto the least of thy brethren ye do it to thy Maker.

For the Lord hath knowledge of thee, for thou art a portion of Him. Yes, each soul is a portion of Him! Thou art not aware of thy pulsebeat until a disturbance arises. So in the mind and heart of thy Maker, thy Creator. When thou art disturbed, He becomes aware of thy disturbing forces. Then keep peace in thy own heart and mind. (1650-L-1)

The more we realize our Divine Nature, the more we are free. Truth does set us free; for karma inspires hope for the future and resignation to the past.

We begin by loving only ourselves, yet we must finish by loving everyone except ourselves. . . .

For reincarnation will stop only through the labor of loving your neighbor.

APPENDIX: THE PHILOSOPHY OF

REINCARNATION

Acceptance of karma necessarily includes a belief in reincarnation. Unless there is rebirth in a physical body—reincarnation—the effects of former lives cannot exist. The material in the following pages deals specifically with conditions of rebirth, which does not logically belong in the previous pages. It does, however, add many interesting facts and gives some of the reasons as to when, where, and why we are reborn. No doubt there are many other questions we would now ask Edgar Cayce, if we only could. The first reading, 294-189, explains much of the philosophy of reincarnation.

The following information was sought by a group of individuals closely associated with Edgar Cayce, after seeing an article in a Los Angeles newspaper dated November 23, 1937: "Arthur M. Hanks, who made a fortune peddling flowers in the Los Angeles financial district, left no will because he believed he would return through reincarnation and claim his life's savings. He has been dead seven months now, and today Judge Joseph P. Sproul opened the way for relatives to divide the flower peddler's $100,000 estate." Edgar Cayce's reading of November 25, 1937, was in response to this question, presented to him in the opening suggestion: "You will have before you the enquiring minds of those gathered here [besides Edgar Cayce, Mrs. Cayce, Gladys, and Hugh Lynn, there were Lucille, David, S. David, and Richard Kahn, and Mary and Thomas Sugrue]. You will give at this time information which will help us to understand the laws governing the selection by an entity of time, place, race, color, sex, and the parents at any rebirth into the earth plane—especially the possibility of Edgar Cayce, present in this room, bringing through in his next incarnation memory of this life. If possible we would like to be advised as to how proof of such memory can be established by leaving a record or money now that may be called for during the next appearance."

Mr. C: Yes, we have the enquiring minds of those present here, as a group, as individuals—and those conditions as may be taken here from the records, the experiences or entrances of soul-entities into the material or earthly plane.

This condition, as has so oft been given, varies as to time—according to developments of entities as related to material expression of spiritual activities, or as to the manner or the character of the removal from the material experience.

As to race, color, or sex—this depends upon that experience necessary for the completion, for the building up of the purposes for which each and every soul manifests in the material experience.

For as is generally accepted, and as is in greater part true, the experiences of a soul-entity in materiality, in the three-dimensional sphere of activity, are as lessons or studies in that particular phase of the entity's or soul's development.

Development for what? That to which the Giver of all good and perfect gifts gave the expressions in materiality when spirit had entangled itself in matter. Thus that which has been given: The will of the Father is that no soul shall perish, but that ALL shall come to know Him as He is. For God IS, and seeks that man should worship Him in spirit and in truth, even as He is Spirit, is Truth; not as a condition only but as an experience, as a manifestation.

As love is the expression for experiences in life manifested in the earth, so is the experience of the soul in the earth dependent upon that plane, that experience, as to its race or color or sex. For if there has been the error in that phase, in that expression, the error must be met. For indeed as has been given, whatsoever ye sow, so shall ye reap. And these are gathered only in the phases of experience in which the associations, the activities, the relations have been. Thus, as there is continuity of life expression, so must it continue.

They who have done error suddenly, they who are advanced, they who have not met a whole expression may suddenly—as you count time.

As for the entity Edgar Cayce, this depends then as to when that experience has been reached in which the union of purposes of entities in materiality has created that expression, that phase, to which the entity's development may reach to find expression through same. How did He give? As the tree falls, so does it lie.

Then as this entity builds in the present experience, creating that activity, that union, that expression of divine love toward the fellow men, then where that is left off—the period of expression is begun where it may take hold.

As to when—it may be perhaps a hundred, two hundred, three hundred, a thousand years—as you may count time in the present. This may not be given. For how gave He? The day no man knoweth, ONLY the Father in heaven knoweth it; and it is provided you so live, as He gave, that "I may sit upon the right hand and my brother the left." These are not to be given; they are prepared for those who have through their meeting with their fellow men manifested that which brings them into that association, that consciousness, that enfoldment as to where they become, may become, that which may in the greater manner manifest that love of the Father to the children of men. As to when—no man knoweth; only the Father. Ready for questions.

Q. Would you suggest any way that a record may be left by an entity?
A. By LIVING the record! For when the purposes of an entity or soul are the more and more in accord with that for which the entity has entered, then the soul-entity may take HOLD upon that which may bring to its remembrance that it was, where, when, and how. Thinkest thou that the grain of corn has forgotten what manner of expression it has given? Think thou that ANY of the influences in nature that you see about you—the acorn, the oak, the elm, or the vine, or *anything*—has forgotten what manner of expression? Only man forgets! And it is only in His mercy that such was brought about. For what was the first cause? Knowledge—knowledge! What then is that cut off in the beginnings of the Sons of God? Becoming entangled with

237

the daughters of men, and the Daughters of God
becoming entangled with the sons of men! As in Adam
they forgot what manner of men they were! Only when
he lives, he manifests that life that *is* the expression of
the divine, may man BEGIN to know WHO, where,
what, and when he was!

That there may be read from the records of God's
Book of Remembrance, as from here, in the keepers of
the records, is true—if thy purpose, thy desire, in heart,
in soul, is for the love of God as may be manifested
among the sons of men; but these may be read only by
those in the shadows of His love. (294-189)

We are through for the present.

It is very difficult to determine what is the reason for a
soul's entrance at a certain time. The readings gave cases
where there was a long lapse of time and other cases where
there was a very quick return to earth life. No doubt the
desire of the entity itself is a large factor. This question and
answer give some details:

Q. In the life readings as given, explain the difference in
   lapse of time between incarnations. Is it that not all
   experience in the earth world are given in life readings,
   or is it that sufficient development in life makes it
   unnecessary for a reappearance until a long lapse of
   time?
   For example: 195's first appearance was ten million,
   five hundred thousand years ago. The next appearance
   was twelve thousand years ago. Did the entity have any
   appearances on earth between these two eras of
   incarnation?
A. His appearances in the earth plane are given in full. In
   the lapses, there are developments other than the earth's
   plane. Hence, as has been given, it is often that other
   systems of our present planetary system are the abode,
   or have had their influence in the entity's life. . . . Then,
   it is nearer correct to say that the development is such
   that there may be long or short periods from one
   incarnation to another. (139-MS-1; 1,2)

Cycles

A little more light is thrown on our ability to work out problems by 993's question.

Q. Was I associated with Jesus Christ when He was on the earth as the son of Mary?

A. As this *is* to become a portion of the experience, this may best be given later.

You were!

This may not be wholly understood. It is as this: Individuals in the earth move from cycle to cycle in their own development, in their relationships with individuals and with the activities having to do with that which may be accomplished in a given experience. They have, as it were, taken this or that road in meeting certain conditions. And *one* experience at one portion of the life, then, is as a lamp or a guidebook. Then when they have come to the crossroads again, as it were, there is another experience or another lesson.

This might be illustrated in a very simple, yet a very direct way and manner as follows:

In training the mind in material things, that pertaining to the care of the body is not that used in meeting a friend; yet it is at times a *portion* of the same, see? Yet in meeting the friend, various portions of the development come to the forefront; as to what has been the manner of activity, the social custom, or the needs of the individual—whether friend or foe.

So, as that association is to be, as it were, the crowning of the efforts, the experiences of the entity in this particular experience or sphere of activity, hold fast that thou hast; and then it may be given thee.

The readings given for 518 seem to give a great deal of information concerning the reason for certain conditions in an earth life of an entity and why and how it progresses or retards during an experience.

518 was a young woman twenty-four years of age when her first reading was given. She said she had studied piano most of her life and had graduated from Chicago Musical College in 1931, hoping to become a music teacher.

Because of the Depression she had been unable to find a position.

From the astrological aspects much may be gathered that will be helpful in the entity's experience in the present sojourn. While the astrological aspects make for general tendencies in many entities' experience, the planetary sojourn in the earth's environ deals more with the mental development of an entity than just because the stars, the sun, the moon, or any of the zodiacal signs are in the aspects at the hour or period of beginnings in this experience.

Rather has that which has been builded in the soul of the entity brought about its influence, and so does the entity become influenced according to its activities in relationships to that which has been the understanding or comprehension of the universal laws, as the entity is related to same. For, without knowledge there is not the comprehension; and without understanding it does not become practical in the material development or manifestation of a soul.

Hence we find these as innate in the inner being of the entity through those sojourns in this environ:

In Venus we find the influence in the present making for the ability for the entity to make self compatible in its environs, and make for those experiences of where there is the will or desire for the entity to influence others as to their association with such individuals capable of being made manifest in the activities of self, as well as in the activities of those to whom such mental reaction may be directed.

This is both good and bad, dependent upon the purpose for which such relationships may be brought about. If it is used for the satisfying of self's own desires, whether material, mental, or spiritual, it may be to the detriment of the soul. If it is used for manifesting in the earth's experience the love of the divine influences that are innate in every active force, or to bear fruits in the spirit, then it may be constructive and for the developments of the soul. Hence, much in the way as the use of those things that may be said to be individualities in the experience of this entity, 518, as known in the

240

present experience, will be as to whether this experience is to be soul development or soul retardment.

The experiences in Jupiter, with Uranus as its aid, make for periods when the entity is very easily influenced in those directions of the emotional side of the life; which also may be good or bad. For it tends towards those periods when there is so little from the material standpoint to look forward to; others when everything is bright, happy, gleeful, and those activities of the body may be such as to bring satisfactory or satisfying experiences in the activities of the entity.

If these emotions are used in a compatible way and manner with those innate from the activities of the sojourn of the soul in Venus, what a lovely life may be experienced by the entity!

If these are turned for aggrandizing of selfish motives, or purely for the material gains, what a mess may be made out of this experience!

For, as we find, Uranian and Mercurian influences that are indwelling in the earth during these cycles of experience, from 1909 to 1913 inclusive in their ends, have been Atlanteans in their sojourns in the earth, and the wiles that may be made for such an activity of emotion, such an activity of mental abilities, such an engorgement of the carnal influences in the experiences of others. For self-indulgences by so many in that land, in that experience in Atlantis, must make in these periods in the earth's sojourn the opportunities in the mental attitudes of individuals respecting what are constructive and what are the basic influences for the activities upon the souls of men when *these* souls may—as may be said—rule or ruin man's association in the earth during their sojourn in the present.

As to the appearances in the earth, then, and those that influence the bodily activities to a great extent in the present, these—as we find—are not all, but are those that in the present have a decided effect; or those that were at the periods in association with those that may be aids in the present; not props, not wholly dependent, for when one begins to depend upon another for all that may mean the experience of its soul in any sojourn it becomes weak in its own abilities, but rather lay that foundation which is Life itself, watered by the water of life from the Christ-Consciousness in the earth that may make for a growing in grace, in knowledge, in understanding of those influences that may be wholly constructive in the experience of every soul. But if there will be sought from time to time those that may be aids that may assist in putting their feet on the right way, much may be given from time to time as to what is being done with the opportunities that are presented to such souls in this experience or sojourn.

This entity, 518, was an Indian maiden in one life. She both gained and lost in that experience:

[She] gave much to her own peoples in making for the associations that brought the relationships that had not existed with these peoples at that time; yet losing in the latter portion of same by the associations that brought activities in material relations that brought harm, in that they produced hate in the associations at the time.

In the experience, then, the entity developed in the mental abilities, it gained in soul development, and lost—for it builded many of those things that must be met in the present, as to whether those things of spiritual origin are of those forces or influences that would be for constructive influence in the soul development of the entity or whether they would be for the aggrandizement of selfish interests in the life experience.

These, then, must be met in the present, and only in and through those ways that have been given; that man may know that the life of a soul must be the manifesting of the glory of the Father, through the Son, in this material plane. For other than that makes for selfishness, that is the basis of all sin in the earth.

Before that we find the entity was in that land now known as the Roman, during those periods when there were the spreadings of the tenets from the soldiery, or through the soldiery that returned from the Palestine land during those periods when the earth was darkened and the foundations of the deep were broken up; for the Son of man, the Son of God, was suspended between earth and the sky.

242

In these experiences, from the lessons that were brought by word of mouth, the entity then—in the name Cleo—was the daughter of one that was sent later to fill those places, and coming with Felix and Agrippa into the land. This made for contacts that brought to the entity the understandings of how souls might gain a vision of the truths that make for life under any environ in the earth. Though the body may suffer, though the mind may be blanked, there is the remaining grace in the faith in Him that gave Himself as the ransom in the earth, despised of men yet without fault, showing forth His love in the manner of doing good among those that sought and that were of the household of faith.

The entity was among those that believed, yet with material persecution, with rebuke, with the sneers of those in power and those that were not of the faith, there was made for the *living* of an experience when the heart cried out from within for a turning to the knowledge that was known, and the feet walked in the ways of death.

This in the present experience makes for those periods when, looking upon the spiritual life, the entity becomes rather a recluse—and as to taking from the living experiences the joys and the pleasures of life; yet if there is the understanding there may be known there can be no joy, no happiness in a material plane, unless founded in truth and light as poured into the earth through those blessings that have come to the earth through the Maker of the earth, the Giver of life, the Giver of hope, the Giver of all that is good and perfect in a material plane. For heaven and earth may pass away, but His words pass not away. And He has given, "Be ye joyous in the service of the Lord." Do good to them thou may meet in the way, and especially to the household of faith. Thou are of that household. Keep thine heritage. Blot it not from thine memory. Make known: For, as He has given, "I will bring to thee remembrance of all that is necessary for thine understanding from the foundations of the earth, if ye will but keep my commandments." Love one another in Christ. (518-1)

518 was told of two other experiences in Atlantis and Egypt where the entity gained by helping those who were ill

either in body or mind. Then this advice was given: "Begin where thou art, using today those abilities in the various fields of activity to demonstrate the love of the Christ-Life that thou knowest innately within thee. But be joyous in all thou doest. Smile often, for *smiling* is catching—but sadness drives away."

A year and a half later 518 had another reading seeking advice and guidance for spiritual development.

The suggestion given to Edgar Cayce was:

Entity: Mental and spiritual reading, giving the original purpose of entrance into this solar realm of experience; trace the mental and spiritual development from the beginning through the various stages of experience, and give such guidance as the entity needs in awakening her psychic soul faculties and in using same for the highest spiritual development in this life. You will answer the questions she has submitted, as I ask them.

Mr. C: Yes, we have the entity and those experiences in the mental and soul forces of same, as may be applicable in the experience in the present; that may make that necessary for the entity's development and to bring the influences that are necessary for the understanding.

In tracing the experiences of the entity, and in giving purposes, aims, desires, let these be set as the law, or as the ideal manner of approach to any of such conditions:

First, the entering of *every* soul is that it, the soul, may become more and more aware or conscious of the divine within, that the soul-body may be purged that it may be a fit companion for the *glory* of the Creative Forces in its activity.

The activity for this entity, then, is the same; that it may have the opportunity. For it has been given that the *Lord* hath not willed that any soul should perish. But with every temptation He hath prepared a way; so that if he or she as the erring one will turn to Him for that aid, it may find same.

Then again, in the appearances, do not look or seek for the phenomenon of the experience without the purpose, the aim. *Use* same as a criterion, as what to do and what not to do. Not that it, the simple experience, has made or set *anything* permanent! For there is the constant change evidenced before us; until the soul has been washed clean through that the soul in its body, in its temple, has *experienced* by the manner in which it has acted, has spoken, has thought, has desired in its relationships to its fellow man!

Not in selfishness, not in grudge, not in wrath; not in *any* of those things that make for the separation of the I AM from the Creative Forces, or Energy, or God. But the simpleness, the gentleness, the humbleness, the faithfulness, the longsuffering, *patience!* These be the attributes and those things which the soul takes cognizance of in its walks and activities before men. Not to be *seen* of men, but that the love may be manifested as the Father has shown through the Son and in the earth day by day. Thus He keeps the bounty, thus He keeps the conditions such that the individual soul may—if it will but meet or look within—find indeed *His* Presence abiding ever.

The soul, the individual that purposely, intentionally turns the back upon these things, choosing the satisfying of the own self's desire, then has turned the back upon the living God.

Not that there is not to be joy, pleasure, and those things that maketh not afraid in the experience of every soul. But the joy in service, the joy in labor for the fellow man, the joy in giving of self that those through thy feeble efforts may have put before them, may become aware in their consciousness, that *thou* has been with, that *thou* hast taken into thine own bosom the law of the Lord; and that ye walk daily with Him.

What, ye say then, was the purpose for which ye entered in at this particular experience? That ye might know the Lord and *His* goodness the more in thine inner self, that ye through this knowledge might become as a messenger in thy service and activity before thy fellow man; as one pointing the way, as one bringing—through the feeble efforts and endeavors, through the faltering steps at times, yet *trying*, attempting to do—what the conscience in the Lord hath prompted and does *prompt* thee to do.

As to thy music, in this thy hands may bring the

consciousness of the harmonies that are created by the vibrations in the activities of each soul; that each other soul may, too, take hope; may, too, be just kind, just gentle, just patient, just humble.

Not that the way of the Lord is as the sounding of the trumpet, nor as the tinkling of cymbals that His might be proclaimed; but in the still small voice, in the hours of darkness that which lightens the heart to gladness, that which brings relief to the sufferer, that which makes for patience with the wayward, that which enables those that are hungry—in body, in mind—to be fed upon the bread of life; that they may drink deep of the water of life, through thy efforts.

These are the purposes, these are the experiences that bring in the heart and in the soul the answering of that cry, "WHY—WHY have I come into this experience?"

Be ye patient; be ye quiet and *see* the glory of the Lord in that thou may do in thine efforts day by day.

Do that thou *knowest* to do, TODAY! Then leave the results, leave the rewards, leave the effects into the hands of thy God. For *He* knoweth thy heart, and He hath called—if ye will harken.

Ready for questions.

Q. How may I attune myself that I may be one with the Creative Forces with Christ that I may find this true relationship?
A. Just as indicated. Let thy patience, thy tolerance, thy activity be of such positive nature that it *fits* thee—as a love—to be patient with thy fellow man, to minister to those that are sick, to those that are afflicted, to sit with those that are shut in, to read with those that are losing their perception, to reason with those that are wary of the turmoils; showing brotherly love, patience, persistence in the Lord, and the love that overcometh all things.

These be the things one must do. And do find patience with self. It has been said, "Have we not piped all the day long and no one has answered?" Seekest thou, as was given from this illustration, for the gratifying of thy self? Or seekest thou to be a channel of blessing to thy fellow man? They may not have answered as *thou* hast seen. They may have even shown contempt, as sneering, for thy patience and thy trouble. But *somewhere* the sun still shines; *somewhere* the day is done, for those that have grown weary, for those that have given up. The Lord abhorreth the quitter. And those temptations that come in such cases are the viewing of thine own *self*. Ye have hurt thyself and ye have again crucified thy Lord when ye become impatient or speak harshly because someone has jeered or because someone has sneered or because someone has laughed at thy efforts!

Leave the *results*, leave the giving of the crown, leave the glory, with the Lord! He will repay. Thou sayest in thine own heart that thou believest. Then merely, simply, ACT that way! In speech, in thought, in deed.

Q. What are some of my difficulties that I have to meet in the present, and how should I overcome them?
A. These ye find day by day. They have been pointed out, and the way to meet them. *Bless* ye the Lord!
Q. Am I choosing that which is best for my soul development?
A. That must ever be answered from within. How readest thou? Read that which has just been given thee, as to how ye shall conduct yourself toward thy fellow man. This will show thee thy shortcomings; this will show thee thy graciousness. And let thy prayer be "MERCY, LORD! HAVE MERCY, THOU, UPON MY WEAKNESS, AND GIVE ME STRENGTH IN THEE!"
Q. What must I do and how to make this experience be for my soul development?
A. It has just been given. Bear in thy activities the fruits of the spirit that maketh for *constructive* creative force in the experience of the body.
Q. What should I do in order to live the lovely life in this earth plane?
A. One and the same as that given.
Q. What are those abilities or talents that lie innate, and how can they be aroused?
A. By the application of that thou knowest to do: And

those that have been intimated ye will experience as ye apply. *Seek*, and ye shall find; knock, and it shall be opened unto you. That thou needest to do.

Q. What phase of music should I study in order to derive the most benefit?

A. That more of the nature which to thine own self creates *harmonious* vibrations in the experiences of self and those about thee. That partaking of the rhymes, the lullabies, the pastoral scenes, which make for such harmonious forces, bring quiet, cheer, hope, and casting out fear. (518-2)

Though it is very rare, a few predictions as to the next incarnation are in the reading. 304 was told he would be a lawyer in his next life.

One cannot help wondering why he was not a lawyer in his present life. Did he make a wrong choice, or was he working on some other condition?

As to the appearances of this entity, we find that before this, this entity was in the court of England, in that of Alfred, called the Great [848(?)—900], and those influences as exercised in the present sphere are seen in the understanding of the law as written in any given state, and in the next reincarnation we will find this entity a lawyer. (304-5)

This next reference seems still more unusual, for the emphasis is on destiny.

One given to be of many days in the present earth's plane, through the enforcing elements in Jupiter and in Mercury, with Mars as the ruling effect of the entity's destiny.

In the conditions, then, as set, irrespective of that which may be made with the will in the next return we would find one in these conditions that have to do with one of power, and of rule over many peoples, yet in the same sex as at present.

The above prediction was given for a woman born in October, 1876. We can only speculate as to the meaning of this. First, the all-important factor of will seems to be of no effect. Then, where is this domain over which she is to rule?

No doubt we all would like to know about our next incarnation. Mr. 416 asked about his and received a rather sharp answer. Probably most people would have gotten a similar reply.

Q. When and where will I next incarnate, and will I be associated with associates of this incarnation and whom?

A. Better get into shape so that you can incarnate. That depends a great deal upon what one does about the present opportunities. It isn't set for time immemorial as to be what you will be from one experience to the other. For, as has been given, there are unchangeable laws. The Creator intended man to be a companion with Him. Whether in heaven or in the earth or in whatever consciousness, a companion with the Creator. How many will it require for thee to be able to be a companion with Creative Forces wherever you are? That is also a law. What ye sow, ye reap. What is, then, that which is making for the closer association of body, mind, and soul to Father, Son, and Holy Spirit? Just as has been indicated in thy physical being—there are those tendencies for auditory disturbances. Ye have heard. Have ye heeded?

In those, then, to be the applications, what becomes disturbing? He that heeds not, then, has rejected, and there is the need for remembering the unchangeable law: "Though He were the Son, yet learned He obedience through the things which He suffered." Shall thou be greater than thy Lord? Where will these occur? Where do you make them? The place where you art is the place to begin. What were the admonitions? "Use that thou hast in hand. Today, if ye will hear His voice, harden not thy heart." (416-18)

Sex

The question as to whether entities always manifest in the same sex is frequently asked. There are several

249

readings which told the person he was not in the same sex as at present, and a few were told they had never changed sex. These quotations give some of the answers as to how sex is determined.

> The entity is one that has never changed sex; thus it is every whit a woman—dependent, and yet free from the needs of the companionship as many. These emotions the entity in others oft never comprehends; nor do others comprehend the emotions or manners or ways of the entity. (2390-1)

Q. Does spirit action ever change the sex of an entity from one incarnation to another?

A. It does at times. It depends upon that which is builded in the entity in the earth's plane, for the force of will in the earth is the ruling factor. . . . That which is builded in the desire determines the sex in a particular incarnation. (136-D-20, 6—7)

Another answer explains it further:

A. How oft has there been the expression heard, "Were I a man—" or "Were I a woman—*I* would do so and so!" They do it! That as is constantly builded in the mental being takes shape in the home of the soul, whether to build that of the man or woman in a material world; for man is so much a portion of the whole as to either be a coworker, or a cobuilder with the oneness of the force called God, or a destroyer—and as these forces then are builded, they take physical form through that experienced by the body of the *entity* (not the physical, but the *body* of the entity—the soul). The soul is that everlasting portion of a body that is either crowded into that (beings that are known as men and women) of small or great stature. As has been studied time and time again as has been given in relativity of force—in the active principle of the atomic conditions that take place in the materia! world—the surroundings of the individual has *its* influence, see? That is, it has been long seen and known by man that the Laplander gradually attains to a

250

certain stature and build. Why? The material surroundings are such that there is constantly implanted in the soul of the entity that which is necessary for the best development through that individual plane, phase, place, position of such peoples. Peoples seek, then, through that same channel through which it (the soul, the entity) may develop that which is necessary for its experiences to bring the perfect understanding of that oneness of which there has much been spoken. (900-MS-6)

This woman wanted to know why she had chosen to manifest as a man.

Q. Why was entity a man or horseman in the Arabian incarnation?

A. That would depend upon those desires as were made by the entity from its appearance in the *previous* incarnation, see? And finding, as it were, the opportunity in this particular period to enter in that capacity as had been desired, so the entity entered in as one who could fill, fulfill, that desire; for, as should be gained by all: Desire brought the earth and the heavens into being from the All-Wise Creator. So man, by his heritage to that creation, may bring through desire, whether of earthly, heavenly, spiritually, those things that they, the individual, the entity, must meet, by creating, making, *being*, that desire! Hence, as we find, all the various phases of changes as may be wrought in man's, or woman's, activities; for by taking *thought* no man may add one cubit; nor can—by taking thought—the head be changed one whit; yet desire, and the fathering and mothering of desire, may change a whole universe! For from the desires of the heart do the activities of the brain, of the physical being, shape that as would be created by same. See? So the entity, in seeking in this particular appearance, found in that appearance the manner of expression so desired. (276-3)

This entity was told when the sex of the incoming soul was determined:

251

The sex is determined at the period of the first movement of the embryo, and it occurs in the first three weeks of conception. (136-D-21, 6)

Q. What causes changes in sex and why do some change, others not?

A. What [is] from the *spiritual* desire. Now—*desire* may be given in a varied form or manner, and in some conditions appear only as wish, or as an expression of a sensing from within. In this there is seen as to *how* that the desire of an individual would *bring* them in under the environ of male or female, while one may appear in the earth as male or female as a regular or at intervals, according to the *development*. In the same *sphere*—that is, in other planets there may be an entirely different sex, *by* the desire or that builded, see?

A little more information concerning the responsibility of the channel and the incoming soul is given in this quotation:

As has been indicated through these channels respecting that which takes place at the moment of conception, as to ideals and purposes of those who through physical and mental emotions bring into being a channel through which there may be the expression of a soul-entity, each soul choosing such a body at the time of its birth into material activity has its physical being controlled much by the environs of the individuals responsible for the physical entrance. Yet, the soul choosing such a body for a manifestation becomes responsible for that temple of the living God when it has developed in body, in mind so as to be controlled with intents, purposes, and desires of the individual entity or soul. (263-13)

The time of soul birth is of importance to many people, especially to astrologers. The readings tell us that there may be quite a difference in the time of physical birth and of soul birth. We get some information on the entrance of the soul from these questions:

Q. Does the soul enter the child at conception or birth or in between?

A. It may at the first moment of breath; it may some hours before birth; it may hours after birth. This depends upon that condition, that environ surrounding the circumstance. (457-MS-4)

Q. Give exact time of physical birth and soul birth.

A. With *this* particular entity, we find there was—in that as would be called time by man—only a period of four to four and a half hours' difference. This mooted question, as may be asked by man, is—as we find—as illustrated here: In the material world life is of the *universal* consciousness, as all development through that known or called evolution of life in a material plane, and is a portion of a body from conception to the transition in what is called death. That which enters, as the soul, is that which would use, or be the companion of, that life-physical through any given period of existence in an earth's appearance. As the variations come, these are brought by the activities of those who through their *own* desire attract or detract those that would manifest in a particular body. See?

Q. Why is there a difference, and what happened in the interim?

A. A physical being, or life, as given, is from inception, and is of an universal consciousness—see? When a physical being, or body, as this body, is brought into being by the birth into the physical world, the interim between that is as of *that* period when the decision is being made by *that* soul that would occupy *that* individual body. See? (276-3)

Q. Does a soul ever enter a body before it is born?

A. It enters either at the first breath physically drawn, or during the first twenty-four hours of cycle activity in a material plane. Not always at the first breath; sometimes there are hours, and there are changes even of personalities as to the seeking to enter.

Q. What keeps the physical body living until the soul enters?

A. Spirit! For the spirit of matter—its source is life, or God, see? (2390-2)

The next questions, while not directly related, do give us more details about reincarnation.

Q. About how much time have I spent in reincarnation up to the present time?

A. Almost in all the cycles that have had the incoming from period to period hast thou dwelt. Thine first incoming in the earth was during those periods of the Atlanteans that made for the divisions. Hence, counting in time, some twenty thousand years. (707-1)

Q. What is necessary for me to attain and retain physical perfection?

A. Perfection is not possible in a material body until you have entered at least some thirty times. (2982-P-1)

Q. When an entity has completed its development, such that it no longer needs to manifest on earth's plane, how far then is it along towards its complete development towards God?

A. Not to be given. Reach that plane, and develop in Him, for in Him the will then becomes manifest. (900-20)

Q. Altogether, how many incarnations have I had?

A. Rather use the ones you know of and have need for, rather than knowing numbers! Know, as there has been indicated, there is a wisdom as concerning incarnations or activities that cometh not from above. Use that thou hast in hand, that more may be given thee in its proper place and sphere. Remember Moses and his doubts when he took hold of the serpent. Would you take hold?

These become not as criticisms, but are the attempt to have the individual entity attain to that consciousness of "using that I have in hand." For know, as He hath given, "*I* will bring to thy remembrance ALL things, since the foundation of the world." Where has HE promised to meet thee? In thine own tabernacle. For thine body—thine body—is the temple of the living God. There ye may ascertain thy needs. These become eventually the consciousness of all who attain complete righteousness in purpose, in hope, in desire. These may be given as ye apply self in making those adjustments, those corrections in that ye have in hand. (1861-12)

Many people ask why we have to go through all this and for what purpose. Here is an answer to that question given in a reading.

Q. Are souls perfect, as created by God in the first? If so, why is there any need of development?

A. The answer to this may only be found in the evolution of life, in such a way as to be understood by the finite mind. In the first cause or principle all is perfect. That portion of the whole (manifested in the creation of souls) may become a living soul and equal with the Creator. To reach that position, when separated, it must pass through all stages of development, in order that it may be one with the Creator. (254-13)

This next statement gives us a little more information as to why we are here.

What influences such a journey of the soul from the unseen into materiality? *Soul development:* That by the lessons gained in physical experience, it may take the place in realms of soul-activity in an infinite world, among others that have passed through the various realms; seeking companionship, which first called every soul and body into experience. Hence we have as much force of heredity and environment in the soul's experience as we have in the law of the earth in respect to parentage, bodily environment, and thought development. (541-1)

That which makes of the development for the soul—which is the purpose for the entrance of a soul into material experience—is ever through the will for the entity to be in accord with that which is its ideal. If the ideal is chosen for material blessings, material benefits, self-indulgence, fame, or fortune, then little may be the soul development; for in these manners there is the deceitfulness of fame or fortune. But rather being sincere to that which is the material manifestation of the spiritual impulses makes for that as may bring in its effectual way and manner the material blessings that are the more worthwhile, and the soul developments which are fulfilling the purpose of entrance into materiality. (1196-2, page 1)

Animals

And finally: Do animals have souls, and do they reincarnate? These questions are frequently asked, and questions about animals do occur in the readings given by Edgar Cayce.

The readings state that animals have group souls, but there is some sort of rebirth even in them. There is quite a little information concerning animals in the readings, but Edgar Cayce refused to give a reading for an animal, though he did often answer questions concerning them. He wrote in a letter to 4525 that he could not give a reading for her dog, as he was too busy with other problems, but said he had been asked several times to give readings for pets.

Mrs. 268 asked about her little dog, Mona, in her life reading.

Q. Where and how have I been formerly associated with the following: my little dog, Mona.
A. In the same experience.
Q. In the Roman?
A. The Roman.
Q. Was she a dog then?
A. A lion!

This woman's niece 405 also asked about Mona and was told that Mona would not always be a dog. Thus it would seem that animals also go through some sort of evolvement.